A NOVEL BASED ON THE LIFE OF
JOHN CABOT

DREAMS
OF DISCOVERY

Jule Selbo

THE
MENTORIS
PROJECT

Barbera Foundation, Inc.
P.O. Box 1019
Temple City, CA 91780

Copyright © 2018 Barbera Foundation, Inc.
Cover photo: Pictorial Press Ltd / Alamy Stock Photo
Cover design: Suzanne Turpin

More information at www.mentorisproject.org

ISBN: 978-1-947431-16-4

Library of Congress Control Number: 2018907721

The Mentoris Project is a series of novels and biographies about the lives of great men and women who have changed history through their contributions as scientists, inventors, explorers, thinkers, and creators. The Barbera Foundation sponsors this series in the hope that, like a mentor, each book will inspire the reader to discover how she or he can make a positive contribution to society.

Contents

Foreword

First and foremost, Mentor was a person. We tend to think of the word *mentor* as a noun (a mentor) or a verb (to mentor), but there is a very human dimension embedded in the term. Mentor appears in Homer's *Odyssey* as the old friend entrusted to care for Odysseus's household and his son Telemachus during the Trojan War. When years pass and Telemachus sets out to search for his missing father, the goddess Athena assumes the form of Mentor to accompany him. The human being welcomes a human form for counsel. From its very origins, becoming a mentor is a transcendent act; it carries with it something of the holy.

The Mentoris Project sets out on an Athena-like mission: We hope the books that form this series will be an inspiration to all those who are seekers, to those of the twenty-first century who are on their own odysseys, trying to find enduring principles that will guide them to a spiritual home. The stories that comprise the series are all deeply human. These books dramatize the lives of great men and women whose stories bridge the ancient and the modern, taking many forms, just as Athena did, but always holding up a light for those living today.

Whether in novel form or traditional biography, these books plumb the individual characters of our heroes' journeys.

The power of storytelling has always been to envelop the reader in a vivid and continuous dream, and to forge a link with the subject. Our goal is for that link to guide the reader home with a new inspiration.

What is a mentor? A guide, a moral compass, an inspiration. A friend who points you toward true north. We hope that the Mentoris Project will become that friend, and it will help us all transcend our daily lives with something that can only be called holy.

—Robert J. Barbera, President, Barbera Foundation
—Ken LaZebnik, Founding Editor, The Mentoris Project

In 1497, John Cabot, born Giovanni Caboto in Genoa, Italy,
sailed to the coast of North America and claimed
the lands of Newfoundland, Nova Scotia, and
northern territories of the United States
for Henry VII of England.

His journey is a testament to perseverance and persistence.

Part One: Genoa

Chapter One

The first days of 1460 had blown into Genoa with very strong sea winds. Energetic Giovanni Caboto, ten years old, flew down the narrow, icy alleyway from Via Banchi towards the harbor. His thick, dark hair fell past his ears; it was flattened to his head under a worn leather cap. His wool scarf left his long nose barely visible and his breath formed clouds in the cold air. "Come on, Piero, the ships are docking—Papà expects our help." Giovanni ran backward for a moment, a huge grin on his face. "We might see treasures, Piero! Maybe even pirates!"

His brother moved his short, chubby legs trying to keep up, but Giovanni was taller, leaner, stronger, faster—everything Piero wanted to be. He huffed. "Mamma's not happy we hurried out of church."

Giovanni shrugged and continued on. "Fra Marco, he sings too much. Even God must tire of it."

Father Marco always frowned at Giovanni's squirming on the flat wooden benches in the medieval Church of Saint Mary

Magdalene. But he had also talked to Giovanni's devout mother about her son's quickness and his adroit understanding of Biblical stories and teachings of the Catholic Church, and intimated that the Caboto family would do well to have one of their sons dedicate his life to God. Signora Caboto would have liked to have a son pave her family's way to heaven—for she feared her husband's interest in the wealth of purse outpaced his interest in the wealth of soul. But she knew that the priesthood would never be for Giovanni; just last week he had confided to her that he saw his future as a pirate.

Piero came to a stop. His cheeks were dotted with red splotches from the biting wind. "Wait, Gio, *attendere prego*." He leaned against one of the massive walls of Palazzo San Giorgio, a large palace built two hundred years before by Genoa's first appointed leader, the doge.

Giovanni relented, pulled his scratchy scarf closer on his neck, and ran back to Piero. "You're right, this is good place to rest for a moment. I've told you that here, in this palazzo's dark and cold dungeons, Marco Polo was kept a prisoner."

"You tell me every time we pass by."

"This is where he told of his adventures in the Mongol Empire." Giovanni pressed his gloved hands against the thick stone edifice and told Piero to imagine the Venetian explorer Marco Polo, captured in the Genoese war with Venice in 1298, and his cellmate, the writer Rustichello of Pisa, talking of the riches of the Far East and of rescuing princesses. "Just think, when they were released after months of sharing terrible food with rats, the book *The Travels of Marco Polo* was published." Giovanni had read the book many times.

"You told me that too." Piero blew his nose into the piece

of cloth his mother had put into his sleeve at church. He felt Giovanni's hand on his shoulder.

"Give me your hand, Piero." Giovanni's voice was kind. "You know I'll never leave you behind."

Piero grabbed Giovanni's outstretched fingers, glad to be guided through the steep, thin streets where familiar metal workers and leather craftsmen worked in their bottegas and into the harbor and its teeming throngs of traders, merchants, sailors, and smugglers.

"Ah, Piero, look at the ships!" Giovanni's large brown eyes became even brighter as he breathed in the salt air and took in the unloading of spices, silks, lutes, swords, harps from the Far East, and fine horses from Arabia. As he and Piero dodged through the crowds, Giovanni longed to stop and listen to sailors' spine-tingling stories of great voyages, colorful bazaars, caves filled with hordes of jewels and ancient statues, palaces of eminent princes, and people with faces the color of honey or dark tea, whose thick, braided hair reached to the ground. Of eunuchs and concubines and men who wore extraordinary turbans like towers atop their heads. Of carts painted in vibrant hues, strange foods that he had never tasted. Giovanni longed to be part of these adventures. He stopped for a moment and sighed, pointing at a gleaming carrack, its massive ropes holding the cargo ship to the largest dock.

"Maybe I should stow away on that ship when it leaves for Constantinople or Mecca or wherever it's going."

Piero shook his head, causing the light curls peeking out from under his knitted cap to shimmy in the cutting wind. His shivering lips pouted. "No, Giovanni, Mamma and Papà and I would be too sad without you."

The boys nearly collided with a stocky, battered, one-legged sailor who limped off a ship with the aid of a wooden crutch. The sailor fell to his knees next to the red and white Genoese flag, the colors once held high by Genoa's patron saint. He shouted, "Saint George, I pray you smite the sea dragon who took my leg." Tears spilled on the broken sailor's cheeks. "Even as I give ye praise for the rest of me reaching shore." He crossed himself and kissed the ground.

Piero was wide-eyed. "Did you really see a sea dragon?"

"I did, little man, I did. Monsters tall as the mast lurk in the open water. And I heard the mermaids singing. Seen birds as colossal as churches. When the fog wraps around your ship, hold on to yer soul—all monsters rise in the thick air."

Giovanni pulled Piero away for the sailor's eyes were wild, as if the demons had gotten hold of him. They hurried on. "Those are just stories, Piero."

Piero jogged to keep up with Giovanni. "But, Gio, stories can be true, can't they?"

Giovanni heard the flat tones of English sailors. One, with a thick and rosy face, dressed in a dark blue wool coat with brass buttons and a broad leather hat, called out to him. "Laddie, you with the ratty scarf! Two coins, one for you, one for the beer you fetch me!"

Giovanni, seeing the opportunity to place a coin in his empty pocket, raced over to take the money and a wooden mug from the sailor's hand. "*Sì, Signor*. Right away." Giovanni eyed Piero, his eyes demanding obedience. "Stay here, Piero." Giovanni raced across the busy dirt lane to the market cart filled with barrels of ale.

Piero stared up at the sailor's eye patch and scraggly beard. "Are you a pirate?"

The florid-faced sailor scoffed. "Not me. I'm a rigger, take care of the sails under the British flag, laddie. England. Best place on earth."

Giovanni, out of breath, was back with the filled mug; he'd been careful not to spill a drop.

"Long live King Edward!" The rigger tilted his head back and gulped the bitter ale.

The boys moved on past wooden docks and a bevy of caravels—the lightest and swiftest ships—just in from the Adriatic Sea. Piero nearly danced with excitement. "What are you going to do with your coin, Giovanni?"

Before Giovanni could answer, he saw a tall, thin dockworker waving to them. The *camalli* wore patched and worn woolen pants held in place by a thick rope, and a moth-eaten sheepskin jacket too short for his long arms. "Look, Piero. Alfio, Papà's friend, wants us."

Alfio's frog-like eyes seemed to protrude from his forehead. He held out what looked like a hard ball, its surface brown and hairy with fibers. "Want to show you something. For your father." Alfio took a long, thick knife from his bag, set the round mound on the stone street, and whacked it with the dull side of his knife. "This ugly thing comes all the way from a golden island far away, near a magical place called Jaffa." The brown sphere cracked open like the thick skin of a nut. Alfio used his knife to wedge a larger fissure. Then he lifted the shell to his lips and drank. A white liquid ran down his chin. Giovanni and Piero were mesmerized.

"What is it?" Giovanni asked.

"I call it a cow nut because inside there is sweet milk." Alfio offered it to Giovanni and Piero, who nervously stepped back. Giovanni took the cow nut and drank. The nectar in his mouth was fresh and sweet.

Alfio appreciated Giovanni's curiosity. "First I seen it. A sailor gave it to me. A merchant like your father might be interested. Could be some good trading in it; a person could make a lot of money. Tell your father to remember who told him about it."

"I shall tell Papà we must trade in cow nuts. *Grazie*, Alfio."

The boys ran off. Giovanni was excited that he had something new to share with his father.

Giovanni and Piero spotted their tall father, dressed in a worn but clean green velvet tunic, thick leggings, and a brown wool cloak. Signor Caboto was well into his third decade, and more than half of his life had been dedicated to becoming a well-respected spice merchant in Genoa. Now, he watched eagle-eyed over the crates, barrels, and ceramic holders being carried off a large ship docked in the harbor. Spices such as cinnamon, cardamom, ginger, pepper, and turmeric were valuable, not just because they were used to flavor food, but they also preserved food from rotting, so nothing would go to waste. Signor Caboto's reputation for fairness was known; he would pay a just amount for the spices he imported from Sri Lanka and the Indies—but not a florin more—so that he could charge an honest price of his clients.

Spices from China and India and other Asian ports were transported over long land and water routes by traders, and at each stage on the journey the merchant would add a little to the price. By the time the spices reached their destination in Europe, their cost had doubled or tripled. Giovanni knew that many merchants were hoping that a new route around the Ottoman Empire could be found so that the price of the spices could be better controlled. Signor Caboto saw the boys approach and immediately motioned for them to move small crates into the cart.

"We're late because of Father Marco, Papà," Giovanni apologized.

Signor Caboto shook his head. "Ah, he sings too much."

Giovanni held out the large brown shell. "At the dock, Alfio let us drink from a cow nut. There is milk inside. From Jaffa, Papà. We could bring it into our trade."

Signor Caboto quickly dismissed the possibility. "We have enough with spices and teas, my sons."

Giovanni did not give up. "No one else has this nut, Papà. We could be the first in Genoa."

Signor Caboto's eyes were on the crews unloading goods. "Ah, there are our jars. Check that the tea is wrapped in thick cloth in the barrels and that the bags are not broken open. We must be vigilant, boys, and not take goods that are damaged." He saw Giovanni's disappointment. "Gio, you will understand, when I am old and you take over the business from me, that your clients must know you are the best in a few things. A bird must fly and a fish must swim."

Giovanni stood his ground. "But Papà, a duck can do both."

Signor Caboto laughed. "Ah, you are very clever, Gio."

Giovanni was frustrated and wished his father were more daring. He also wished he had the courage to tell his father that the merchant life was not for him, that he was going to be an explorer and an adventurer and discover wonderful things, such as cow nuts and gems as big as his foot.

Traders moved the thick ceramic jars of spices and barrels of tea into waiting carts. Signor Caboto confirmed the tallies and Giovanni counted out the florins. Giovanni listened to his father and the other merchants grumble about how the Turkish leaders of the Ottoman Empire were making the sea and land routes of the Silk Road more difficult and dangerous. The men sighed. If only there were another way to get to India, China, Jaffa, and other markets in the Far East.

"Prince Henry the Navigator, God rest his soul." A merchant crossed himself because the famous Portuguese patron of exploration had recently died. "He funded sea routes to Africa. So now we can trade for Africa's ivory and gum from the acacia tree—and the prized pepper—but these goods do not compare with profits to be made on the Far East's silks and gems and spices. The pottery and rugs."

Another added, "Now the Turks are adding more taxes on each ship and each caravan. And they insist of keeping a portion on the goods. The fees get larger, the looting more aggressive."

Giovanni ventured a question. "If the Turks keep making it more difficult for the traders, will we at some point not be able to reach the Far East at all?"

Signor Caboto said, "Someday, someone will find a new route."

Giovanni was fascinated. "But, Papà, what other way could there be?"

A wrinkled merchant pulled his fur coat tighter around his bulbous middle and puffed on an ivory pipe. "What shape is the earth, boy? What did the Greeks tell us?"

"Round. The earth is round like a ball," Giovanni answered.

The fat merchant nodded. "And that being so, there are those who suggest a new direction. Toscanelli, the mapmaker, thinks we can sail west into the Ocean Sea and eventually— because the earth is round—find the East."

Another merchant, wearing a hat made of rabbit fur and

rings on every finger to alert all to his success, argued, "Many sea captains have tried. Their ships have never returned and many think they've fallen off the edge of a flat earth."

Piero gasped and nestled closer to his father. "Off the edge? Where do they go?"

The rich merchant grimaced. "Some say to nothingness. Some say to hell for their hubris."

Giovanni blurted, "But the world is not flat, Piero. Today, we know the world is round."

The rich merchant sniffed and shrugged.

Giovanni turned to his father and asked, "What do you think, Papà?"

Signor Caboto, always one to avoid an argument with a potential customer, rubbed his hands together. "I think it is time to take our goods and your brother indoors—he will soon turn to ice."

Signor Caboto and his sons pushed the cart up the stone streets toward the bottega.

Giovanni asked him, "Papà, what if that is true, that you can sail west into the Ocean Sea to get to the East?"

Piero chimed in. "You'd be sure to meet pirates, Giovanni. You want to be a pirate. That's what you told me."

Signor Caboto gazed seriously at Giovanni. "Is that true?"

"I do think about sailing the seas to find treasures. A pirate does that."

Signor Caboto said, "Pirates, son, are a sorry lot. They take what is not theirs. If they're caught for their crimes, they're hung from their own masts. Are you the kind of person who takes what it not yours?"

Giovanni looked at his father. "When I sail into the Ocean Sea, Papà, you will be proud of me."

~

The sun had completed its descent in the winter sky. The wind kicked up. Giovanni and Piero blew on their cold fingers as they put the last of the Caboto goods in place and locked the family's stall near Piazza De Marini. Their father had gone off to enjoy wine and discussions of outsmarting the Ottoman Turks, the Sea Consuls' rising tariffs, the vagaries of Genoa's merchants, and the expected war with the Republic of Milan.

Giovanni and Piero headed toward home, passing a shop that sold honeyed nuts. Piero's eyes grew wide as he imagined the crunchy, sweet taste. "What about the coin you got for getting the sailor's beer, Giovanni?"

"The coin must be used for something more important than sweet treats," Giovanni said, and led his brother down a street dotted with the storefronts of furniture makers, bookbinders, and weavers, and pushed open the door of his favorite shop. The bell over the door sounded. Signor Antonio Fallio, his shoulders in a perpetual hunch, his beard long, and his tunic dusty, was surrounded by books and rolled-up maps. He sat at a long table near the small fireplace, deep into reading a letter.

"*Buonasera*, Signor Fallio." Giovanni took a burlap bag from his pocket. "My father sends you turmeric from Burma to relieve the pain in your hands and cardamom for your digestion." Giovanni saw that Fallio's lunch of salted fish and dried fruit was untouched. "Did you forget to eat again?"

Fallio looked at the food on the table as if seeing it for the first time. "I had to read an important letter from a friend in Venice. A monk of the Camaldolese order, Fra Mauro, has completed, after many years, the most comprehensive world map."

Giovanni was excited. "A map of the whole world? Do you have a copy?"

"No, no. It is too large—two meters by two meters. And commissioned by the Portuguese court. For the eyes of royals."

Giovanni nearly shouted his frustration. "But everyone needs to be able to see it, Signor Fallio."

"You and I agree. Ptolemy's ideas of the world, a thousand years ago, helped sailors and explorers change how we thought about the world. And we must keep learning more. Toscanelli's world map is now a decade old—and it leaves so many questions. Fra Mauro's map may answer some of them." Signor Fallio patted Piero's head. "And it shows where sea monsters have been sited."

Piero hungrily eyed Signor Fallio's dried plums. "Sea monsters bite your legs off when the ship is in the fog. I heard that today at the wharf."

Giovanni settled onto a stool near Fallio's desk. "How did Fra Mauro get all his information?"

"From his own explorations, before he became a monk. From reading the writings on Marco Polo and others. Talking to sea captains and sailors who sailed for Prince Henry the Navigator. Ones that told of rivers, mountains, islands, villages, and cities. Castles. Palaces. Peoples. Hills. Tides and currents. Gates and harbors." Fallio sighed. "I would very much like to see this map."

Giovanni longed to see it too. "One day, Signor Fallio. I wish to see it with you."

Fallio shook his head. "That might be impossible. The doge in Venice is promised a copy. We can hope he will display it. But, alas, perhaps only for his circle of nobles and the tutors of their children."

Giovanni groaned in exasperation.

"*Calma*, Giovanni." Fallio knew of Giovanni's desire for more education. The boy had finished the rudimentary lessons available to him at the merchants' school, gaining minor tutelage in Latin, reading, and writing. But as a merchant's son, other avenues were closed to him. Only the sons of nobles had access to the best tutors, to the best books and maps. Fallio smiled at Giovanni. "One day, perhaps you'll find your way into Prince Henry the Navigator's library, the one he set up for ship captains and astronomers and cartographers in Portugal."

"The Portuguese don't like us because Genoa has a more important port than Lisbon."

"Anyone with something to offer can find a welcome," Fallio said gently. "Remember that. And now, Gio, let me see you teach Piero what I have taught you." Fallio unrolled a map and positioned it on the table with iron weights on its corners to keep it flat. The map included outlines of Europe, the Mediterranean, the Ottoman Empire, China, and eastern islands. "Show Piero the route Marco Polo took to the Bosporus, and how he traveled the Silk Road overland to the deserts of China."

Piero's brow furrowed. "Papà talked about the Silk Road this morning. Is it really made of silk?"

Fallio chuckled. "No, no. And it doesn't even look like a road much of the time. The trade route stretches almost seven thousand miles, over mountains and deserts and waters. The traveler, to follow it, must know how to navigate by the stars. The Silk Road is built on dreams and hopes and the idea that by forming a connection of all peoples, we can learn from one another."

"Piero, I'll show it to you," Giovanni said.

Piero leaned into the table and his nose followed Giovanni's finger as his brother pointed to a city on the Adriatic Sea. "This port here is called Venice. It's a great seafaring city like Genoa. It's where Marco Polo lived. He was seventeen years old and finally got permission from his father and uncle to travel with them to here, Constantinople." Giovanni traced a trajectory to the most important city in the Ottoman Empire. Then his finger moved east on the map. "The Polos traveled east to the Empire of Trebizond on the Black Sea, and then south and inland, reaching Jerusalem." Giovanni's finger pointed further east. "Piero, you've heard Father Marco talk about the city of Jerusalem in church."

"That's where the Last Supper was. Jesus ate with his Apostles and people called him the Prince of Peace. Before he was betrayed."

Giovanni nodded and tapped his finger on the map. "See, it's here, above Egypt." Giovanni guided Piero's eyes to another area on the map. "Then the Polos traveled to India and Kashgar, a stop on the Silk Road at the border of a very large country called China. It is where fur caps and spices can be traded."

Fallio unrolled a map of China and weighed it down over the world map. "This shows China, Piero. Marco Polo also called it Cathay. A land so large that it makes the boot of our Italian Peninsula look very tiny."

Giovanni pointed to areas in China. "The Polos found their way on the Silk Road to Lanzhou in China's Gansu province. They saw ancient temples." Giovanni's finger moved. "Then to Cambaluc, the capital of the Yuan Dynasty. There they met the wise and sometimes scary Great Kublai Khan of the Mongol Empire."

"Scary?" Piero's eyes were wide.

Fallio ate one of his dried plums. "If the khan did not like you, he could make your journey very difficult." Fallio took a copy of *The Travels of Marco Polo* from his shelf. "But the khan was also a very curious man, which is admirable. After meeting Marco Polo, he wanted to know more about Christianity. He asked the Polos to travel back to Rome to ask the pope to send holy water and one hundred learned priests. But the pope was not as generous as the khan hoped and refused the request. The Polos had to convince two friars to travel back with them. But as they approached the Gobi Desert, the friars became frightened of the arduous path. They turned back to return to Rome."

Giovanni shook his head. "How could anyone deny adventure? They could have seen snow leopards and giant camels and moveable tents that are kept as warm as houses."

"When Marco Polo told the khan the bad news, the khan was not pleased. He had been told that those of the Catholic religion were generous—or at least interested in him or his people. But because Marco Polo told him the bad news in the khan's own language, the khan's anger fell away."

"Marco Polo could speak many languages, Piero," Giovanni said. "It was one of his talents."

"Why don't they speak our language in China?" Piero asked.

"There are thousands of languages in this world, Piero. A person who can speak to someone in his native tongue has a prized talent. This ability brought Marco Polo great favor and the khan insisted he travel to new places to represent the Mongol interests." Fallio pointed to Tibet, Burma, and India. "Polo traveled to these wonderful places."

Giovanni grinned. "You love history very much, Signor Fallio."

Fallio sipped his tea, nodded. "If we do not know the past, how can we move forward with intelligence to not repeat mistakes?"

The door opened and two boys near Giovanni's age entered the shop. They were short and sturdy, with wide legs and necks wrapped in rough wool scarfs. Giovanni noticed that their gloves were threadbare and their faces dry from the winter air.

Fallio greeted them. "Bartolome. Cristoforo. Come in and warm yourselves."

Bartolome, the younger of the brothers, his face full of freckles, took a map from under his arm and spread it on the table. "I brought it to you first, Signor Fallio. I told you I will be a mapmaker. Will you sell this in your Shop of Maps?"

Cristoforo's piercing eyes crinkled and he smirked. "It is only of the harbors of Genoa and the near islands in the Ocean Sea. And what he imagines beyond—scratches in thin ink."

Fallio looked at the map, whistled. "*Alora*, the first Bartolome Colombo map."

Giovanni and Piero peered over Fallio's bent shoulders. There were cartoons of sailing ships heading west from the Republic of Genoa's rugged coastline. In the open water of the Ocean Sea, there were sea serpents, mermaids, and colossal mermen wielding tridents. On the left side of the map, Bartolome had drawn a land mass filled with cartoons of Asian temples, fireworks, and gold mines.

Bartolome jutted out his chest, proud. "Toscanelli believes that the Far East can be reached by sailing west into the Ocean Sea. This is a map of that possibility."

Cristoforo looked at Giovanni and explained, "Toscanelli is a cartographer of great importance."

Giovanni bristled. "I know. I have studied his map."

Cristoforo eyed Giovanni. His look was interested—but not friendly.

Bartolome smoothed out his work. "No one has sailed far

enough west to find out what is out there, how far away Asia really is when going that direction." He looked at his brother. "Cristoforo thinks he will be the first one to find out."

Giovanni challenged Cristoforo. "You need money to afford a ship. Or the support of people who are very rich."

Cristoforo nodded. "Or the backing of a king or queen."

Bartolome grinned proudly. "My brother thinks big."

Giovanni had never imagined a possibility of a lowly merchant's son gaining royal patronage. Despite himself, he was impressed by Cristoforo's boldness.

Bartolome turned to Signor Fallio. "Will you sell my map in your shop?"

Giovanni pulled the coin he had just earned from his pocket and put it on the table. "Is this the price of your map?"

Cristoforo hooted. "Ah. My brother's first customer."

Bartolome roared with celebration. He rolled up the map and handed it to Giovanni. "Sold. You have fine taste."

The Colombo boys raced out, calling to Signor Fallio that they would stop by again soon. Signor Fallio settled back in his chair and smiled. "The Colombo boys share your dream, Giovanni. Their father weaves cloth and wants his sons to be in his business. But he, I think, will be disappointed. His boys want to captain ships and steer them to places no man has sailed."

Giovanni moved to the open doorway. He looked after Cristoforo Colombo as he ran down the street, and made a promise to himself that he would be the first—not Colombo—to go on an adventure into the Ocean Sea.

That night, in the small room that was used for cooking, eating, and his mother's stitching, Signora Caboto served anchovies and *baccala*, a soup made of salted codfish, olives, and dried toma-toes. "I added our last potatoes tonight, because it is the New Year and my boys are growing so big." She kissed the top of Piero's head but her serious eyes met her husband's. Giovanni noticed the look and wondered what secret his parents shared. He waited, hoping he would find out. Patiently, he watched his mother pour a Ligurian wine, diluting it with water for himself and Piero. She bowed her head and said the family grace, asking for the Holy Father to shine his kindness on them and watch over them. Giovanni saw another look pass between his parents. It was unusual for his father to be so quiet.

Piero bubbled over with news of their stop at the Fallio bookstore and Fra Mauro's new map of the world. "There is even a land of green on it."

"It is called Greenland," Giovanni corrected him. "Signor Fallio told us a Viking named Erik the Red discovered it when he had to flee a very snow-filled Iceland because he murdered someone."

Signora Caboto frowned and looked at her husband. "Are these proper stories for young boys?"

"It is history and a reason for new geography and naviga-tion," Giovanni said, defending Signor Fallio. "That is the most interesting part."

Piero continued, "Don't worry, Mamma, the Garden of Eden is drawn on it too."

"God's first garden." She crossed herself. "And we have other things to talk about."

Giovanni saw his parents' eyes meet again. What were they holding back?

Signor Caboto put down his spoon and pushed back his chair. "Sons, I have shared very important news with your mother and now I'll discuss it with you."

Signora Caboto nodded. "God has given us an opportunity."

Giovanni knew his mother thought all flowed from God. Not so for Signor Caboto. He believed in hard work. Giovanni wondered if they both were right.

"An aged merchant has offered me an arrangement. The Cabotos will take over his interests in his successful business after I'm acquainted with his most deep-pocketed clients. This merchant also has contacts with traders of goods that can expand our specialties . . ."

"You could consider cow nuts, Papà." Giovanni added.

Signor Caboto raised his hand, did not want to be interrupted. ". . . such as rugs and pearls that fetch high prices. This merchant's concern is in Venice."

"Venice, Papà?" Giovanni was stunned.

"*Sì*, Gio," Signor Caboto said. "The family will move to Venice."

"But Genoa was at war with them, Papà," Giovanni said.

Signor Caboto shook his head. "That is the past and we live today and must look to the future. It is time for us to think of our best interests. The Republic of Venice is the richest port in Western Europe, closer to the Silk Road and the trading posts in the Mediterranean. For a man who wants a fine future for his family, this is all very good. I have asked your mother to pack our belongings. We will leave after the next Sabbath."

Piero's eyes filled with tears. "But Papà, this is our home."

Signora Caboto opened her arms and Piero climbed onto her lap. She whispered in his ear, "Piero. Wherever our family is together is home."

Signor Caboto turned to his older son. "Gio?"

Giovanni felt an excitement well up inside him. "Papà,

Venice is the birthplace of Marco Polo. It is where the Fra Mauro map is. It will be a great adventure."

Part Two: Venice

Chapter Two

As the calendar turned to February, Giovanni and his family crossed the border into the Most Serene Republic of Venice. After traveling overland more than two hundred miles, they left their rented carriage in the small town of Jesolo in the northern part of the Republic and boarded a flat-bottomed transport ferry made of oak; it had a single mast and square-rigged sail. The salty air of the Adriatic Sea was warm and sweet. Giovanni lifted his face to feel the breeze and the winter sun; he imagined he was on his way to Constantinople or Baghdad or Mecca.

Giovanni's mother held tight to the rail of the sturdy ferry. "I prefer solid earth below my feet, my husband."

Signor Caboto's voice was calming. "Wife, I'm here by your side. The passage will be calm today, the wind steady."

Giovanni knew his mother did not like to be on the water. Her brother had been lost at sea when she very young, and her fear was rooted in a sadness that she rarely talked about. He tried to distract her. "Mamma, I read there are over one hundred islands that make up Venice. It's sometimes called the Floating City."

Signora Caboto groaned and laughed, not sure this was good news. "Ah, a floating city."

"You will be happy, my wife," Signor Caboto said. "A hundred thousand people live there just fine."

Piero hugged his mother. "Gio says there will be lots of new kinds of fish to eat."

"And it will be warmer than Genoa," Giovanni added. "You like warm air, Mamma."

The sail on the barge filled with a sudden wind and Giovanni spotted the outline of islands on the horizon. "Look, we're almost there!"

The ferry sailed into a wharf in the Cannaregio district. The family climbed into a smaller rowboat, this one manned by two oarsmen. They ventured down a dark canal; the buildings on each side were close to the water, causing the narrow canal to be in constant shadow. Signor Caboto told them that canals were used as streets in Venice, and that citizens hopped from boats to streets whenever they wanted to move around the city. Signora Caboto shivered and frowned, looking at the water lapping at the doors of the buildings. "I heard there are times when there's not an inch of dry ground in Venice."

"Rain can cause the canals to overflow. That is true," Signor Caboto said. "But the city has been here for hundreds of years. Everything returns to its proper place."

Signora Caboto put on a stolid face. "I'm sure I will get used to it."

The tight avenue of water soon fed into Venice's Grand Canal and Giovanni gasped at its bright, bustling festival of color. Seagulls sailed high above their heads. There were long narrow boats painted in gold, pink, and green floating past carrying women and men in vibrant silk clothing edged with fur. Pastel-painted palazzos and storefronts seemed to rise out of the water. Musicians stood in some of the narrow boats, strumming guitars and singing Venetian ballads. Giovanni thought of Genoa, its duller grays and browns and dark, cold alleyways. On this day in February, Venice was the most exciting place he had ever seen.

The family disembarked at Campo San Silvestro, one of the city's squares. It was filled with market stalls set near the water's edge; fishermen sold baskets of fish, and bakers, wine-sellers, and butchers hawked their products. The citizens, in high spirits, seemed to glide across the *campo*, waving to each other; the timbre of the conversations was light and teasing as they tasted breads and olives and wine.

Signora Caboto sighed with relief when she set foot on the stones of the *campo*. Two violinists played next to the fountain. Children ran, playing tag. Giovanni helped unload their belongings onto a laborer's cart. He walked next to his father as the cart was pulled by the strong laborer.

"Father, Piero and I can push the cart," Giovanni said.

His father leaned down to him. "Gio, you must remember, a merchant must make a good impression. Looking successful will help people trust you. That is why I have arranged for us to move into a home in this *campo*—it is a very respectable address."

They moved through an archway to a small iron gate. Ahead was a compact two-story building with a bright green door and flowerboxes at the low windows. Giovanni saw his mother take it in, a smile on her lips. "Very nice, my husband."

The door opened and a small, round woman, old enough to be Signora Caboto's mother, stood in the doorway, drying her hands on a cotton towel. Her face was sweet and her eyes kind.

"Wife, this is Signora Ceci. She lives nearby and will help you make this house our home."

Signora Caboto now beamed. She looked at her husband, eyes glowing with gratitude for his thoughtfulness. "Shall we go inside?"

Giovanni noticed their new neighbors watching as his father led his mother inside. They looked impressed.

Signora Caboto happily settled in with the help of the aged Ceci. Giovanni and Piero were soon heading out with their father to explore the narrow stone streets and canals. As Piero danced near the window of a bakery, Signor Caboto put his hand on Giovanni's shoulder. "Gio, it is important for the family to make good with this venture. Going backwards, back to Genoa, is not what we want to do."

"Yes, Papà."

"You are old enough now to understand and be at my side. Let us go and find our store."

Piero pointed at the buildings rising from the water. "Papà, how do they build stone buildings on top of the water?"

"They are built on top of wooden platforms," Signor Caboto explained. "The platforms are supported by special pilings made of the strongest timber and driven into the earth, deep below the water."

Giovanni asked, "But doesn't the wood rot in the water?"

Piero sidled up to Giovanni's side. "And fall into the water and float?"

"This is the story I have been told," Signor Caboto said. "About two hundred years ago, a great sickness—a plague called the Black Death—spread over many places in Europe. People could get sick by just breathing the air near those that were infected."

"Black Death, Papà?" Piero's eyes went wide. He took his father's hand, wanting to hear every world but nervous about the details.

Signor Caboto continued. "It caused many to leave their homes in Eastern Europe and head toward the sea, where they thought the air and winds would be cleaner, fresher. Some of the people were from places like Slovenia and Croatia and they ended up in Venice. Here, they were blessed with good health. To thank the Lord, they arranged for the strongest wood from their home countries to be brought to Venice so they could build the Santa Maria della Salute Church. It took many thousands of wooden pilings, and the grateful foreigners pounded them into Venice's shallow lagoons. These people knew when their wood was submerged in saltwater and did not come in contact with the air, it would petrify and become rugged and almost as hard as stone. The Venetians who had lived in the city for a long time took notice and soon wanted to use this wood for their homes and businesses. It has made for a strong city." He looked around. "Venice is not going to wash away."

Signor Caboto waved to one of the colorful long boats; he wanted to hire it to take them south on the canal to the Rialto *sestiere*.

"The language is different, Papà. Some of it sounds strange," Giovanni said.

"*Sì*. Even though we're still on the Italian Peninsula, the Venetian tongue is a bit different. You must listen to the people around us, hear the pronunciations, and learn to speak as a Venetian as soon as possible. To be prosperous, our family must be seen as Venetians."

One of the long narrow boats, painted golden yellow, glided up to the dock. The oarsman, dressed in a yellow tunic and cloak and burgundy-colored leggings, stood at one end, using the oar to steady the boat.

"Are we going to get into this, Papà?"

"Sì, Piero, be careful . . ."

But Piero sprung onto the boat, lost his balance, and landed on his backside on the boat's flat bottom. Giggling, he apologized to the oarsman, who looked down his nose at Piero. "You don't pounce into a gondola. You must step lightly."

Giovanni sat on a low bench in the narrow boat. "This is called a gondola? And why do you only use one oar? Why do you steer while standing?" Giovanni's questions piled on one another.

The oarsman eyed him, assessing the young passenger. "You are not Venetian."

"We're from Genoa." Giovanni looked apologetically at his father; they had already been found out.

"You wouldn't use a boat like this in the Genoa waters," the oarsman said. "Genoese waters are too open, too rough. Gondolas are made for Venice. Why do I stand? Because the sandbars in the canals constantly shift, I have to be able to see where they are so I do not run aground."

Their gondola floated past a robin's-egg-blue gondola full of ladies whose hair was piled high on their heads and dotted with feathers and jewels. Giovanni thought their faces looked painted—blue on their eyelids, pink circles on their cheeks, red on their lips. Their fur shawls barely covered their brightly colored gowns that were cut low and adorned with ruffled lace on the bodice and sleeves. Their skirts were flounced and trimmed to show their legs in white and gold stockings and their high-soled shoes were painted in bright stripes. The ladies called out, singing and fluttering their fans. Piero's mouth was agape. "Papà, those ladies look like the clowns from the circus."

The gondolier laughed. "Don't let them hear you say that."

"Keep your eyes forward, my sons," Signor Caboto admonished.

But Giovanni, struck by the gaiety and freedom of the ladies, continued to stare. Women in Genoa did not act like this, and his mother did not act like this. He watched their gondola veer off towards the dock of a pastel-colored palazzo.

"You're tourists?"

Giovanni brought his attention back to the gondolier. "We're new citizens."

"If you're new here, maybe you don't know it takes fifteen years to call yourself a citizen in Venice. You have to earn it."

Giovanni looked at his father. "Fifteen years, Papà? What does that mean?"

Signor Caboto's face was set. "It means we can work here, belong to the merchant guild at a very low stature, and make our way. We will pay taxes, but we cannot vote or have a say in city matters. For fifteen years."

Giovanni was taken aback. "But Papà . . ."

"Our family business will prosper, Gio. And in fifteen years, it will be yours and Piero's. We are doing this for our family's future. For you boys."

Giovanni felt the tightening in his stomach. His father's

expectations were so clear and Giovanni did not want to disappoint. But what if he didn't take over the family business? What if, one day, he walked up a gangplank and sailed to Jaffa?

The gondola glided to a pier in the Rialto neighborhood. Signor Caboto paid the oarsman and they stepped onto the dock. "Sons, our store is located in this neighborhood, near the gold and silver merchants and the rug and spice merchants. It will be the advantageous location."

They passed storefronts of craftsmen who produced fine fabrics—the silks, damasks, and satins for Venice's wealthy residents and also for export. They passed storehouses fragrant with the exotic scents of the Orient, stores full of goods piled high waiting for the ships that would take them to the markets in the East or to merchants and clients in Portugal, Genoa, or England.

They reached a small *campo*. Pigeons strutted on the stones. Piero chased them, laughing as the birds waited until he was only a foot away before taking to the sky.

Signor Caboto stopped in front of a small storefront. "Gio, the Chabotto Trading Company is here."

Giovanni looked at the sign painted on the door.

"Chabotto?" Giovanni was confused. His father was pronouncing their name in a new way.

Signor Caboto put his arm around Giovanni's shoulders. "It is the Venetian way to write and pronounce our name. Your name, in Venetian, translates to Zuan."

"So now I am Zuan?"

"*Sì*. We are now the family Chabotto. Here in Venice, you are Zuan Chabotto."

Chapter Three

Over the next year, Giovanni kept busy at the wharf, unloading goods and helping his father in the storehouse. He also delivered goods from Chabotto Trading and explored the tangle that was Venice, with its many canals, stone streets, and hard-packed dirt alleyways. He knew all the various *campi* where market stalls stood and where parades, public meetings, and impromptu musical concerts were held. He knew the locations of the shops of the shoemakers, tanners, woolworkers, painters, and gold and silver beaters that filled the narrow streets off the *campi*. He knew the meeting halls of guilds—the bankers, the merchants, the doctors and apothecaries, the leather workers and other craft guilds. Few bridges connected the small islands that made up the city; many were nothing more than floating planks of wood tied to stakes on either side of a narrow canal. The family had invested in a small rowboat and Giovanni painted it sea-green. He became the family's helmsman, doing errands for his mother and taking Piero to his small school in the morning. On the way to school, they passed near the Convent of San Lorenzo and waved to the nuns at work in the vegetable gardens. The convent's cemetery held the remains of Marco Polo; when they passed it, the brothers took their hats off in respect.

Soon after they arrived in Venice, Giovanni had found his way to the doge's palace. He had asked the guards if the Fra Mauro map of the world was on display. The answer was yes. He asked if he would be allowed to see it. The answer was no and the guards' assessment of Giovanni's less-than-noble attire made the reason evident. Disappointed, he sat on edge of a nearby fountain and watched politicos, leaders of the guilds, friends of the doge, and the sons of nobles with their tutors, all in fine boots and gloves and velvet hats, enter. He knew he could never sneak in by blending with those sons of the wealthy.

But he wanted to see that map. He had sighed, wondering when—and how—that day would come.

A week before Christmas, almost a full year after arriving in Venice, rain fell in a constant drizzle. Giovanni was on his way home after delivering goods from Chabotto Trading. He pulled his wool cap lower on his ears, bent his head, and tucked his nose into his scarf. He grabbed his gloves from his pocket and headed back to the canal where the family rowboat was moored. Suddenly, a bevy of wild cats darted out. Giovanni dropped his gloves and lurched to the side to let the cats—and the lean stray dog yapping after them—speed by. As he picked up his gloves, he found himself looking down a narrow, cropped alley. A sign that read *Charts* swung in the air next to a low door.

Giovanni peered through the dirt-crusted window. The shop looked like it was one square room, a path cleared in its middle. A small iron stove in a corner held a flicker of flame. A man with a chiseled, square jaw and sandy hair and short beard, wearing a worn sailor's shirt and a thick, moth-eaten coat, sat behind a lone desk. An imposing, broad-shouldered man sat opposite him, his brocaded silk vest bright under a long frockcoat festooned with gleaming buttons. A sea captain's tri-cornered hat rested on a table nearby. Giovanni watched the two pore over a map. The sea captain's thick finger landed on a point on the map. The men nodded. A particular spot seemed to have been identified, and the sea captain clapped his hands sharply, signifying he was pleased. He reached for his hat and headed for the door. Giovanni slipped to the side of the building, out of sight, and watched the sea captain stride down the alleyway toward the *campo*.

"You can come in." The words were shouted from inside the shop. "I see you there."

Startled, Giovanni bent his head to peek into the window again. The man, who seemed to be in his late twenties even though he had bags under his tired eyes, motioned to him. Giovanni gave his apology. "I'm sorry, Signor, I don't have money to buy a map."

"Come in. Don't stand in the rain."

Giovanni stepped inside and shut the door. The air inside was toasty, filled with the scent of books bound in leather and the wood burning in the stove. "Thank you, Signor."

"Name's Rizo. Don't need the signor. I'm just a rigger—well, I used to be—climbing up masts and setting sails." His eyes darkened for a moment. "But not the same able-bodied sailor anymore."

Rizo turned his wooden chair to the side and rolled it out into the small open space. Giovanni saw that two large iron wheels had been attached to it. He took in Rizo's wide shoulders and intense blue eyes, and also noticed the rough wool blanket

33

over his lap that did not disguise the fact that Rizo's two lower limbs were missing.

Rizo saw Giovanni's stare. "Sea monster took 'em for his lunch."

"Your legs?" Giovanni said.

"Ain't seen 'em for three years."

"My little brother believes sea monsters exist."

Rizo sensed Giovanni's curiosity went beyond hearing macabre horror stories. "You don't?"

Giovanni was serious. "Did you see the monster?"

"It happened during a storm. Might've seen the monster's maw but the rain was thick and cold. Like sleet in my eyes. So, didn't get a good look."

Giovanni was disappointed. "I haven't talked to one sailor who has actually seen a sea monster."

"Ah. Seeing 'em is one thing. Hearing them another. We can hear 'em. Over the screech of the creaking wet rails and flapping sails on the spars, over the crack of a broken mast. There's the sea monster's wail." Rizo, a glint of humor in his eyes, shrugged. "But then that wail might be coming from the sailor next to me, calling to his mamma to save him."

Giovanni tipped his head, looked more closely at Rizo. "You don't believe in sea monsters either."

Rizo breathed out, as if he were glad to give up the tall tale. "Fact is, the terrifying wind broke the mast and it fell on my legs. That mast is a full-sized, very heavy tree trunk, if you didn't know. But the truth is just not as good a story."

"The mast cut through your flesh? And your bones too?"

"The ship's carpenter did the final cut. He's the surgeon when he has to be. When my legs turned green and tripled in size 'cause they were full of pus, he said he had to get rid of the poison. The legs had to go or the whole of me would go."

"I read that's called gangrene."

Rizo raised his eyebrows. "You like facts more than myth, young man."

"Are your maps fact or myth?"

Rizo chuckled. "I like the truth, just like you. What's your name?"

"Gio . . . I mean, Zuan Chabotto."

Rizo wheeled his rolling chair back behind his desk. "I specialize in charts. I find them more interesting than maps." Rizo pointed to a map on the wall of the shop. "Maps give you an overview of a place. But the chart . . ." He pointed to a chart on his desk. "This is what the mariner needs. Charts help you get somewhere—give you specifics—step by step, sometimes. They're working documents. You can identify your starting position and mark where you want to go, draw the lines for latitudes . . ." He tapped the chart where the lines were drawn. "Those are the lines east to west. The north-south lines—can't get as precise, information is spotty there. So, I add coordinates for navigating using the stars. That helps."

Giovanni moved closer to the chart to get a better look. "Did you learn where everything is—the islands, bays, rocks, and inlets—when you were a sailor?"

"And from others sailors. Their diaries, if they're lucky enough to know how to read and write. Sea captains will bring in their log books and I'll update charts for them, document where there are deep enough bays for harbors or shallow enough to anchor—or flat beaches for resting." He showed Giovanni a drawing of a tree. "I draw pictures of fruit and trees and animals where it's known the ship's crew can hunt and forage for food. Charts help the sea captain stay the course. Or sometimes, if he studies 'em, might find him a shorter route."

"I thought ship's logs were secret."

"Captains know I'm good at keeping secrets. And the sailors who want to be captains one day trust me too. They know how important it is to have your own charts. A captain without charts is no good to anyone."

"Could you teach me how to make a chart?"

Rizo snorted and rubbed his bearded chin. He was clearly taken by surprise. Finally, he said, "Why would I do that?"

Giovanni looked around at the small shop, at the piles of books and pamphlets. At the unwashed pottery with food caked on it. The dust. The dirty windows. The cot at the back of the shop with thin blankets tossed over it. "I could help you here. Run errands for you. Would that be a good exchange?"

Piero, chewing on a piece of dried beef, pointed at the wall of the bedroom he and Giovanni shared. "This one's better than the one you did last month. Signor Fallio might think it's okay."

Giovanni and Piero gazed at the charts tacked to the walls. Giovanni said, "Rizo says I'm getting better."

Piero used his teeth to tear into another piece of dried beef. "Did you read Fallio's letter from Genoa? He wanted to know if we'd seen the Fra Mauro map yet."

"I'll write. Tell him I'm still working on it." Giovanni was interested in Piero's opinion. "Why do you think that one is better than the other?"

"More places to stop for food." Piero smacked his lips,

tasting the last of the salt of his chew. "Shows where to get fruit and nuts and lots of fish."

Giovanni laughed. "All you think about is food." He tossed a small ball at Piero. It was filled with sand and strips of cloth; they used it to practice their football skills. Piero ducked and laughed, scrambled over the low bed that they shared, and picked up the ball. He kicked it up in the air with his knee, aiming it back at Giovanni. Piero hadn't lost his chubbiness, but he was getting taller and his kicks were usually right on target. Giovanni deflected the ball with his shoulder just as the door opened. The ball was headed right toward Signor Caboto's unprepared face. "Papà! Watch out! Catch!"

Signor Caboto, thinking fast, caught the ball. The boys breathed easier. Their father said, "Your mother and Signora Ceci have supper on the table." He looked at Giovanni's charts. "I see you continue to challenge yourself."

"Yes, Papà." Giovanni answered.

His father pressed, "For what purpose? Our goods come to us, we unload and sell them." Signor Caboto tossed the ball to Piero and bid them to hurry to the dining room.

Piero tucked the ball onto a shelf. "You have to tell Papà."

Giovanni sighed. "Tell him what? That I'm now almost fifteen and others my age have already sailed on carracks and caravels to the great ports of the world? That I want to be on the ships too? I know what he will say."

Piero saw Giovanni's frustration. He looked to the map tacked on the wall above the doorway. "I like this one the best. It sends me dreaming."

"But that one's not even mine," Giovanni said. "It's that boy's map from Genoa. Bartolome Colombo. We met him and his brother in Signor Fallio's shop." He laughed. "You like it because there are sea monsters in it. You have to grow up, Piero. There are no such things."

"What do you know? No one's been out that far in the Ocean Sea, or if they have been out there, no one's come back to tell about it. I know you want to find out yourself, Gio. I know you'll figure out how to make that happen."

Work at Chabotto Trading fell into a routine. When his father went to a café in the mid-afternoon to meet with clients and traders, Giovanni would finish the shop's inventory and leave Piero, whose head was deep into the account books. Sometimes he would attend public lectures on navigation. He'd experience a familiar envy at seeing the nobles' sons with their tutors, knowing they spent much of their time learning history, languages, and other subjects he ached to learn. Most days he headed to Rizo's chart shop.

It was a day in February and Giovanni had arrived with a pile of vellum and bottles of ink. "What's the latest news?" Rizo's eyes were dark-rimmed because he had worked by candlelight through the night.

"The merchants on the wharf say the Muslim Turks continue to make things difficult," Giovanni said. "Higher tariffs, more looting. And Argos, in Greece, wants Venice's protection, for the Turks want their territory. There is also talk that Hungary may become our ally."

Rizo shook his head, gazed at the map on the wall. "What we need is for Persia to be on our side."

Giovanni organized the books Rizo had taken down from the shelves. "And a new route to the Far East."

Rizo rubbed his eyes and looked at the chart of North Africa on his desk. "Portugal may be the only one making headway. But they haven't reached the southern end of Africa yet and their plans of going around seem to be stalled."

Giovanni dusted a shelf. "What if there is no end to Africa?"

Rizo sighed. "Know your history, Gio. The Greeks wrote about rounding Africa thousands of years ago."

"Too bad they didn't chart it." Giovanni sat heavily onto the extra chair in the room. His shoulders slumped.

"Why so glum, Giovanni?"

"My father will never give me permission to sail. Because my mother is afraid for me and he doesn't want to upset her."

"I predict you will captain your own ship one day," Rizo said.

"But not if I never get the experience," Giovanni reminded him.

"We will make sure you're prepared, so once you are on a ship, you'll know more than a lot of sailors. I thought today we'd get you acquainted with using the compass rose."

"What's that?" Giovanni wondered.

"The compass rose is also called the mariner's compass. A sea captain uses it for orientation." Rizo pulled open a drawer in his desk and brought out pieces of vellum. "Here are drawings of how one works." Each piece of vellum had an intricate drawing on it. On the first was a four-pointed star; north was designated as the top, south at the bottommost point, east to the right, west to the left. Rizo moved to the next sheet of paper. This drawing had intermediate points marked between the main directions—northeast and southwest. "The more exact you can make your charts, the better," Rizo said. "Make sense?"

Giovanni nodded. The next piece of paper showed even more

exact markings such as north-northeast to the right of true north, and north northwest to the left of true north. The last drawing showed even more specific orientations. "There are thirty-two markings on a compass rose," said Rizo. "It's called that because a rose has a lot of petals and layers. Like this compass." Rizo showed Giovanni a metal compass with the magnetic needle and how it landed on the directional location of the chart shop.

"It's beautiful," Giovanni said.

Rizo took out a map of the Italian Peninsula and used a quill to trace the eastern coast. "Let's say you are sailing from Venice to Sicily, Gio. You'd head south in the Adriatic Sea, yes?"

"Of course, a captain would have his pilot steer south."

"But if you headed straight south you'd run aground in Ancora, so you have to sail south-southeast to pass it—and Foggia. Once past Foggia, you'd have to change course to southwest to go around the heel of our peninsula to get to the toe of Calabria. Continue true west and you'll find Sicily." He looked up at Giovanni. "You see the importance of breaking it down to more specific steerings?"

Giovanni pointed to the thin lines Rizo had drawn on the chart on his desk. "So, these are lines that will align with the directions on the compass rose?"

Rizo rubbed his eyes, stretched his arms. "Took me all night. I like to be as exact as I can. Let's see you put the compass markings onto this old chart of North Africa."

Giovanni bent to the task and concentrated. He copied the chart illuminating the coast near Cape Bojador on the northwestern bulge of Africa's landmass. Rizo watched as Giovanni worked. "One thing to remember. The earth is round, and our portolan charts are drawn on flat pieces of paper. Accuracy on a chart can only go so far. The sea captain must have other skills to be truly successful."

"What are they?" Giovanni asked.

"Experience. Judgment. Intuition."

Giovanni sighed. How was he going to get experience?

Chapter Four

"Gio, be careful with the flowers. Father Rodrigo notices if the petals are bent."

"Mamma, I'm being careful. The flowers are fine."

The family moved toward the church in Campo San Silvestro. The rains were pounding. Signor Caboto held a makeshift leather umbrella over his wife's head; it grew heavier with every step as the material became soaked with water. Giovanni and Piero wore wide-brimmed hats and heavy cloaks. Signora Caboto was happiest when she was walking with her family to church. She practically sang, "It's Easter, time of new beginnings."

Signor Caboto grumbled, "And the time of spring rains."

"The sun will shine on us soon, my husband. God always has a plan."

"Is God's plan to retrieve the ships lost in the storm?" Signor Caboto worried about losing his investment. "Let me know. I must tell my clients."

They entered the church. Its stone edifice kept out the rains but not the biting cold. Giovanni imagined the ships out in the storm, riding the high and mighty waves, the sailors scrambling, maybe even tying themselves to the masts or iron eyebolts that secured storage and equipment. Maybe the pilot, at the wheel, was straining against the elements. The captain could be shouting orders, using his charts to try to find safety. Giovanni felt his mother's elbow in his side. He had missed the priest's call for prayer, so he quickly moved to his knees and prayed for all sailors' safety. And a way to join them, even on dangerous waters.

Chabotto Trading was growing, but Signor Caboto chafed under the family's noncitizen status. He couldn't make major improvements to his storefront without permissions that were slow in coming. He could not approach certain nobles to interest them in his business, for they were connected to confraternities— these were like exclusive clubs of Venice—and he did not have access. He knew if there were to be any disputes regarding his wares, the jurists of Venice would most likely find in favor of the full citizen. Piero's early schooling would be finished soon and his younger son would not be allowed into any of the better confraternity schools that provided advanced education.

Days later, the rain had turned to a soft drizzle and Giovanni and his father were at the harbor. Signor Caboto was still worried about the possibility of lost ships. Giovanni caught up with sailors; he had been quick to learn the Venetian dialect and was adding Greek and Arabic words to his vocabulary. Finally, the sun claimed the skies. A cheer went up when several ships appeared in the distance. His father's mood lightened. "Gio, go to the market, and get your mother's favorite fish for supper."

"Yes, Papà."

Giovanni, breathing in the warmed air, raced towards the market. He joined a group of young football players near the

Campo San Marco and kicked a leather ball, scoring one of the first goals. As Giovanni stopped to catch his breath, he saw a cluster of young men his age with confraternity sashes over their cloaks following a tutor in a long, oxblood-colored robe.

Giovanni recognized Signor Penzo, Venice's noted scholar of geography and cosmography. His likeness was drawn on many of the pamphlets Giovanni organized at Rizo's chart shop—Penzo's eyes were large and deeply sunk and set above a hooked nose, his gray hair reached his shoulders, and his dark beard was peppered with silver. Giovanni waved goodbye to the football players and, at a distance, followed the students. They soon entered the school doors of the stately San Giovanni Evangelista, one of the most elite confraternities in Venice.

Giovanni longed to join the classroom, to listen to Signor Penzo. But he couldn't barge in; he knew he'd be turned away. Just then, he noticed a worker come out a side door, pail and broom in hand, and head toward a shed to the side of the courtyard. Giovanni rounded the corner of the building, and saw the door had been left slightly ajar. He slipped in and padded up the narrow staircase, trying not to make a sound. At the landing was a door on his right and on his left. He pushed one open—it was a storage space. He pushed the other door open, and saw it led to a balcony overlooking the lecture hall. Relishing his great luck, Giovanni slipped into the shadows. He could see Professor Penzo moving to the front of the room and the students, in their fine tunics, taking seats at long tables with inkwells, quill pens, and parchment at the ready.

The professor's assistant opened a large satchel and lifted out a sandglass, a piece of wood, a chart, an astrolabe, a compass, and an abacus. They were arranged on the long table.

"Students. What do these items have in common?"

Professor Penzo waited. No student raised his hand.

Giovanni wanted to call out that those items could all be used on a sea voyage. How could the students not see that?

Penzo continued, "These are instruments necessary for what I would like to call the European Age of Discovery." He paced in front of the class. "In the first century, after the birth of Christ, a Greek explorer named Hippalus found a route—over water and land—from Greece to the Red Sea and on to India. He wrote about it and the world was suddenly thought of differently. Larger. More expansive. Full of different ideas and different people. In addition, new trade routes were opened and this meant there were new pathways to knowledge and riches."

A few of the students straightened with interest. They had been raised to know the importance of riches.

Penzo tapped a tapered pointer on a map tacked on the wall. "And then there are the tales of Marco Polo, our native son, who helped to make maps more exact. And other explorers added to our knowledge. Let us talk about the age of discovery that we Europeans are now experiencing. Who is leading this new age?"

A round student, with puffy lips and pink cheeks, wearing a hat trimmed with feathers, waved his hand. "Venetians?"

Penzo shook his head. "Unfortunately, no." He paused. The students sullenly waited for him to inform them. Penzo formed another question. "Did you know the Portuguese developed excellent ship designs—like the caravel and a sturdier carrack—that can sail to windward through the rougher, more open seas?"

Some of the students yawned. Giovanni leaned forward, forgetting he should stay hidden. His foot banged against a copper spittoon, and it rumbled forward and pinged loudly against a column. Students turned and looked up. Giovanni, heart pounding, slipped behind a column, hoping he was out of sight.

Penzo continued. "Approximately one hundred years ago, King Alfonso IV of Portugal sent out expeditions that reached the Canary Islands, off the coast of North Africa. These islands were claimed for Portugal. However, there was a dispute, for the Genoese had sailed to the Canaries previously. But the Portuguese were more organized and they arranged for settlers to build homes and ports on the islands. They invested there, and felt their rights were stronger. A rivalry began." He looked at the students. "Who do you think should have the harboring and trading rights to these islands?"

An interested student called out, "The republic—or kingdom—that got there first?"

Giovanni peered out from behind the column to see a student who sat slightly away from the others. His long hair was tied back with a dark ribbon, like a pirate. Signor Penzo walked over to the young man. "What is your name?"

"Fernando di Sera, Professor."

Giovanni recognized the name. It belonged to one of the shipbuilding families in Venice.

"Fernando di Sera," Penzo continued. "What about the kingdom—or republic—that spent more time, energy, and money in the territory and built ports and villages? Or is there a third option? What about any natives on the land that have lived there for generations? Even if the military and intellectual might of a more advanced kingdom has invaded them, is their land free for the taking?"

Fernando leaned back, not sure. "What do you think, Professor?"

Penzo smiled. "I don't give answers. Only questions." Penzo paced again. "In the last five decades, Portugal has sailed to—and claimed—lands on the western coast of Africa. Where they eventually found natives, with gold rings in their noses. So, what did the Portuguese begin to look for?"

"Gold," the students responded.

Penzo took a small leather bag from his satchel and poured small glittery pellets onto a ceramic plate. Several students stood, wanting to get a better look at the raw gold, the metal that was so coveted by all Europeans.

"And did they find gold?" asked the round-faced, pink-cheeked student.

"Name?"

"Benito Gravi, sir."

Penzo continued. "Well, young Gravi, the source of gold—used in the nose rings—was not found. Explorers had to be content with collecting plants and roots to make spices to sell and export. And then capturing pagan slaves to be brought back to Portugal for sale. By 1434, the Portuguese had reached as far as Cape Bojador and found a great and formidable desert that seemed to stretch forever. That stopped them for years for they wondered if the rest of Africa was all desert. Finally, an explorer pushed further south, the desert ended, and sailors saw seals on the rocks along the coastline. These seals were slaughtered for their oil and their skins. More profits."

"But did they find gold?" Several students demanded the answer.

Penzo was in no hurry to answer that question. "After more than a hundred miles, the mouth of a river was found. Along its trajectory, they found elephants. Which could be taken for what?"

"Their tusks. For ivory. But what about the gold?" The students were impatient.

Finally, Penzo gave them the information. "Inland, near the river, the Portuguese found loose gold on the ground and a few strains of dull yellow pebbles in the hills. They quickly planted the Portuguese flag. They left soldiers to explore the hills and defend their claim. Other kingdoms were envious."

Fernando raised his hand. "But no other kingdom had risked their own expeditions. So their envy is worthless."

"But still, the Portuguese can't claim everything." Pink-cheeked Gravi pouted, looking like he found this very unfair.

"For now, they do." Penzo smiled, leaning back against the table. "The Portuguese continue to search on the river, and who knows where large quantities of gold can be?" Penzo took a breath. "Another question for you. Who here is the most competitive at football? Who likes to kick in the winning score?"

The students, almost in unison, said, "Silvio."

"Ah. Who is this Silvio?" Penzo asked.

A student, the only one with a fox fur lining his cloak, raised his hand. "Silvio Balbi, Professor." His voice dripped with entitlement, as if his participation in the class was a favor to the professor.

"Silvio Balbi, would you compete with the Portuguese?"

Silvio shrugged. "I don't want to spend time on stinky ships."

The others laughed.

"Silvio," Penzo continued. "The coffers of Portugal could fill with gold. But there are other advantages. We must remember that some explorers journey for riches, and others journey for knowledge." Penzo looked out at the group. "What is of most importance?"

Silvio crossed his arms. "Knowledge doesn't provide a fine

home or costumes for the Venetian balls. Or fine food. I like fine food."

Another round of laughter.

"What do you think, Professor?" Fernando asked.

Penzo dipped his head to the side, wanting to get his message clear. "Remember, students. My job is to urge you to think for yourselves."

Silvio Balbi's thin mouth pursed, and he rolled his eyes and yawned.

Suddenly, Giovanni heard footsteps on the staircase. He realized he had left the door to the balcony open. He heard the banging of a pail. He flattened his lanky body against a wall.

Signor Penzo was speaking. "Next class, we will talk about navigation. How it is built on science—and leaps of faith."

Giovanni heard the storage door close and the worker descend the staircase. He waited a moment and quickly slipped out. At the bottom of the stairs, he looked outside. No sign of the worker. No sign of anyone. He raced across the courtyard. His heart was soaring. The lecture had given him much to think about. How he wished to be able to talk to the professor. He reached the *campo* and waited. But when the group came into view, he saw Professor Penzo deep in conversation with the student named Fernando and the other students were walking behind them.

Giovanni slipped off to the market to get the salted cod for his mother's *baccala* soup.

By August of 1465, Chabotto Trading had added rugs from Arabia and pearls from Asia to its products. Giovanni had learned to talk to the foreign merchants and check the undersides of the rugs for signs of shoddy construction and expert dyeing of the wool. He and Piero weighed and sorted the pearls according to size and shape. Piero made columns of the numbers; his eyes gleamed for he enjoyed the challenge.

A warm day had settled on Venice, and the sky was soft blue, not a cloud in sight. Signor Caboto called out, "Gio, I need a keen eye here, son."

Giovanni saw his father with a well-known antiquity trader. The trader had just come off a large ship and he carried a long, narrow object wrapped in canvas under his arm.

"It has arrived, Signor Chabotto," said the dignified trader.

Giovanni was intrigued. "What is it, Papà?"

"An antique, procured at the request of Signor Balbi, a man who has the doge's ear. He lives in the Castello and is anxiously waiting for it." Signor Caboto motioned to the object. "We must inspect it before it is accepted, Signor Rengio, as you know."

The eyes of Giovanni and Signor Caboto were riveted on the unwrapping of the canvas. A plain, unpolished wooden box was revealed. Giovanni was perplexed. This did not look to be of much worth.

Rengio lifted off the top of the box. Inside was a narrow ebony container, highly polished and decorated with ivory and jade. Giovanni whistled in appreciation.

"Ah, but this is not the real treasure." Rengio smiled and pressed an invisible clasp and the ebony holder sprung open. Giovanni's eyes grew wide.

Moments later, Giovanni raced on a path near the Grand Canal, searching for a boat to hire. The wooden box was in a leather pouch secured across his body. The small family rowboat could not be relied on to make it through the more open waters to the Castello and his father had given him coins to hire a transport. When Giovanni reached the docks, his heart sank. It seemed as if the warm day had invited all of Venice to take to the canal. The waters were crowded with gondolas, batellas, light and speedy carolinas, skiffs, and larger sailboats. Some of the boats ferried nobles conducting business under the pleasant sun. Married women and chaperones glided by in covered gondolas. Painted courtesans, showing off their latest fashions, flirted from brightly festooned open boats. Giovanni saw poets spouting verses. Musicians played mandolins and nodded their appreciation of coins tossed into their gondolas. Frustrated, he scanned the docks; not one boat was available for hire. He noticed a fisherman in a small skiff organizing his catch. He pushed his way through to him and called out to get his attention. "Hello. It appears you've completed your catch for the day."

"What is it to you?" The fisherman, not much older than Giovanni, wore a threadbare green cloth hat. He did not even look up.

Giovanni pressed. "I need transport to the Castello."

"I'm a fisherman, not a ferryman. About to take my fish to market."

"And then?"

"Then my day becomes my own." The young fisherman finished rolling his net. He deposited it in the stern of the boat.

Giovanni saw the name *Felicita* written on the boat. He wanted to ingratiate himself. "You named your boat after Saint Felicita?"

"The saint known to bring happiness and luck. What every fisherman needs."

Giovanni held out his palm, and silver flashed under the sun. "I have coins to hire your happiness and luck. Just as far as the chapel of Francesco della Vigna."

The fisherman's green eyes were on the coins. "You'll pay that much?"

"It's important."

"What's your name?"

"Zuan. Of the respected merchant Chabotto family."

"I'm Carlo, of a lowly fisherman family." Carlo laughed in a way that sounded like a bark of glee. He pocketed the coins and moved his spear and bamboo rod to one side. "Market first."

Giovanni, tucking the leather pouch carefully under his arm, leapt into the skiff before Carlo could change his mind. He sat on an overturned shackle box near the square bow, noticing baskets filled with silver-skinned sea bass. Peering out from under a damp cloth, a dozen cuttlefish, with their strange eyes, lay motionless. "Looks like a good catch," Giovanni said.

Carlo fit his oars into their holds. He rowed cross-handed, his rhythm steady. "It's my job. It was my father's job. And my grandfather's before my father's. It's what I do."

Giovanni eyed the sail that was low on the mast. "Shall we raise the sail to go faster?"

"Not in the narrow canals. Have to control the speed."

Giovanni nodded. "My family has a rowboat. I'd like a boat with a sail."

"It became mine when my father died."

Giovanni heard the sadness in his voice. "I am sorry for you."

Carlo shrugged. "I take care of my mother now." He looked over his shoulder. They were nearing the marketplace. Giovanni saw the stalls hung with fresh and dried meats, peppers, and artichokes. Carlo steered the skiff close to the small pier and tied a sailor's hitch to a pollard to keep the boat in place. He gave a loud whistle. A fishmonger and his two muscled sons, all wearing long aprons and linen caps, strode towards them. Carlo handed off his bounty and they grunted and lumbered back to their market stall.

Carlo turned to Giovanni, grinned. "My cousins. Don't talk much." He sat at the oars. "And now, I'll earn your coins. Off to Castello."

Moments later, the skiff entered the Grand Canal. When they passed the doge's palace, Carlo reached forward to release the main halyard and raise the sail. The winds caught quickly in the rugged sailcloth and Giovanni thrilled at the added energy. "This is yar!" He yelled. Carlos grinned too and as they raced past the marshlands that, at low tide, formed the southwest line of the city, both young men hooted with exuberance, feeling the freedom that comes with the wind on one's back.

Unlike his cousins, Carlo liked to talk. As they moved through the water, he told Giovanni of digging into shallow sand to find the best green-shelled shrimp, and of the importance of the fisherman's net. "If you wait to catch one fish at a time, you'll never have enough for market and your family will starve. Each of us fishermen—we have our own spots. We don't poach into other's territories. I have my father's spot, the same spot his father had before. It's not large, but it's enough." Carlo pointed to a sandbar and shouted. "One day, I found a dolphin there. It got stuck here in low tide. I nudged it out with my oar till he could swim off!"

"A dolphin! I would like to see one close!" Giovanni scanned the waters and couldn't help but feel envious of Carlo and his adventures on the water.

"I swear the dolphin smiled at me. Big, silver–green fish smile!" Carlo's attention was now on the sail. He called out, "Mind your head. We're coming about." Giovanni bent, head to his knees as the sail swooshed over his head. Exhilaration filled him.

Carlo steered north and they passed the Porto Magna, the main gate of the Arsenale, where the large merchant ships were being built. Carlo waved towards the ships. "Biggest shipbuilding yard in the Adriatic. Did you know that?" A row of single-masted cogs was dwarfed by the larger carracks that were outfitted with double or triple masts. Giovanni admired the sleeker, more handsome caravels that were moored nearby.

"I want to travel on a caravel. They're the fastest," Giovanni said. "I want to go someplace. Some day."

Carlo shook his head. "Not me. I'll stay here. Venice is big enough for me. My fish would miss me." Carlo allowed the wind to sweep them into the rougher waters of the eastern edge of the city. Giovanni looked north. "Have you been to the island of Murano?"

"No reason to—can't fish there. It's a small island anyway. Not a lot of markets."

"Have you heard of Fra Mauro?" Giovanni asked. "He lives in a monastery on Murano."

"The mapmaker. Sure. He's famous."

"I've written letters to him, asking to meet him. But I never got a response."

"The Camaldolese monastery follows the teachings of a hermit saint—Saint Romuald. Hermits don't talk to people. Maybe don't even answer letters. It's all about solitude." Carlo laughed. "Why be in group of people if you don't talk, that's what I want to know."

"I promised someone in Genoa I'd try to meet Fra Mauro," Giovanni said. "And see his map of the world."

"Well, my new friend, it won't happen. Hermits don't see anyone."

A burst of wind filled the sail and the skiff raced forward. Giovanni and Carlo shouted with excitement, lifting their chins to feel the salt spray on their faces.

"I have something for Signor Balbi," Giovanni called out.

Giovanni assured Carlo his errand would be swiftly accomplished and Carlo agreed to wait. Giovanni had raced to the chapel of Francesco della Vigna and through the massive gates of the nearby Balbi palazzo. He'd stopped for a moment to catch his breath just as a young nobleman, glaring at him, moved out of the palazzo onto a wide terrace.

"Signor Balbi is my father." The young man's voice was high and supercilious.

Giovanni recognized him as one of the students in Signor Penzo's class. The one who suggested fine costumes were more important than gaining knowledge from explorations.

"I am Silvio, his eldest. I'll take whatever it is."

Giovanni knew he could not relinquish his duties. "Thank you, but my father, Zilio Chabotto, insists I deliver it in person."

Silvio looked at Giovanni's red, sweaty face. He almost sneered. "My father is busy."

The doors to the palazzo swung open and an imposing man with a sharply trimmed beard stepped out. Signor Balbi stood on the terrace. "Silvio? Who is this?"

"Only someone who delivers, father."

Giovanni bowed. "Zuan Chabotto, Signor Balbi. I'm from

Chabotto Trading. My father says you are most anxious for the arrival of your treasure."

Signor Balbi eyed the pouch under Giovanni's arm. "Bring it inside." He turned to his son. "Silvio, join us. You may find this of interest."

Silvio frowned. "I'm sure it will be edifying but there is a dog race I've planned to attend." His voice dripped with disinterest and he sauntered off.

Giovanni took off his cap and smoothed his dark hair. He followed the elegant Signor Balbi inside into a massive marble entryway. Servants hovered, ready to be set to task. The air smelled of lavender. Fine tapestries warmed the walls next to statues worthy of the doge's palace. Signor Balbi continued through thick oak doors into the library. Giovanni, close behind him, took in the fine furniture upholstered in soft leathers and silks, the full bookshelves, and the draperies that framed the windows. Giovanni thought of the plain walls of the Chabotto home, the thick shutters on small windows, and the family's main room that was used for cooking, dining, and comfortable gatherings around the fire at night. What does a family do with all this space?

A thin, dark-haired girl was nestled, nearly dwarfed, in a large corner chair, reading a book. She looked up. "What is it, Babbo?" She bolted out of the chair to join her father at a long library table. She did not look at Giovanni; her only interest was the mysterious box he set on the table.

Signor Balbi nodded to Giovanni. "Open it, please."

When Giovanni lifted the top of the rough wooden box and revealed the thin ebony case with its jade and ivory pattern, he heard the young girl sigh with delight.

"*È carina*," she whispered.

"This case holds something more spectacular," Giovanni said.

The girl pressed her hands together in anticipation.

Giovanni touched the hidden spring. The top of the ebony case lifted. An awed silence followed. Then Signor Balbi lifted the jewel-encrusted scabbard from the ebony box. The silver and gold gleamed. Rubies and emeralds sparkled. As he pulled the sword from the sheath, the sound was like a crack of lightning echoing in the room. The hammered blade glowed.

"Daughter, this is a scimitar. Used by a Mongol chief of Central Asia more than three hundred years ago."

The young girl leaned in, studying it. "Why is it curved?"

Giovanni knew the answer. "Scimitars were used to advantage in battles on horseback. The Mongol, while riding a horse, could slash at an enemy more easily than stab him. That is why the swords were curved."

Signor Balbi raised a cautionary hand. "Perhaps some information is not suitable to share with a young girl."

The girl sniffed. "Babbo, I have read of the Arabian Knights and their battles. And you promised you wouldn't keep things from me just because I'm a girl."

Signor Balbi kissed the top of his daughter's head. "Very well, *cara ragazza*."

"Signor, may I also add another bit of information?" Giovanni asked.

Signor Balbi, taking in this self-possessed young man, gave his permission. "Very well."

Giovanni pointed to the scimitar. "Some call it the sword of truth."

"Why?" The girl's eyes were bright.

Signor Balbi, admiring the intricately carved hilt of the weapon, said, "Because when battles are fought, it is often the truest heart that emerges victorious." He turned to Giovanni. "Do you believe that, young Chabotto?"

Giovanni replayed the words in his head. *The truest heart emerges victorious.* After a moment, he nodded. "I think that—I hope that is so, Signor."

Signor Balbi put the scimitar back into its scabbard and laid it on the table. "I'm most pleased. I'll give you a letter for your father." He crossed the room to a magnificent walnut desk, opened a drawer, and took out a piece of thick ivory-colored notepaper.

The girl looked up at Giovanni. "I'm reading a book now on China, about its temples."

"Not many girls are taught to read."

"My babbo thinks no one should be ignorant." Her words challenged, as if she expected an argument.

"How old are you?" Giovanni asked.

She tossed her hair. "How old are you?"

"I am fifteen."

"In five years, I'll be fifteen."

"So, you are also good with numbers," Giovanni observed.

"You sound disapproving. Like my brother. You don't think a girl should know these things."

"I do not think that."

"I'll have great adventures one day. Boys can't have all the fun." She picked up her book and flounced out of the room. She called back to her father, "Babbo, I want to know more about scimitars. I want to know everything. Please."

Signor Balbi laughed. "Very well, Mattea, we will discuss

Mongols and China and their military tactics later. I'll find you another book."

Giovanni watched Mattea skip up the massive staircase.

Signor Balbi chuckled, watching as a servant scrambled after his daughter. "She is my joy. Curiosity is a very strong virtue." He moved towards Giovanni, holding the note. "This contains my signature and instructions for payment to the Banco Medici on Calle Cavalli."

"Thank you, Signor Balbi. My father will be pleased that you are satisfied."

"And let him know the deliverer also impressed, for he had knowledge of the antiquity." Signor Balbi smiled. "Well done."

Giovanni's chest swelled with pride. He nodded his head in respect, and followed a servant out of the palazzo. As he jogged towards the end of the property, he couldn't stop thinking of the words of the young girl named Mattea, who seemed so sure of her future. Sure of the adventures she would have one day.

Chapter Five

In the deep heat of a late summer day, Giovanni again scampered up the back stairs of the San Giovanni Evangelista confraternity. He'd come to every lecture he could, sometimes holding his breath to remain undetected. Now he took his place behind a column in the balcony. He saw the students below; among the regulars were the round-faced Benito Gravi, Fernando di Sera with his hair pulled back like a pirate's, and the disagreeable Silvio Balbi. Professor Penzo began his lecture. "Navigation. Navigation is one of the greatest scientific challenges of our time."

Only a few students used their quills and ink to scratch notes on their parchments. Giovanni paid close attention for he always had to write his notes in his diary from memory late at night under candlelight.

Signor Penzo continued. "Let us start with a simple aspect. Dead reckoning. Who knows what it is?"

Fernando raised his hand. "It's calculating the swiftness of the ship by using a knotted rope and a timing device, measuring the wind and currents. Dead reckoning is figuring out how the ship is moving so that it can be adjusted to head to a specific destination."

Silvio yawned. Gravi leaned back and closed his eyes.

Signor Penzo nodded. "Let's start with speed. The captain of a ship has procured a rope that is, let us say, one hundred feet long. He orders knots to be tied in the rope every six feet— the length between the wooden ribs of his ship. The captain has tied to one end of the rope a good-sized piece of dried wood that will float. The long, knotted rope is then coiled on deck so that it will easily release as the ship moves through the waters. When the sails are full, the captain orders a sailor to heave the log from the stern of the ship and let the rope flow out freely. When the sailor feels the first knot pass through his fingers, he shouts to another sailor, who turns a one-minute sandglass. Why one minute?"

Fernando rushed in, "That's one-sixtieth of an hour?"

Signor Penzo turned the one-minute sandglass on the instructor's table. The students watched as the sand trickled into the bottom compartment. "So, the first sailor continues to shout the number of knots that play out, and when the timings have been recorded, they calculate the speed of the ship in nautical miles per hour. That is why speed is referred to in knots."

Penzo continued. "The captain must also take into account the specifics of wind direction and currents. He must use skills in mathematics to calculate. I'm assuming you are all well-trained on your abacuses?"

Giovanni leaned forward, listening carefully. He wanted to understand the mathematics of dead reckoning. He thought of Piero and his ability with numbers and realized he'd have to work with him more closely. Signor Penzo pressed on. "The results are recorded in the ship's logbook—speed and time and direction. These calculations will be valuable information for the making of the captain's charts."

Giovanni thought of his time at Rizo's and was even more determined to better his skills. Signor Penzo paced. "However, dead reckoning, by its nature, can only be an estimate. That is why navigators also use the sun, the moon, and the stars to make their way."

After the lecture, Giovanni waited until the students and Signor Penzo filed out. After a few moments, he headed down the stairs and slipped out. He was not prepared to see four students waiting for him.

A thin student with a bobbing Adam's apple, wearing a bright orange coat, glared at him. Beside him was round-faced Gravi, Silvio Balbi, and Fernando di Sera. Gravi sneered, "I told you someone was hiding up there."

Silvio eyed Giovanni with a bored expression. "I've seen him around. Someplace. I don't know where."

Giovanni was relieved that Silvio did not recognize him as the person who delivered the sword to his father. Gravi clicked his tongue, his fat cheeks jiggling. "You can't sneak into our school. Maybe you're a spy."

Giovanni, who had decided to remain silent, heard himself blurt, "Spy?"

Gravi's eyes were like a lizard's—narrow slits. His voice was mean. "Other schools are jealous of us. And every confraternity has secrets."

Fernando's voice was low and reasonable. "Maybe he just wants to learn something, Gravi. Not like you."

"I'll be a banker, like my father. So will Trifulo." He patted the skinny student with the prominent Adam's apple. "What do we care about ships' logs and knots and stars?"

Trifulo shoved a finger into Giovanni's chest. "This is our school. Just stay out."

Gravi shoved Giovanni. "You hear that?"

Giovanni almost lost his footing. He wanted to push back, but he knew Gravi had numbers behind him: four against one.

"Come on, Gravi. No need for the assault," Fernando said.

"I say he got our message. Let's go," Silvio said and headed off. Gravi waddled after Silvio. The witless Trifulo followed.

Fernando hung back. "Don't waste your time worrying about them."

"Easy for you to say," Giovanni grumbled, tense.

"My name is Fernando." Fernando scratched his thin nose. "If you want to know, the one with the fattest flesh is Gravi. He's really afraid everyone will realize he's stupid. Trifulo, the one with the two-colored leggings, is ruled by his mother. She even decides what he wears every day." Fernando laughed. "And Silvio, he only thinks of himself. He won't give you another thought."

Giovanni snapped, "Why are you waiting around? Making sure I leave the school grounds?"

Fernando was in no hurry. "I want to know why you come to listen to the lectures."

Giovanni thought it was obvious. "Because, like you said, I want to learn."

Fernando nodded. "Signor Penzo is my favorite. Other lecturers talk more about kings and emperors. Politics."

Giovanni breathed out, his frustration high. "Navigation and geography and politics and rulers of the world are all connected."

"What do you mean?" Fernando asked, curious.

Giovanni realized that Fernando was actually waiting to hear his opinions. "Rulers are powerful because of their geography. Don't you think the doge of Venice is more powerful than the doge of the inland Modena or the Captain General of inland Mantua because Venice has water access and is a great port? We can have our own navy because of that. So our doge has more power. So it's evident that geography can bring power."

"I suppose that's true. Venice is considered the greatest power of the Italian Peninsula." Fernando was used to his friends talking about dog racing or the latest festivities or football games. Giovanni's interests were different.

Giovanni continued. "The same with Portugal and Spain, because of their ports. And their exploration on ships. They can find new trade routes; that brings them wealth and power. I know that Genoa, where I was born, is stronger than many republics because of its location. Water on one side and mountains on the other. A country that has no port or mountains, or rich land for animals to graze, is more likely to be a country that struggles and is easier to attack."

"Who is your father?" Fernando asked.

"The merchant Chabotto. I'm usually with him at the wharf or at our storehouse. When I can, I attend lectures."

"You sneak into lectures."

"When the doors are closed to me."

As the weeks went by, Giovanni realized Fernando was making a point of finding him at the wharf. They compared the merits of the various ships, identified the flags of Spain, Portugal, England, France, and the Middle Eastern countries. They shared their hopes of one day traveling the world and talked of Giovanni's chart-making. Fernando asked to meet Rizo, and when they arrived at the chart shop, Piero was there, helping Rizo with his account books. Carlo arrived at almost the same moment with a basket of fish and was soon preparing a sizzling lunch on the iron stove. Giovanni introduced everyone. "This is Fernando. His father builds ships."

Fernando sat on a pile of books and shared the midday meal, looking very happy to be with this mix of sea-lovers. He asked Rizo about his days as a sailor, when he had first gone to sea.

Rizo licked his fingers, savoring the olive oil that had been used to cook the fish. "At your age, I was on my third voyage to Baghdad. Already been to Argos, Sicily, even Constantinople."

Piero looked to Giovanni. He knew how his brother was aching to get onto a large ship and head into the seas. "Gio, it is worth asking Father again."

Giovanni shook his head. "He has asked me not to. He's tired of the question."

Fernando asked, "Why is your father so against it?"

"Two reasons. He wants Piero and me to take over the business he has built for us," Giovanni said. "And my mother is too fearful, for she lost a brother at sea. She thinks it's too dangerous. And my father will not make her unhappy." He vented his impatience. "I don't want to disobey or disappoint. My family is important. I don't want to make my mother sad."

Fernando nodded. "But what about you? Will you live your life to make others happy? Or to make yourself happy?"

Giovanni shrugged. "It is too difficult to think about sometimes."

As Giovanni and Fernando were heading out, Rizo asked Giovanni to stay for a moment. "One more thing, Gio. Andrea

Bianco, a sailor and chart-maker who has worked with Fra Mauro, was in yesterday. He told me the monk is very ill." He handed Giovanni a letter. "He was not able to deliver your latest letter to him."

A week later, Giovanni tried to peer through the large wooden gate of the monastery. Carlo, who had brought him out to the island of Murano in his skiff, had told him he had only an hour before he had to get back to take his mother to evening church service, so Giovanni did not have much time. He could see only slivers of the monastery's bare stone walls, a lone lizard scampering up toward the hot tiles of the roof. Giovanni heard deep voices in a unified and mellow song. It was a monophonic chant.

"May I help you?"

Giovanni felt a large hand on his shoulder. He turned to see a giant monk with high, skeletal cheekbones and a pale face. The monk's bulbous eyes were steady. He spoke in a deep voice. "No visitors allowed."

"I am Gio . . ." Giovanni gulped and caught himself. Sweat broke onto his forehead. "I am Zuan Chabotto and I hope to give Fra Mauro my respects."

The monk repeated. "No visitors allowed."

"I heard of his illness. That is why I don't want to delay my hopes."

The look on Giovanni's stricken face interested the monk. "Why is seeing Fra Mauro so important to you?"

"Because of his most wonderful world map. My friend, who told me about the map—Signor Fallio of Genoa—he is also old and very ill. I wanted to be able to tell him that I met Fra Mauro."

"Genoa?" The monk's deep voice rumbled.

Giovanni, feeling miniscule next to the monk, swallowed loudly as he looked up and said, "I was born in Genoa."

"I am a Genoese. My father is a fisherman."

"So, you know how different Venice is. You know how wonderful Genoa is." Giovanni, to his own surprise, felt his eyes fill with tears.

"You are homesick." It was if the monk could see into his soul.

"Sometimes." Giovanni realized it was true. "For the heavy waves of the ocean and the cold air that's not filled with the scent of flowers and Venetian perfumes but the smells of simple salt and fish. For people who do not judge you by your clothing. For Signor Fallio, who taught me to love maps. For where I first dreamed of knowing the world and where I thought it was possible."

"And do you still dream?"

"Now I dream that I will not lose my desire."

Moments later, the giant monk ushered Giovanni into a small cell. A small, thin monk sat at a wooden table, his back to the door. The monk's neck was permanently bent, and a woolen shawl was draped over his hunched shoulders. Giovanni noticed pages of parchment in piles on the desk. Maps and drawings were tacked onto the walls, and jars of brushes and quills and paints lined makeshift shelves.

The large monk's voice echoed in the cell. "Fra Mauro, you have a visitor who I could not turn away."

Fra Mauro turned his head. His hooked nose was prominent on his thin face; it extended outward farther than the jut of his chin. He wore a baggy cap low on his forehead. He coughed, bringing a piece of cloth to his mouth. He looked old and worn out, yet his large brown eyes were bright and clear.

"What do you want, young man?" His voice was raspy, as if he hardly used it.

"Your understanding of the world, Fra Mauro. To know of places far different than here."

Fra Mauro gazed at Giovanni, taking in his bright, inquisitive face. "Give us some time, Fra Tono."

The giant monk nodded and left.

Fra Mauro used the desk to support a rise to his feet. His back remained bent like a curved needle used to repair fishing nets. His robes hung heavy on his emaciated frame. He waved to Giovanni to follow him into a small room that was adjacent to his cell; it was the monk's cartography workshop. Giovanni breathed out in appreciation, taking in the shapes, colors, and details of the sketches and maps on the wall. Sketches of European, Indian, Turkish, and Chinese ships. Renderings of castles, temples, and walled towns. Of explorers on horseback trekking through deserts. Islands in large and small bodies of water. Rivers and mountain passages. He moved closer to a large map where the names of villages, trading posts, and kingdoms were hand-lettered and their histories explained in short passages. "This was a study for the world map," Fra Mauro whispered. "I expanded on it, of course. More details."

One of the maps included a rendering of the solar system according to Ptolemy. Beside it was a drawing of Eden; Adam and Eve on a blue-green island, their perfect garden surrounded by ivory walls. Giovanni turned to Fra Mauro. "The garden was included in your map of the world."

Fra Mauro nodded. "God's first nod to us, his gift of life.

Many think the garden was situated in the Far East, but God has not told us for absolute."

Fra Mauro waved to the maps. "We worked with the accounts of explorers like the Greek Hippalus; the Moroccan Battuta, who traveled to Mesopotamia, Jaffna, and China and wrote down his observations. Nicolas Conti, Marco Polo. My good friend Andrea Bianco, a sailor and mapmaker who visits me to this day, helps me." He moved to a chart with detailed compass markings. "Andrea's work. His navigation includes details using the compass rose."

"My friend Rizo has a chart shop. Andrea Bianco is the one who told him you were ill. Rizo is teaching me to do charts."

Fra Mauro dipped his head to one side so that it almost rested on his shoulder. "Yes, I am ill. But I do not fear death. God has given me a good life on this earth. Why should I question his plans for me in the future?" He smiled, the thin skin on his face creasing. "I have memories. My own adventures. I was once a soldier—I left home when I was near your age. I traveled to the Byzantine Empire—now the Ottoman Empire—and to India and the Maldives. And then I traveled as a trader. When I heard God calling me, it was a voice that told me to come back to Venice. God chose me to settle on Murano, to write histories and draw maps."

"Signor Fallio, a man with a map store in Genoa, told me about you when I was only ten years old. He is in Genoa still and wanted to see your world map one day. But he has gotten too old to travel."

Fra Mauro's buckled hands lifted a drawing from a pile. It was a rough sketch of the Garden of Eden. Fra Mauro quickly signed his initials to it. "Send him this. With my regards."

Giovanni's eyes filled with tears. He knew what this would mean to Signor Fallio. "That is generous, Fra Mauro."

The towering monk entered the doorway. Fra Mauro held up his hand before the monk could speak. "*Sì*, Fra Tono, I will rest now."

Giovanni helped Fra Mauro to his small and narrow bed. Fra Mauro's voice was kind. "You are a brave young man. You must not let anything or anyone stop you." His tired eyes studied Giovanni. "I do not think that is your nature. For you found your way to me." Fra Mauro put a hand on Giovanni's shoulder. "Bless you, young man."

Moments later, Giovanni walked to the Murano pier to meet Carlo. Fra Mauro's drawing was secure in his tunic's inside pocket. The sun was warm on his face. He felt inspired by the faith of Fra Mauro. He wanted to believe that his destiny included exploration. He looked forward to getting home and writing his letter to Signor Fallio.

Chapter Six

The next day, Giovanni arrived at Rizo's chart shop to find Fernando there, standing next to a man in a hooded cloak. Rizo met Giovanni's eyes, his look warning him to be cautious. Rizo's voice was overly bright. "Gio, I expected you a half hour ago."

"I had an errand for my father," Giovanni said, wondering why Rizo looked concerned. "Did I miss something?"

The hooded man turned around. It was Signor Penzo. Giovanni felt his throat tighten.

Signor Penzo pointed a thin finger. "You. You used to stand in the balcony to hear my lectures."

Giovanni stammered, "Signor Penzo, I thought I was hidden. I admit, I did sneak in. I apologize. But I no longer do that."

"Why?" Signor Penzo snapped.

Fernando answered for Giovanni. "Because some of the students forbade it."

Giovanni, his heart pounding, continued, "I know only citizens are accepted into San Giovanni Evangelista, and my family are not yet citizens of Venice. It was right that I was warned off."

"There is no 'right' at work here," Signor Penzo contradicted Giovanni.

Giovanni gulped, "Well, you see, my family could never afford the price of the Scuola Grande. It is too high. Even if we were citizens."

"Fernando di Sera tells me you have studied quite a bit," Signor Penzo said. "Here. With Signor Rizo."

"Don't need the Signor," Rizo growled.

Signor Penzo looked at the charts on the wall. "Why not, Signor Rizo? You are clearly accomplished and deserving of respect."

Giovanni saw Rizo's jaw set squarer, his shoulders straighten. He appreciated Signor Penzo's words.

"And I understand," Signor Penzo continued, looking at Giovanni. "That you've made some of these charts."

Giovanni nodded. Rizo added, "He started just copying, but now he's working from sailors' diaries. See what he can do from a source."

Fernando lifted a book off Rizo's shelf. "Giovanni has read all these books." He joked, "I think he can quote all of *The Travels of Marco Polo*."

"What is it that you are driven to learn from my lectures?" Signor Penzo's eyes were piercing, his voice sharp. As if he did not approve.

"All I can about ships. Navigation. About people in exotic places. What they think, how they live. Their poems and philosophies. Reading alone is not enough for me. I want to be able to ask questions and get answers."

"I see," Signor Penzo said. "You are interested in history?"

"And languages. And ways of thinking."

Signor Penzo harrumphed. Stroked his long gray beard.

Giovanni bowed. "I apologize for sneaking in. But Fra Mauro predicted I was one who would always try to follow my heart."

Penzo looked at him, surprised. "You met Fra Mauro?"

"*Sì*. Last week."

"How did you do that?"

"I went to Murano. And asked to see him."

"Determined. Brave." Penzo looked at him more closely. "And your name is Zuan Chabotto."

Giovanni nodded to his Venetian name. "Yes, Signor."

Signor Penzo looked at Giovanni for another minute, then headed to the door. "Fernando di Sera, thank you for this interesting outing. Now let us not be late for our next meeting. Good day, Signor Rizo."

Penzo and Fernando moved out. Fernando shot Giovanni a look as if to promise an explanation for the visit later.

Giovanni took a deep breath, willing his pulse to slow. Rizo coughed, "Well, let's get to work."

Heat saturated the stone streets and buildings of Venice. Venetians, in gondolas and all shapes of boats, traveled the canals, many letting their hands slide into the water, hoping to transfer its relative coolness to their limbs. Giovanni and Piero sweated inside the Chabotto Trading storehouse. Piero was going over the account books and Giovanni sorted pearls. Signor Chabotto organized spices.

There was a knock on the open door. "For merchant

Chabotto." A messenger, dripping with sweat, stood at the transom holding a letter.

"That is my father. I'll take it." Giovanni said.

The messenger headed off, calling over his shoulder. "It is from Scuola Grande di San Giovanni Evangelista."

Giovanni's heart skipped a beat. He stared at the letter. What could it be? A reprimand for darkening its doors? A reminder that only citizens are allowed on its premises?

"What did the messenger bring, my son?" Signor Caboto asked.

Giovanni handed Signor Caboto the letter. "I did not mean to cause any trouble, Father."

The family celebrated in grand style that night. There was a roasted rabbit, fennel, carrots, tomatoes, and un-watered wine.

"To my son, Gio, who has opened a very heavy door for the family. To the Chabottos, who now belong to the best confraternity in Venice."

Piero crowed with joy. "I told Gio he was smart, the smartest in Venice." He raised his glass. "*Salute!*"

Giovanni beamed. "Now I'll be able to study with the most excellent tutors in Venice." He had met with Fernando earlier, and found out that Signor Penzo had petitioned the school to accept Giovanni. And Fernando had convinced his father to lend a noble's signature. He raised his glass. "To friends."

Signor Caboto clinked Giovanni's glass and nodded. "Yes, yes. To learning. But it is more than a school, it is a fraternity of five hundred of the highest nobles in Venice and their sons. We are now part of this guild because of you, Gio. This could mean more clients for Chabotto Trading. More traders wishing to speak to us. I'll tell everyone my son is at the best Scuola Grande of Venice and they will know they are doing business with a family of worth."

Giovanni's smile was wide. His father might have been thinking of the growth of business and trade relationships, but Giovanni was imagining sitting on the main floor in the lectures on geography, navigation, and world politics and not having to hide behind a column.

It was the end of May, Corpus Christi Day, 1467, and Giovanni sat in Carlo's skiff. They were traveling to a pier bordering the high-rent Rialto district. Giovanni hopped out of the skiff. Carlo encouraged him, "You wanted this. Stop looking so nervous. And if they give you grief, we'll ram their fancy gondolas on Venice's next sunny day. Take names, my friend." Carlo laughed and pushed off.

Giovanni walked past the five-hundred-year-old church, San Simeone Profeta, and entered Campo San Stin. A young noble, with books under his arm, darted past and pressed open the heavy gates.

"Let's follow him in," Fernando said, racing up to join Giovanni. "I'll show you the Sala delle Colonne. You'll see why it's called that—it's a room full of columns. Not too imaginative," he laughed. "Students meet in there for special occasions."

Giovanni was tense. "You helped make this happen, Fernando. If I sink, it's going to make you look bad."

Fernando shrugged. "I don't expect to look bad."

They entered the school and Giovanni took a deep breath. A glass chandelier, its candles unlit, hung from the ceiling. A massive curved staircase wound its way upward. "Up those stairs is the jewel of the confraternity," Fernando told him. "It's where they keep a sliver of wood. It is believed to come from the true cross." Fernando quickly touched his forehead, heart, and both shoulders in the sign of the cross. "Part of the wood that Jesus Christ was nailed to. A Chancellor of Jerusalem gave it to the school years ago and it's supposed to bring blessings. Maybe it does because so many members here become rich and powerful."

"Really?" Giovanni suddenly felt even more pressure.

Fernando grinned. "Let's hope so. Right?"

An hour later, the students of San Giovanni Evangelista, wearing the robes of the school, marched in Venice's Corpus Christi parade. The horns and drums were loud. Colorful flags waved from all the windows. They passed the doge's palace. Giovanni marched next to Fernando and waved at Piero and his ecstatic parents. He thought he saw his father's eyes filled with proud tears. He could hear Gravi and Trifulo behind him, muttering just loud enough for their voices to carry. "Zuan Chabotto. His family can't even pay the full school fees. He doesn't belong here." Giovanni could feel his blood heat as his pulse quickened.

"Ignore them," Fernando hissed.

At that moment, Giovanni determined to be first in all his classes. To show all who thought he did not belong.

The class bell sounded and Giovanni took a seat in the lecture hall. Signor Penzo was at the front of the room. "Today we will talk of sailors and stars. Many stars act as torches for those on sea voyages. One must know where to look for them in various seasons of the year. But there is one star that stays in one place all year long. What is the name of that star?"

Giovanni raised his hand. "Polaris."

"That is correct, Chabotto. It is also called by another name. What is that?"

Giovanni raised his hand. "The North Star, Signor Penzo."

"Correct." Signor Penzo nodded towards Giovanni, giving a small encouraging wink. Then he pointed to the celestial map tacked to the wall. "A sailor can find the North Star by finding the plough—a group of seven stars. It creates a shape like a ladle, like a dipper that you use to gather water."

"The new student is a Big Dipper," Gravi sneered, his voice loud enough for all to hear. Trifulo laughed.

Giovanni's eyes narrowed. Signor Penzo ignored the comment and continued, pointing to a spot on the celestial map. "At the far edge of the bowl of the Big Dipper are two stars called pointer stars. The brightest of them is the North Star."

Fernando raised his hand. "What if there are clouds in the sky and you can't see the stars? Then how do you navigate?"

Signor Penzo pointed to another constellation. "A group of stars, named after a very vain Greek queen, Cassiopeia, is on the opposite side of the North Star. If clouds obscure the night sky and the North Star is hidden, you can look for beautiful Cassiopeia for it is more determined to shine brightly and can often be seen through cloud cover."

"But if a storm is raging?"

"Then the sailor has to wait it out. And hope he is not blown too far off course."

Giovanni raised his hand. "That helps us with north. What about east and west?"

"Excellent question," Signor Penzo said.

Giovanni heard Silvio groan and yawn behind him. But Signor Penzo continued. "For east and west you must find

Orion's Belt. Three bright stars that rise in the east and set in the west . . ."

Giovanni reveled in his classes—mathematics, philosophy, languages, literature, and all areas of maritime study. Discussions of the wars and battles, of the increasing aggression of the Ottoman Empire and the Venetian Navy's attempts to stay the Turks' taking of ports closer and closer to the Republic. Of how the dangers had increased for merchants and crews sailing east and trekking overland on the Silk Road to exotic India, Arabia, and Mongolia, seeking their coveted resources. There were discussions of the Ottoman Empire's exacting of even higher fees and its allowances of more looting. He learned that the Turks had captured Argos and other Venetian holdings. He came to a deeper understanding of why the people of Venice were on edge. He learned more about Portugal's sea explorations—how their hopes to find a path to the east around the Ottoman Empire's reach were still frustrated. No explorer had found the southern end of Africa. The desire—the need—for a new route to the Far East was paramount.

Giovanni discussed with Signor Penzo Toscanelli's map and his theory that traveling west into the Ocean Sea would bring a ship, eventually, to the Far East continent. Giovanni was full of questions. Why had no one undertaken the voyage? Wasn't the risk worth it? Signor Penzo explained in his usual way, by asking more questions. "Giovanni, where is the kingdom that could support such a sea exploration? How much would it cost? If no one knows how far the journey might be, how could we know how many provisions must be stored on a ship? What is known about the uncharted waters? What stars would show the way? What is the way? How would an explorer convince a crew to put their lives in danger?" Giovanni admitted he did not know the answers. But he wanted to find them.

Juggling schoolwork, his duties with the family business, chart-making with Rizo, and keeping up with the changing landscape of power and Venice's position in the world, did not leave Giovanni much time for anything else. But one day, a fifteen-year-old Venetian girl crossed his path. And turned his head.

Chapter Seven

Giovanni rarely missed one of the special late afternoon lectures at the Scuola Grande. One this day, Signor Penzo was speaking on the recent scientific thinking on rainbows and their formation in the sky. Signor Penzo's voice rang out over the gathered crowd. "Aristotle, nearly four hundred years before the birth of Christ, noticed that rainbows in the sky appear opposite to the sun. That they can also appear in water sprayed into the air, either by a rower of a boat on the water or in the drizzle of a sun shower. Imagine. The sun is reflecting in each waterdrop . . ." Giovanni was settled against the wall, listening. His eyes grazed over the other attendees and up to the balcony where he had snuck in, years ago, to first listen to lectures. There in the shadows, he could make out two feminine figures. Fernando was next to them.

Signor Penzo continued. "More recently, Roger Bacon in England calculated angles in rainbows and experimented with crystals of glass. Bacon shined light through those crystals while spraying water, and as the water droplets formed, he saw that the crystal reflected colors in the moist air. His work was used by a German, named Freiberg, who . . ."

Giovanni moved along the side of the room and out the door. He accessed the outside stairway to the balcony. Fernando was startled when he slipped in. "Gio. Close the door."

Giovanni, aware that light was shining into the balcony, quickly shut the door. He bowed to the ladies, one younger, the other in her thirties. He whispered to Fernando. "Who have you brought with you tonight? There are no other women here."

"Mattea Balbi wanted to hear about rainbows," Fernando groaned. "I can never say no to her."

Giovanni recognized the name. He looked at the younger woman. Mattea Balbi had grown; she was tall, the top of her head at his shoulder's height. Her hair was the color of chestnuts, her olive skin smooth, and her sea-green eyes sparkled, just as he remembered them.

Mattea leaned in towards Giovanni. "Isn't this fascinating? Rainbows and magical colors. I've been reading about the newest scientific findings. Have you?"

Giovanni could smell the light lavender fragrance in Mattea's hair. For a moment, his head felt light.

Anxious, the older woman put a cautioning hand on Mattea's arm. "Ssshhh. Do not gain attention, niece. We don't want this to get back to your father."

Mattea frowned and continued whispering to Giovanni. "My Aunt Sofia—she is my chaperone—she and I are on our way to a dinner party at the Gravi palazzo. I didn't see anything amiss at stopping here for a short schooling."

Aunt Sofia called for quiet again. Signor Penzo continued to talk about rainbows, but Giovanni was not hearing a word. He was aware of Mattea's slim figure under her heavy dark blue cape, its hood lined with green satin, and of the toes of her leather boots peeking from under her full skirt. She was not looking at him; all her attention was on Signor Penzo. Giovanni glanced sideways at her profile. He had never seen anyone so beautiful.

After the lecture, he and Fernando escorted Mattea and her aunt to a waiting gondola. A soft wind, cool and vibrant, felt fresh on their faces. Autumn leaves, red, purple, and yellow, swept off the trees and through the air.

Giovanni fell into step with Mattea. "We have met before. I brought a scimitar to your palazzo—to your father."

"Oh. I remember. From the Mongol Empire. You were fifteen then and now I'm fifteen years old. Not a child anymore." She raised her chin. "I remember, after you left, I asked my father to buy an elephant—and to have you deliver that too."

Giovanni laughed, picturing the headstrong girl demanding the near-impossible.

"You have not told me your name," Mattea said.

"In Venice, I am called Zuan Chabotto." He was not sure why he wanted this young woman to know him fully.

Mattea looked confused. "You say you are *called* Zuan? But is that not your name?"

"I was born Giovanni Caboto. In Genoa."

"What name do you prefer? Giovanni Caboto or Zuan Chabotto?"

Giovanni hesitated. He had never been asked this.

Mattea thought for a moment. "I like the sound of Giovanni. It is like a trill on the tongue. Very musical." Mattea forged on. "I have heard my brother talk about you with his friends. They say you are a student of distinction at the Scuola Grande di San Giovanni Evangelista."

"That is generous."

Mattea shook her head. "They were not being generous. They resent you."

"I try not to give offense." His heart sank. Why did he want her to approve of him?

"They say you should not get the best tutors because your family does not pay the highest fees."

Giovanni, angry, defended himself. "I do not choose my tutors."

"But the tutors choose you. They choose the students they think have the most potential." She looked over at her aunt, who was deep in conversation with Fernando. "I know that because my Aunt Sofia is in love with a tutor. He tells me these things." Mattea told him that Sofia was a young widow and promised herself she would never marry again. But that she had met Massimo Faber, a third son in a noble family. "I have seen them talking and the way they look at each other. It makes me wonder if Aunt Sofia will be able to stay true to her promise."

Giovanni recited. "'Love is a great thing, yea, a great and thorough good. By itself it makes that which is heavy, light.'"

Mattea's eyes widened. "Did you compose that?"

"No, Signorina," Giovanni said quickly. "A monk named Thomas à Kempis, a German, wrote it. We read poetry at school and are told to memorize it. To sharpen our wits."

"And you have the wit to use it now. While speaking to me."

Giovanni felt color in his cheeks. It struck him that Mattea said exactly what was on her mind.

They reached the canal and Fernando helped Mattea and Sofia into the gondola. He took a moment with Giovanni before joining them. "Mattea is strong-minded. Our families have known each other as long as I can remember. She's very smart. She's helped me all the way through school. If Silvio knew I did her this favor, he would not be happy. Can you keep this between us?"

Giovanni nodded and the gondola glided off. Giovanni sighed; he understood why Fernando found it difficult to deny Mattea Balbi.

Later that week at Chabotto Trading, Giovanni examined a beautifully carved miniature statue of elephant, its trunk curled upwards, its body thick, and its legs sturdy. He moved his fingers over the smooth, cool ivory. "Piero, what is the best price we can expect for this ivory?"

"It's from India, possibly a hundred years old. It has passed through ports in Baghdad. To make a profit, we must ask . . ." Piero checked his account books and showed the figure to Giovanni.

Giovanni opened the safe and deposited some florins. "It is now mine."

Piero snorted in surprise. "Why do you want a tiny ivory elephant?"

Giovanni placed the small statue in a tufted velvet pouch, then wrote a note and placed it inside. "I know someone who wanted a real one," Giovanni said as he strode out of Chabotto Trading.

"When did you start giving gifts?" Piero called after him. But Giovanni was already out of sight.

A week later, a sealed envelope addressed to Giovanni arrived at Chabotto Trading. He tore it open.

I treasure my tiny elephant. It rests beside my favorite chair, where I sit in my room and look out at the sea. You are very kind and thoughtful.

—*Mattea Balbi*

"Who sent you a letter sealed with gold-flecked wax?" Piero wanted to know.

"Pay attention to the business at hand, my brother. This, I would like to keep to myself." Giovanni put the letter into the inside pocket of his tunic. Close to his heart.

It was just after Christmas; the nights were cold and most Venetians spent their late afternoons before fireplaces. But Signor Penzo's lectures were popular and today he was in the middle of speaking on currents and tides. Giovanni kept his eye on the balcony. Moments after the lecture began, he saw the door open. It was Fernando and he ushered in Mattea and Sofia. Giovanni moved out of the lecture hall and into the outdoor stairway. In a moment, he slipped onto the balcony. He thought he could see a small smile move onto the corners of Mattea's mouth. He used his handkerchief to dust off two chairs and—as gallantly as he could—offered them to the ladies.

Fernando shook his head, wondering at Giovanni's exaggerated good manners. "What's gotten into you? And do you live here in these lecture halls? You're always here."

"You would get better marks if you spent more time here too," Giovanni joked.

Mattea's aunt leaned towards her niece, subtly nodding towards Giovanni. She whispered, "That young man is interested in you, niece. Don't give any encouragement."

An hour later, Giovanni walked next to Mattea. He enjoyed looking at the fur hat that framed her face and the heavy velvet shawl that wrapped around her thin shoulders. They were heading to the canal, where gondolas waited with blankets and heated braziers for their customers' feet.

"Shall I see you at the Carnevale?" Mattea queried. "The doge's ball, where everyone wears the most fantastic masks?"

"The doge's ball? No." Giovanni shook his head. "I will not be there." Giovanni knew that the Carnevale Ball at the doge's palace was Venice's most elite event. It was held the night before Ash Wednesday, the beginning of the forty-day period of Lent, when all Catholics were expected to give up luxuries and vices to atone for their sins before the Easter season. "My family does not receive such invitations."

Mattea stopped and smiled up at him. "The tradition of wearing the mask is for the purpose of denying strict social rules, for at least a night. It's supposed to make us feel free." She heard her aunt call to her that the gondola was waiting. Mattea leaned in and spoke quickly. "I'll request Fernando bring you as his guest. He is your friend, as well as mine. And besides, he owes me. Come with Fernando."

"I don't want to cause trouble."

Her sea-green eyes challenged him. "You must come to the doge's Carnevale Ball. It will be an adventure. Let's make it our first adventure."

Giovanni could not resist her smile, her excitement. He entered into the plans of subterfuge. "If I wear a *bauta*, a full mask, to cover my face, you will know me because of the pirate's hat with skull bones and a red band."

Mattea laughed. "My mask will be the color of pearl and I'll wear a crown of blue peacock feathers. And we'll have a secret code, like I read about in books." She whispered into his ear, and her closeness made Giovanni feel intoxicated.

Mattea pulled back and looked at him. "So, we have our code."

"I'm not sure if this is a good idea."

Mattea saw her impatient aunt motioning to her again. "I have to go. Promise me you'll come." She hurried off.

Piero leafed through the book illustrated by the dancing master Domenico da Piacenza. Giovanni had found it on the shelf at the Scuola Grande, brought it home, and announced he needed Piero to come to their room, for he needed help.

"It's not likely they'll be dancing the piva," Piero said. "That is too common; it's the one we do at Christmas with our friends. You must learn the newly popular *bassadanza*."

Giovanni slumped on his bed. "Does it have leaps?"

Piero shook his head and opened Domenico's book. "No. You stay low. It is danced to a slower tempo than the piva. Stand up. Let's try it." Piero and Giovanni followed the steps shown in the text, first stepping forward with the left foot while leaning in with the hip and the shoulder at the same time. Then stepping back and doing the same with the right side. Piero read as they followed the drawings. "Then you do a *doppio*, which is feet together, rising high on the toes, and lowering back to the floor. Then you give your partner your arm and lead her forward three steps. That's it. And you repeat it all again."

"I think I can do that."

"Oh, wait." Piero's voice dropped. He had bad news. "Seems there are variations. Sometimes you lift a knee and skip as you go forward. Sometimes you move in a circle. You'll have to do your best to see the style of those dancing next to you."

Giovanni groaned. "I don't want to make a fool of myself."

The night of the doge's Carnevale Ball arrived. Giovanni trailed into the palazzo behind Fernando wearing a tall and wide mask that covered most of his face and a high ruffled shirt and dark ruby red cape. Over his unruly hair he wore a pirate's hat. They entered Sali del Maggiore, the main hall, and blended in with the hundreds of guests flowing towards the ballroom.

They passed a large group of musicians. Giovanni saw the conductor signaling the players of the spinet pianos, violins, lutes, flutes, harps, crumhorns, bells, and long tabor drums. Fernando spied the young woman he'd been courting; he turned to Giovanni. "You're inside. Have fun but don't call me if you're found out!" He laughed, slapped Giovanni on the back, and hurried off.

Giovanni moved around the perimeter of the ballroom; he took in the gilded ceilings, the painted walls. He soon realized that no one paid him any attention; his mask totally obscured his face. He recognized Signor Balbi, unmistakable because of his height and elegance, but also because he wore a mask that only covered his eyes. He was talking to a group of men, deep into conversation of Venice's politics. Next to him were two women; the slimmer one wore a mask the color of pearl and a crown of peacock feathers. She was looking over the dancers and guests, as if she expected someone. Giovanni moved behind them. He heard Sofia chiding Mattea. "I know who you are looking for. And if he is wise, he has not come."

Mattea shrugged. "If he has not come, then I will know that he is not the daring man I think him to be."

Sofia continued to caution. "Your father is making plans for you, niece. You must do nothing that will complicate considering the best marriage proposals."

"Aunt Sofia, were you happy in marriage?" Mattea said, fanning herself.

"A woman's place in marriage is not focused on happiness, my niece," Sofia said. "I did not consider my well-being, only that of our family."

Mattea noticed a man dressed as a Harlequin moving towards them. "I recognize your Signor Faber, Aunt Sofia. He is coming our way." Sofia flushed as he approached and bowed.

"Signora and Signorina," he said. "Good evening." They replied with low curtsies. He held out his hand to Sofia. "May I escort you to the dance floor?"

Sofia lifted her skirts to join the dancers. Giovanni stepped forward and bowed in front of Mattea. "Signorina, may I have this dance?"

She barely glanced at him. "I'm sorry, I have promised this dance to . . ."

Giovanni spoke their code. "The adventurer Marco Polo who has come back to life this very night."

Mattea's eyes, behind her dove gray mask, grew wide. She smiled. "Yes, it is Marco Polo to whom I have promised this dance."

She put her hand on Giovanni's arm and they moved onto the dance floor. Giovanni, nervous, apologized before they settled in among the others. "I will not be worthy."

Mattea sniffed, "We will see, Marco Polo."

Despite hours of practice with Piero, Giovanni moved right

when he should have moved left and turned when he should have stayed in place. He was sure that Mattea regretted her choice to invite him to the ball, to deign to dance with him. But as their steps brought them closer together for a moment, she whispered, "You are doing well, Giovanni."

The dance called for them to tour the floor, stepping lightly to the music. Giovanni motioned to the marbled walls, the gilded mirrors, the chandeliers filled with candles. "Maybe this palace is designed after Marco Polo's Xanadu."

Mattea nodded. "Perhaps it is. It was written that his paradise was a 'marble palace, the rooms of which are all gilt and painted with figures of men and beasts and birds, and with a variety of trees and flowers, all executed with such exquisite art that you regard them with delight and astonishment.'"

Giovanni congratulated her. "I remember you said you had read the book about his travels."

"Yes," Mattea teased. "And I wanted to show you that I could memorize too."

Giovanni looked at her. "You would have gotten top marks in any school."

Mattea smiled. "I know. But I've learned on my own. Reading is my Xanadu—my paradise."

As they swung back into the center of the dance floor, Giovanni felt more confident, swaying in at the right moment, dipping back when expected.

When the music came to an end, Giovanni bowed to Mattea and offered his arm. They walked towards the tall, windowed doors that led to a balcony.

"Do you know what I'm thinking, Giovanni?" Mattea asked.

"No, but I would very much like to know."

"My mother and aunt tell me a woman's place in marriage

is not focused on happiness. It is about duty, to connect wealth and property. But as I told you, my Xanadu is reading and I have read books about great love. My favorite is about the princess Psyche and her love for Cupid. She could not even see his face for he stayed in the darkness. He told her that light would be too dangerous for them. She was fearful at first, but fell in love with his kindness and tender feelings for her. The sad thing is, she began to listen to the wrong people—the people who said they cared about her—who questioned this mysterious love. When she betrayed Cupid's trust in her and lit a candle to see his face, he left her. She had to journey to great lengths—even to the Underworld—to convince him and the gods of her love. She wasn't perfect, but their love was."

Mattea spoke softly. "My aunt says these are fantastic tales. That the gods have liberties that we mortals do not." Her lips turned downwards. "There are times, Giovanni, when I wish I were my brother. A person who isn't expected to live as others see fit. Silvio has such freedom, he can do things. He can make plans. He can make decisions in his own life."

"I wish freedom for you, Mattea."

"Oh, no." Mattea's hand went to her mouth. Her eyes had suddenly become wary.

Giovanni turned and saw Silvio approaching, clearly wondering about the identity of this stranger who was dancing with his sister. "I see your brother too. It is time for us to part," Giovanni said. He quickly led her to a group of women near the orchestra.

"Good night, Giovanni," Mattea whispered. "Thank you for fulfilling your promise."

Giovanni slipped off, moving quickly through the thick groups of nobles and fine ladies. He looked over his shoulder and saw Mattea raise her head in defiance as she talked to her brother. Giovanni knew he would have to wait for his next chance to be near her—and he knew it would not be tonight.

Chapter Eight

The customary breezes of Venice were absent. Summer was approaching and the season's first heat hung in the air. "Gio, you've entered the information on the rugs in the account book three times. What's the matter with you?"

Giovanni didn't hear Piero. He was looking out the window of the Chabotto storehouse towards the wharf, his thoughts miles away. He could not get Mattea out of his mind. The way she smiled when he faltered during the dance at the doge's ball, the way she raised her chin whenever she became stubborn— which was whenever her brother Silvio crossed her path. How she lingered in the bookstore near the Campo San Marco, filling her chaperone's satchel with poetry and tales of travel. Her laughter as she waved from a gondola, heading to a party at a nobleman's home.

That morning, in language class at Scuola Grande, he had failed to remember that there were over a hundred unique varieties and dialects in the Chinese language, and that in India, a traveler might be able to get by if he knew Hindu and Bengalese, but even then, there were areas in the large country that only spoke Kashmiri or Odi or Punjabi. The professor had frowned, unused to Giovanni's lack of attention. Gravi and Trifulo had smirked.

"Gio. Gio." Piero put his face inches in front of his brother's. "Gio."

Giovanni was startled. "What?"

"Papà expects the *Magnifici* in port tomorrow. Arriving from Baghdad." Piero closed the account books for the day. "I've arranged workers and carts to get the goods to the storehouse and . . ."

Piero was interrupted by the door to the storehouse banging open. Silvio Balbi barged into the hot and seemingly airless room. His chest was puffed out, his jaw tight. "Who do you think you are? How dare you think you are worthy to even speak to my sister."

"Silvio." Giovanni scrambled to his feet, taken aback by Silvio's aggression, for in the past Silvio had completely ignored him. "No reason to be upset."

"There is reason," said Silvio, the heat causing his face to redden. He waved a note card in the air. "I found this, a note she has written to you."

Giovanni's temper sparked. Silvio had no right to seize Mattea's things. "Did she give you permission to grab it?"

"Don't tell me how to treat my own sister. I am the eldest and a son. One day I'll be head of the Balbi family." Silvio's spittle flew into the air.

Piero, behind the desk, stood. He was ready to act, if needed.

Silvio, enraged, pointed to Piero. "You stay out of this."

Piero was silent, but took another step closer to Giovanni. Two against one.

Silvio continued, vehemently pointing at Giovanni. "My father is not pleased. He would send Mattea to a convent if he hears of another meeting, without his permission, between you and my sister. You will write to her. State that you know your low position in Venice and that you will not bother her anymore."

Giovanni returned Silvio's bitter stare without revealing his churning emotions. Wretched, he wanted to punch Silvio. He wanted to rage that it was unfair if Mattea faced unhappiness in her own home.

Silvio sneered. "I have now given you a warning. Do not try to latch yourself to the Balbi name and fortune. Our family has influence in Venice and I'm sure Chabotto Trading would not like to lose clients. The Balbis can ruin your family." Silvio turned and strode to the door. "Stay away from my sister. It is for her own good. And yours." He was gone.

Giovanni sank back into a chair, his hands shaking. There was a long silence. Piero, stunned by the turn of events, finally said, "Silvio Balbi's face gets quite red when he's angry." He waited for Giovanni to laugh, to relax a bit.

But Giovanni was deep into worry with the knowledge that he must make a troubling decision. Finally, he turned to Piero. "I will keep my distance from Mattea Balbi." His voice was low and sad. "Regrettably, it seems to be the way it must be."

Piero had seen his brother put aside his desire to be a sea captain and explorer of oceans for the family. He realized he was now witnessing Giovanni deny his love—to protect the family's station in Venice.

~

Months later, the Cabotos sat at the supper table and celebrated their fifteenth year in Venice and their official citizenship in the Republic. "I told you it would happen, family," Signor Cabot said. "And it has. All is open to us now."

"And a birthday dinner for Giovanni to go with it." Piero had noticed Giovanni's low spirits of late, and wanted to lighten the moment. "Since you are now over twenty years old, Gio, I suggest we curtail the football games in our room."

Giovanni laughed. "Especially now that I have my own rooms next door."

"Rooms of your own?" Piero was taken aback. "Italian families live together forever."

"It's the adjoining house, brother. We're growing our own palazzo," Giovanni joked, knowing that their humble home would never be considered grand.

Signora Caboto handed Giovanni a wrapped gift. "For our son, who dedicates himself to his family."

Giovanni opened the package and lifted out an intricately carved rosary. It was made of precious boxwood from the Netherlands. He knew the merchant who imported this religious item and the high prices he charged devout Venetians.

"This is very dear, Mamma. I don't know if I deserve . . ."

"You've brought honor to the family," Signora Caboto said. "You should have a fine rosary for meditation at Scuola Grande. May it stay in the family for generations."

Signor Caboto added. "It is important, at times, to show success. Others notice."

Piero cut into the roasted duck covered with thyme and rosemary. "To citizenship! To birthday dinners! I wish we could celebrate like this every night. But we live in unfortunate times, as we know. It is unfortunate that the Sultan and his Ottoman Empire have now taken the Peloponnesus and unfortunate that our allies, Persia and Albania, are at war with them. The Turks may take Venice on next, and we may not have the opportunity to be Venetian merchants with a successful business much longer."

"I think the Albanians will rally," Giovanni said. "The traders report that Antonio Loredan is there, leading the citizens of Scutari. But of course, their battles will keep them too busy to come to the aid of Venice, should we need it." He thought of Mattea in the Balbi palazzo, and wondered what Signor Balbi planned for the Balbi family's protection.

Signor Caboto put his fork down. "The Venetian army is strong. And our navy has, in the past, thwarted the Ottoman ships on water. I've pledged financial support, as have all the merchants. But I have made a decision. Chabotto Trading will stop sending goods on ships heading east; there is too much danger of losing entire cargoes to warships—or pirates. The Venetian banks are charging too much for insurance, if they agree to insure cargo at all. For a while, we must concentrate on trade with Portugal, Spain, and England."

Giovanni knew this decision would severely curtail Chabotto Trading's profits. But there didn't seem to be a way around it. He wished, again, for a different route to the Far East. Earlier that day, he and Rizo had talked of how an English ship had left the coast of England and made its way north and west as far as Iceland. The ship had planned to steer west from Iceland's shores in hopes of finding a way to the eastern coast of Asia. But it faced violent storms and frigid waters—gigantic islands of ice floating on the water's surface. The ship's captain decided not to venture further into the Ocean Sea, afraid of unknowns that could spell more peril and death.

The meal over, Giovanni kissed his mother's cheek and bid her good night. "Thank you for the celebration. I'm going for a walk. The moon is full."

Signora Caboto held on to his hand for a moment and whispered so only he could hear. "Gio, I have noticed lately that you are quiet. Not eating much. Sometimes you are not as cheery as you always have been. A mother wonders, is there a young woman you are thinking of?"

Giovanni marveled at her insight, but did not want to talk about his feelings for Mattea. He shook his head. "Mamma, when there is a young woman who would have me—and to whom I would give my heart—you will be the first to know." He squeezed her hand and moved out into the night.

As he walked into the *campo*, Giovanni looked up at the stars. He identified Polarus, the North Star, and Orion's Belt. He wondered, for the thousandth time, what it would be like to navigate a ship—westward—by these stars. Was he meant to be a merchant in this city his whole life? Just a week earlier, the Caboto family had received a letter from Genoa telling them of Signor Fallio's passing and the closing of his Shop of Maps. Giovanni tacked the letter to a wall in his new rooms, next to Signor Fallio's letter of gratitude for sending the Fra Mauro drawing and the Bartolome Colombo map that he purchased in Signor Fallio's shop fifteen years ago. He thought of his youthful plans, how he had bragged about his ideas on exploration and his intention to become someone extraordinary. Would Signor Fallio be disappointed in him?

~

In 1479, the Republic of Venice signed a treaty of peace with the Ottoman Empire. The doge of Venice, with advice of his council, signed over the Republic's oversight of the ports of Argos, Negroponte, Lemnos, and Scutari. In addition, Venice agreed to pay an annual tribute of 10,000 golden ducats, just for the ability to trade with the cities in the Middle East. Venetian merchants and traders were, in turn, taxed by their own city council to help cover the costs. Profits, for all, were cut into—and no one was happy.

At Rizo's chart shop, as Carlo fileted a dozen small mackerel and put the oiled cast iron skillet on the fire grate, Giovanni fumed. "All we do is complain about the Ottoman Empire and its ever-growing control of the waters and the Silk Road. The Turks have us by the ears. They will continue to raise tariffs. The Ottoman Empire will always want more and more."

"It is probably true, Gio," Rizo said, breaking a thin loaf of bread into pieces. "We need the bravest sea captains to challenge themselves and find a new path to Asia."

"But first, we eat," Piero said, taking a piece of bread.

Giovanni continued. "Venice is not investing in its future. We have no ships dedicated to exploration."

"Gio, what would you have Venice do?" Piero asked. "The Italian Peninsula is not united. Each of the republics—standing alone—is not capable of financing sea voyages like a unified kingdom such as Portugal. The Portuguese royal coffers are filled."

"Because they're finding new territories filled with resources—spices, gold, precious stones in Africa. Their exploration is one of the reasons they are rich. Maybe the Italian Peninsula should unite," Giovanni said. "Perhaps we would be stronger together."

"That will never happen. We enjoy fighting each other too much," Piero joked.

"This is serious, Piero. Stop making light of it," Giovanni snapped.

Piero sighed. "Gio, you must stop complaining. Would you move to Portugal and beg to be let into the Royal Court to seek support and leave the family?"

Giovanni waved off Rizo's offer of bread, his anger boiling. "Maybe I was born into the wrong family. In the wrong place."

Carlo, surprised at the outburst, looked at him. "Gio, what is this bug under your shirt today?"

"How could you not want to be born as my brother?" Piero laughed, trying to lighten the tension. "Maybe if you were a king, you could make things happen. But none of us are kings."

Carlo tested the iron skillet with a drop of water, and the liquid sputtered on the heat. Carlo drizzled olive oil onto the fish and slipped them into the pan and topped them with grains of salt. Soon the fragrant smell of the meal filled the room.

"But a king is not eating better at this moment, I can tell you that," Piero said as he licked his lips.

Giovanni was exasperated. "Piero, there are more important things than food." He moved to the back of the shop to concentrate on his latest charts.

Piero called after him, unwilling to let Giovanni's mood dampen the gathering. "Not many, Gio. Not many."

The door opened and Fernando entered, dressed in an ornamented velvet frockcoat, vest, and striped hat. His leather gloves were dyed to match the yellow trimming of his boots. "Why are you so elegant today, Fernando?" asked Carlo.

"I'm going to an engagement party." He called to the back

of the room to Giovanni, "Benito Gravi, your fellow student, has gained more weight and a fiancée."

Giovanni's throat constricted. "To whom is he engaged?"

Fernando answered, "He has won the hand of the daughter of a rich Austrian banker. She is also of great flesh."

Giovanni was relieved; he had heard that the insipid and manipulative Gravi was among the many who visited the Balbi palazzo in hopes of gaining Mattea's favor. He did not mean for his voice to sound harsh, but his feelings were clear. "I imagine this is another coming together of fortunes?"

Fernando nodded. "A coming together of monies and appetites."

Carlo laughed as he slipped the hot and fragrant mackerel onto a platter. He picked up a nearby basket of long anchovies, and turned it over so that the small fish landed in the hot skillet.

Fernando puffed out his chest. "And I have news. I, too, will be a husband in the spring. Do I get an extra anchovy for that?"

Giovanni, happy for his friend, got up from his work to congratulate Fernando. "You finally won your noble lady's heart. She realized, at last, that you're worthy?"

Fernando blushed and joked, "It could be I deceived her."

"You are one of the wealthiest young men in Venice. I see more fortunes uniting," Piero said.

Giovanni joined his friends for the meal. He thought that everyone's life seemed to be coming together—everyone's but his.

A harsh winter was soon upon Venice; thin icicles clung to stone walls and the canal waters were dark under gray skies.

Signor Caboto was taken with influenza, and stayed at home while Giovanni and Piero sought medicine for him from Venice's best apothecaries. They ran the business in his absence. At the midday meal, the brothers sat with their weakening father and told him the news of the wharf, the traders, and Chabotto Trading's profits. Then Giovanni and Piero headed to the bank to go over the accounts. The steady income was there, but the profits lost by Signor Caboto's decision to curtail trade going east were less than encouraging. Finally, as the sun lowered in the sky, Giovanni headed to Rizo's chart shop to pore over charts and talk of the cogs, carracks, and caravels that he saw leaving the port every day.

One night, as Giovanni left the bank and headed into the *campo*, he heard his name being called. He turned and saw Sofia, Mattea's aunt, motioning to him. Sofia was wrapped in a heavy woolen cloak and was with a servant from the house of Balbi. The servant's arms were filled with hat boxes.

Giovanni joined her and bowed. "May I be of assistance, Signora?"

Sofia's eyes bore into his, as if what she had to say was of great import, but she did not relish her task. "Signor Zuan Chabotto," she hedged. "I'm not saying that I want to ask this great favor of you."

Giovanni was confused. "You've stopped me *not* to ask a favor?"

"Yes. But matters of the heart can cause one to see things in a new light."

Giovanni found it hard to follow her logic. "I have heard you are now married to the tutor," he said. "I admire him, for he has chosen a field that is of great use to many people. Accept my congratulations."

Sofia nodded and her voice softened. "It has brought me much happiness. And that is why I'm speaking to you today."

Giovanni was even more baffled. "How may I be of service, Signora?"

"I would like to trouble you to check the small courtyard behind the shop for me. I may have dropped my hanky."

Giovanni wondered why she was asking for his help. The servant stood nearby.

Sofia continued, "It would be most appreciated."

He bowed. "Of course, Signora. It will take but a moment."

Giovanni headed down the narrow stone alley to a courtyard. What he saw caused his heart to stop for a moment. It was Mattea, her head covered with a woolen shawl. Quickly, he went to her. "Signorina Mattea, what are you doing here? Are you in need of help?"

Mattea's words were rushed. "I didn't care about the weather. I wanted to get out of my home. I want to see the ships, to dream that there could more for me than entertaining suitors that think more of the Balbi fortune than of me."

Giovanni was surprised by the anger in her voice.

"My aunt and I walked by your shop. The doors were locked."

"Piero and I had an appointment with banking concerns." He was touched. "You sought me out? What may I do for you? I will do anything."

She pulled her cloak more tightly around herself. She seemed nervous, as if searching for the right words.

He tried to put her at ease. "But of course, it is unnecessary that you visit me in my shop. Ladies of Venice are encouraged to ask the merchants to bring goods to them, for them to peruse in their own home before purchase."

"But I cannot ask you to come to me. As you know."

Giovanni nodded. It was true. Silvio had made that very clear.

Tears of frustration sprung to her eyes. "Sometimes I feel as if I cannot breathe, Giovanni. I don't want to live by rules that I think are unfair. Just because I'm not a man, others feel they can run my life."

He wanted to take her hands, to calm her. "Mattea, you cannot displease your father."

"No, I cannot. I love my father." Mattea said, her shoulders dropping in despair. "To displease him would bring me great sadness."

"Silvio told me if he found out we met, your father would send you to a convent."

Mattea gave a tiny, frustrated laugh. "Not a place I would look forward to spending my life."

Giovanni could not hide his disappointment and anger. "So, I must face it. There is no hope."

Mattea looked at him closely, as if measuring his mettle. "Perhaps there is another option."

"Another option?"

"That my father could be persuaded."

Giovanni was perplexed. "But how?"

"In the past, you delivered many antiquities to our home to add to his collection of swords. My father thought highly of your knowledge."

"But not of my purse."

"But Chabotto Trading is doing well. Is it not?"

"We are a young company with satisfying profits, but not stellar by the standards of Venice's most successful families."

Her eyes challenged. "Should we be denied by the absence of trying?"

"Trying? What do you mean?"

"For even greater profits for Chabotto Trading. I know you, Giovanni. Somehow, I know, if you decide to act, you will achieve great things."

Giovanni ached to take Mattea into his arms. "Your faith means so much to me. I have spoken in the past to my father about expanding our trade. I have even given him plans. But he has decided to remain conservative."

Mattea's shoulders slumped. "Perhaps my dreams are just that. Dreams."

"I never wish to disappoint you," Giovanni said, hating to see her unhappy. "I will try again to convince my father to give me the freedom to cultivate new trading options, to add to our spice trade and to our trade of pearls and rugs. But even if I'm successful, I would need time to show profits. There are other suitors hoping to find favor with your father. Would I have the opportunity to outshine them?"

Mattea put her gloved hand on Giovanni's arm. "My father loves me. I don't think he will force a marriage. I'll do my part to secure you the time you need."

"Then I will do my part." Giovanni looked down the narrow stone walk, and he could see Sofia looking in shop windows. "Your aunt, she has been most kind."

"Yes," Mattea said. "Love has changed her."

Giovanni gazed into Mattea's sea-green eyes. He dared not talk of his love, of the overwhelming feelings of excitement, ache, and exultation he experienced when he was with her.

"Giovanni," Mattea said softly. "What are you thinking?"

"Only that I want to be worthy of your faith in me."

She smiled. "I was thinking that you may be thinking of kissing me."

Giovanni's heart soared. Mattea moved gracefully behind a stone column to hide them from eyes of passersby. Her gloved hand stilled the swaying of her full skirts. Giovanni took the few steps to join her.

Mattea leaned into him. Their lips met.

That night, Giovanni sat next to his father near the family's fireplace. "Papà, I'm your eldest son. It is my duty to care for you and Mamma. I want your permission to take our family business to even more success."

Signor Caboto put a frail hand on Giovanni's arm. "You've done well during my illness, Gio. You and Piero. I'm pleased." He coughed, then took a sip of warm wine. He had grown weaker in the past months and rarely left their home.

"Thank you, Papà. We've kept up with the news at the port. We think it's time to trade again with Constantinople and in goods from the Silk Road. Many of the traders believe the conflicts and dangers have lessened. There's much profit we're not accessing, Papà."

"We must stay conservative, Gio. We don't want to lose everything we've built."

"And I want to become our own representative in foreign markets."

"What?"

"To travel on board the ships myself."

"Your mother would not like that, son."

Giovanni pushed on. "This will cut out our need to hire

traders to negotiate with craftsmen and growers and foreign merchants on our behalf. We'll no longer need middlemen. By my presence, in the most important parts of the trades, our profits will increase. You know I have an eye for good quality and fair pricing. My plan is to raise our fortunes to greater glory. Trust me, Papà. Let me try to do more."

Signor Caboto coughed, holding his hand to his chest. His voice was raspy. "What has changed that you now have this new idea?"

Giovanni confessed, "I want to marry, Papà. I need to be worthy of a family that has long been part of the doge's circle."

"Gio. Never say you are not worthy." Signora Caboto's voice was angry. Giovanni turned to see his mother in the doorway. She continued, "Where we were born, and to what social class—those happenstances have nothing to do with character. It is honesty, it is hard work, it is taking care of family. You've proven yourself in all areas."

Signor Caboto pressed his frail hands together and frowned with concern. "Giovanni, your mother is right. The way others perceive us should not hold us back. We don't want to give small-mindedness power over us." He exchanged a look with his wife. "At the same time, it is not advisable to hold on to hopes that are too high. Marriages of the rich in Venice are made for business and status. Love is not a consideration."

Signora Caboto took her husband's hand. Giovanni noticed that hers were now thin, the veins prominent, the fingers permanently bent with age. "But, my husband, think. Isn't striving for true love important? Gio's desire is testament to us. Our love has seen us through many things together."

Signor Caboto kissed his wife's hand and sighed. "I do not want Gio to be disappointed."

Signora Caboto nodded. "The heart is tender, Gio." Her voice was soft and caring. "Protect yours."

Giovanni took his time, thinking about his answer. "'The truest heart emerges victorious.' It is what is said of the soldier who wields the scimitar, the mighty sword of Mongolia." He thought of all the nights he had seen his parents sit, heads together, talking over the events of the day and planning the future together. The warmth of their love had brought comfort to their home. "In this desire, my heart is true. I'm willing to work to achieve a happiness like yours." He turned to his mother. "Mamma, I know you have fear of me boarding a great ship and traveling through deep waters away from home. I have never wanted to cause you distress."

Giovanni could see his mother struggle to diminish the fear that rose in her heart.

"I must not stand in your way," Signora Caboto said. "I will pray for your safe return."

Giovanni took his mother's hand. "Mamma. I'll come back to you. I promise. This will be good for the family."

Chapter Nine

Rizo wrapped thin leather ties around the binder that held Giovanni's charts of the coast of the Italian Peninsula and maps of the waters leading to the coasts of Anatolia, one of the largest holdings of the Ottoman Empire. "After all these years, you know as much as the ship's navigator, I'm sure of it."

"A ship's navigator has seafaring experience. I do not," Giovanni said.

"You have to start sometime. You are twenty-seven. Still young." Rizo wheeled his chair over to Carlo, who was preparing the midday meal. "Shrimp and mussels? You could have gotten a good price for your catch in the marketplace."

"Our friend will be eating dried beef and beans once they're into the open water." Carlo slid the meal onto a large plate. Piero and Fernando gathered around; Piero popped a shrimp into his mouth and chewed. "Rizo, I'll be taking over all of Gio's errands for you. We talked about it. You're covered."

Rizo glanced at Giovanni gratefully. He wheeled to a nearby

shelf. "Don't forget the celestial charts. I want you to note every movement in the sky." He handed Giovanni a rolled-up piece of thick paper. "This chart is the Adriatic's winter sky—you're sailing in summer so you'll be observing a different sky. The stars are in different places, as you know, depending on the season. Mark your charts."

Fernando handed Giovanni a small leather notebook. "Use this as your rutter—your diary of your journey. Every seaman who can read and write and who wants to remember the waters and storms and adventure keeps a rutter."

"Did your new wife pick it out?" Giovanni asked, covering his gratitude with humor.

Fernando shook his head. "I chose it myself."

Giovanni felt the soft leather covering. "Too dear for seawater marks."

"It will have many," Fernando replied. "And we'll treasure every one when you return. And all the details you write in it."

Rizo continued to give instructions to Giovanni. "Include the date and time of your entries. Talk to the pilot; if he shares information, write it down. The boatswain will be using the lines to check depths when necessary. Stand next to him and record his findings. Captain Russo has assured me that you'll be given access to information, but don't hesitate to ask questions."

"Hesitate?" Piero chuckled. "Gio has never been shy when it comes to learning about ships and their travel."

Giovanni was touched by their excitement for his opportunity. He teased, "I promise I won't think of any of you once I'm aboard the ship. Be assured of that—for I won't be wasting a moment."

They laughed and relished their shellfish. Giovanni knew he would miss this camaraderie, but he looked forward to the new world about to open up for him. He had his plan—to make Chabotto Trading one of the finest businesses in Venice.

Giovanni and Piero had decided that Giovanni would take Venetian wine, Murano glass, salt, and crates of prized Venetian lace to the Middle Eastern marketplaces for trade. First stop would be Nicopolis, then on to Thessalonica, and finally Constantinople. At every port, Giovanni would have to pay 10 percent, or more, of both his sales and acquisition prices to the Ottoman Turks. His plan was to search out the best rugs, prized spices, antiquities, and tapestries. A portion of the savings accrued because Giovanni was traveling as the direct representative would be passed on to their clients, and the rest would go into the bank accounts of Chabotto Trading to be used for investment in new avenues of trade.

The brothers now gazed at the *Santa Bella*. Giovanni knew the ship had weathered many storms. It was solidly built and was a favorite among Venetian traders. The ship was a wide galley, three levels deep. It was fully rigged with sails and also retained space for man-powered oar transport—for ships that did not carry oars were at a disadvantage when the winds were not cooperating. And any lost time at sea represented lost profits.

The brothers hugged, pounding each other on the back. Then Giovanni looked Piero in the eye. "Take care of our parents—and the business. I'll be back soon."

Piero handed Giovanni his leather satchel. It contained rolled charts, a sandglass, a compass, a diary, quills, and bottles of ink. "You've waited a long time for this day, Gio. Sometimes, not so patiently."

Giovanni moved up the gangplank, a heady exhilaration propelling his feet forward.

Giovanni's cramped quarters, charged to Chabotto Trading, seemed magnificent to him. A narrow bed was attached to the wall, and a small desk and chair were bolted to the floor. He unrolled his charts and looked over the proposed route. He knew Captain Russo would steer the ship down the east coast of Italy, move from the Adriatic into the Ionian Sea, head southeast towards Crete, and then change direction to east-northeast, round the many islands in the Aegean Sea, and then make way towards the Sea of Marmara. The trip to the famous markets of Constantinople and the return to Venice should be completed in two and a half months, depending on weather. He was eager to get underway, to sail under the stars and smell fresh sea breezes. He knew he had to make a success of this, to forge relationships that would be profitable and earn him the right to be considered by Mattea's father.

Giovanni moved to the deck and stood near the pilot. The boatswain blew his whistle; three sharp staccatos and one elongated sound pierced the air. "That calls for the anchor to be hauled up and stowed," said the pilot. "The captain is ready to find the wind." The pilot pulled on thin leather gloves and moved into his helmsman position.

"First shift! In place!" The boatswain shouted and used his whistle to blow another alert to the crew. The hour sandglass, on the captain's deck, was turned over. The boatswain nodded to Giovanni. "Four turns of this equals one shift." Giovanni watched the boatswain use chalk to mark the number 1 on the wooden board near the sandglass. The first shift was now officially at work.

Giovanni could hear the anchor's chains rolling over the iron windlass as it was hauled up and stowed. Oarsmen moved the ship out into the open waters, where the sails were unfurled. The *Santa Bella* was underway.

Captain Russo came out of his cabin and surveyed the scene. Giovanni nodded to him, "I'm looking forward to sailing under your command, Captain."

Giovanni knew of Captain Russo's reputation; he was a stickler for preciseness, cleanliness, and keeping to schedule. He told Giovanni, "I have a good crew. They understand what is expected. When sailors are prepared to do their jobs, when they are dry, well-fed, and warm, there is an excellent chance of a successful journey."

Giovanni slept only a few hours each day for he wanted to learn everything he could about the ship. He watched the boatswain, captain, and pilot consult the traverse board every hour. Along with the information on speed, depth of water, and wind direction, the traverse board added to exact dead reckoning. It was a circular piece of wood with compass rose points painted on it. There were eight holes along the edges of the circle and eight pegs that were attached, by string, to a large nail in the center of the board. Every half hour, the compass was checked and pegs would be moved to align with the direction of the ship. The captain and the boatswain recorded the information in their rutters. Giovanni, having worked from these diaries while in Rizo's chart shop, understood the importance of the information for it would be used in future voyages to keep a ship on course.

Giovanni thrilled in seeing navigation in action, of charting the celestial codes of the night sky. He'd never felt so at peace. This, he thought, was where his soul lived.

The *Santa Bella* docked at the smaller ports. Giovanni was able to sell half of the Venetian lace in Nicopolis, and the

Thessalonican merchants coveted the Murano glass. Even after the tariffs, Giovanni was satisfied with his profits. The ship continued into the Aegean, and soon Constantinople was only days away. Giovanni talked to another trader, Signor Braga, on the boat. Braga had traded in the famous city for decades, but ten years ago, during an uprising, he had faced great danger.

"My goods were confiscated, my personal belongings burned. The city was in frightening unrest. Christians versus Muslims. So many factions wanting control. I had to flee." Braga's aged face was worried, but he was determined. "This is my first time back. I have heard it has calmed now, but in Constantinople, always watch your back."

Finally, days later, Giovanni stood on deck and watched the seven hills of Constantinople come into view. Soon he could see the city's towering walls and parapets. As they glided into the harbor, he realized the wharf was the largest he had ever seen— larger than the ports of Venice and Genoa. As the sailors readied the ship for docking, Giovanni could hear the buzz of different languages in the harbor. "I hear languages I didn't know existed," Giovanni said to Captain Russo as they moved off the ship.

"Yes, merchant Chabotto. Didn't you learn languages at the Scuola Grande di San Giovanni Evangelista, your confraternity?"

"I did, Captain, but rarely had the chance to practice. I'll now try to put my lessons to good use."

"Best of luck," said Captain Russo. "We'll depart for our return trip to Venice one week from today."

The walls of the city were massive. Giovanni stepped through one of the gates and passed large guards who looked fierce and cunning. Giovanni kept his cloak and his money close. He passed beautiful Muslim mosques and heard the calls to prayer. There were still a few Christian churches, their bells ringing, and nunneries with statues of Mary the Mother of God carved above their doors. Camels and packhorses were loaded down with pots and baskets of goods. Crowded market stalls were filled with barrels of brightly colored and aromatic spices—the favored curries, zenzero, timo, zafferano, and peppers. Sellers shouted from stalls filled with silks, rugs, metalwork, jewelry made with pearls, and gold and precious gems. Tables piled with books. Women were few, and those who did venture out or helped in the stalls kept in the shadows. Most had their faces covered.

Giovanni inquired about hiring a guide and soon a wiry Turk with a wide grin presented himself. "I am Opilio. I know everything and every place. You would be wise to hire me."

Giovanni wanted to test this guide. "First, I'm hungry. I'll judge your abilities by where you lead me to fill my stomach."

Opilio ushered Giovanni to a kiosk and instructed him to purchase a *penapato*—a flaky, spiced confection drenched with honey. Opilio watched Giovanni take a bite to see how this Venetian found the taste. Giovanni's eyes grew wide with pleasure and he licked his lips. Opilio laughed. "There. Now you know you must hire me. Tell me what you want to trade and I will get you to the best people and places, and get you the best prices."

Giovanni, with Opilio's help, quickly arranged for trades of the remaining Chabotto goods. Then they focused on products for Giovanni to take back with him on the *Santa Bella*'s return voyage. Opilio pointed to the barrels filled with colorful peppers. "Kings and nobles and peasants believe peppers can cure gout, aching bones, chest pains. Many of the rich and poor have silk pouches filled with pepper in their pockets; they will inhale the scent to ward off disease. Pepper enhances food. It is also good for love." Opilio winked. "It is hard to go wrong with pepper; it has great value."

Giovanni laughed. "I'll purchase the best pepper. Put that on our list, Opilio."

Giovanni was drawn to the bright, deep colors of the brocades and satins in the bazaar. He noticed beaded velvet slippers, imagining how his mother would laugh, delighted by their extravagance and beauty. Knowing the Venetian penchant for luxuries, he stopped to talk to the craftsman. He pointed to the slippers with golden tassels and added them to his list.

Days passed and Giovanni followed Opilio into smaller streets filled with shuttered shops and negotiated for intricately carved Russian samovars, mother-of-pearl fans, and handwoven rugs from Persia. They moved into alleys off the main market areas where washing hung from lines stretched from building to building. In these humbler areas, Opilio introduced him to weavers of colorful linen and silk wraps, blankets, and table-cloths. Giovanni chose carefully and asked Opilio to lead him to the jewelers. Giovanni knew gems were a big investment, but the profits could also be large. Each negotiation took time; there was always tea to drink and compliments to be exchanged, and Giovanni's growing language skills were an asset.

On Giovanni's last day, he and Opilio sat at a cafe. Groups of men sat nearby, breathing in spices and tobaccos from Bagh-dad through large, intricately decorated hookahs.

Opilio asked, "Signor. What else is of interest? Perfumes, oils, Chinese ceramics? Perhaps you are interested in the slaves. I can show you."

Giovanni had seen the slave markets. Men and women in chains, standing on wooden platforms; merchants bid on these unfortunates, taking into consideration each slave's stature, strength, beauty, and health. Giovanni shook his head. "It is not for me, Opilio. It may be profitable, but Matthew, in the Bible, wrote, 'Do onto others as you would have done unto you.' I would not wish their plight on anyone. I believe all humans should be free and paid for their services and talents."

Opilio looked at Giovanni. "You differ from many people. Many Christians believe that those who are not of their faith are not worthy to be treated as fully human. Or that by enslaving them and converting the captured to Christianity, their souls will benefit—for they will be made ready for the Christian's heaven."

Giovanni shook his head. "I do not agree with that philosophy."

"The Muslim Turks have forced Christians into slavery and taught them to be Muslim soldiers. They use them to control the Silk Road—while promising them everlasting life with Allah."

"I'll concentrate on spices, silks, gems, rugs, and antiquities," Giovanni said. "I will trade objects. Not people."

Back in Venice in late August, Piero and Giovanni accounted for the goods sold in Venice. Giovanni reached for his hat and gloves. "I'll leave tomorrow then—on to the kingdoms of Granada, Castile, and Catalonia."

"Queen Isabel has dedicated herself to taking Granada back from the Moors. Be careful in Malaga—the battles continue."

"I'll move quickly on to Valencia and Barcelona. We've got merchants ready to take possession of the jewelry and rugs I've brought back with me." Giovanni headed to the door. "See you at home, Piero. Tell Mamma not to keep supper for me."

"Where are you going?"

Giovanni was gone before Piero had his answer.

Giovanni hurried to Carlo's fishing shed and borrowed the skiff. Soon he was rowing toward the Grand Canal, where he unfurled the sail and steered east-northeast to the Castello district. Years ago, he had mastered the use of *Felicita*, and now he tacked to catch the best winds. He knew how to avoid sandbars and rocks and shallow waters. He stayed close to the coastline of the city, but in waters deep enough to afford *Felicita* the swiftest passage.

He tied the skiff to a pollard and leaped onto the dock near the Francesco della Vigna Chapel. He knew Mattea and her aunt often went to end-of-day mass. He found a bench in the chapel's garden and watched the sun move lower in the sky.

The bells of the chapel sounded. Giovanni could hear leather soles on the pebbled paths. Churchgoers were approaching. And then he heard her voice. Light and airy, discussing her day's reading of Dante's poetry with Sofia. He moved behind a tree; its full bloom shaded him. He watched as Mattea walked into view. She was more beautiful than his mind's eye remembered.

And then Mattea glanced his way. Startled, she stopped. Their eyes held for a long moment and he finally gave a small bow. Sofia joined her waiting husband and they continued on to chat with another parishioner. Giovanni and Mattea realized they had a moment that was theirs alone. Giovanni put his hand to his heart, letting her know he had not forgotten his promise to her. She touched her lips, and he remembered their soft touch on his own.

And then Sofia called to Mattea, encouraging her to move into the chapel. He waited until the church doors closed and she was completely out of sight. Elated by the sight of her, Giovanni boarded *Felicita* and sailed towards home, rounding the Arsenale and into the Grand Canal, aware of the cooling sunset breeze, and now pushing ahead with his plans to win the woman he loved.

Chapter Ten

The following year, Giovanni made several more trips to the ports of the Ottoman Empire and also to Sicily and the Portuguese port of Lisbon. His reputation as a successful trader with a deep knowledge of sailing grew. Chabotto Trading became the storehouse to query for the best spices and rugs and jewelry, but also for the unique items that Venetians coveted.

Summer arrived and Giovanni and his brother walked a swampy section of a neighborhood on the east side of the city of Venice. It was low tide and they looked at the dilapidated fishermen shacks that stood on stilts. The shacks were used for storing nets and fishing paraphernalia. "This land has been put up for sale, Piero."

"Who would want it? It is under water much of the day." Piero scoffed. "Why are we here, Gio?"

"I've noticed how some low areas of Venice are being filled in with enough sand, shells, rocks, and soil to allow for homes and storefronts to be built."

"Those are city projects, Gio. It takes great investment to change nature."

"I have been thinking it is time to add a new arm to the Chabotto business. I've put an offer in on this land."

"What? Without consulting me?"

"It is only an offer—and I'm consulting you now. I want you to see—and agree—that with proper draining and deep pilings from the Slavic countries, we can build homes to sell or rent. The population of Venice is constantly growing. People need places to live."

"Gio. We are merchants. Now you want us also to be property developers?"

"I feel sure we can make big profits, Piero."

"But don't we have enough now?"

Giovanni thought of the families of Benito Gravi, Zanobi Trifulo, Silvio Balbi, and others who held important positions in Venice and how their wealth brought them prominence. "Why not shoot for the stars?"

"What will we do with more money, Gio?"

"Go to the Arsenale and request Fernando's shipbuilding concern to construct our own ship. I could sail it across the Mediterranean and control even more of our trading profits. And one day, perhaps, sail across the Ocean Sea."

"You don't think these plans are too big?" Piero worried that Giovanni had become obsessed with financial gain, of keeping up with the richest and finest of Venice.

"My dream is not dead, Piero. But I need your agreement. It is the Chabotto family's business and we, as brothers, must agree."

Over the next year, Giovanni and Piero oversaw the new construction projects in the swamps of the San Paulo neighborhood. They were able to drain the land, strengthen the soil, erect desirable buildings, and sell the properties for excellent profit. The brothers purchased property in Chioggia, a section south of the Rialto, at the southern end of the lagoon. When the Chioggia property was developed and sold, the brothers tripled their investment.

Giovanni hired a new tailor, and now he and Piero wore fine velvet coats. The softest leather was used for their gloves and boots. Giovanni arranged for the Chabotto home to be painted a soft sage green and added more flowerpots to adorn its windows and doors.

While the real estate developments were in progress, Giovanni continued to travel. On a voyage to Bristol in England—one of the country's busiest and most important ports, known for trading with North Africa, Portugal, and Spain—Giovanni noticed a diminutive Italian friar in black woolen robes. His young face was chapped and dry from the winds, and the top of his head was shaved to reveal a patch of bare skull. Giovanni knew this bald patch was called a tonsure and was requisite of the monks in the Augustine order, for they emulated St. Peter, the apostle of Christ who had his head shaved by those who wished to humiliate and mock him.

Giovanni heard Captain Ferra, one of the oldest sea captains sailing the waters to England, behind him. "Chabotto, may I introduce Fra Carbonariis?"

The friar extended his hand. "It is a pleasure. Do you speak English?"

"I have some knowledge of it and hope to get better," Giovanni said.

"Good," Fra Carbonariis returned. "I have been appointed, by the Duke of Milan and the pope, to be the papal tax collector in England. The Vatican owns about one third of the English lands and the pope expects a ten percent profit of all income generated on the property. And, as money is never a friendly topic, I will have to approach it softly as I bless men's souls." He added, humbly, "Therefore, I need to speak in their language. Would you agree to practice English with me on this voyage?"

"That would be excellent." Giovanni was pleased, glad for the opportunity. He knew how important it would be in negotiations in the often cold and inhospitable northern country.

Fra Carbonariis's bright blue eyes crinkled in delight. "Then we shall both be more prepared to deal with the English." His eyes betrayed his opinion. "I have heard they're very sure of themselves and their superiority. Yes, they have Chaucer's work. And Francis Bacon in science and philosophy and cardinals of the church who hold sway over royalty. One of my favorites is Sir Thomas Malory—he wrote of the adventures of legendary King Arthur and his Round Table. His tales have been adopted as a kind of truth and many now believe that England is a fantastically honorable place." He laughed. "We shall see. Did you know that even women have published literary works in England?"

"You disapprove, Fra Carbonariis?" Giovanni queried.

The friar shrugged. "I believe all of God's creatures should be heard."

Giovanni chuckled and leaned on the rails, loving the motion of the ship. "But no one can compare to our Dante. And his *Divine Comedy*."

"You are absolutely right," Fra Carbonariis agreed. They looked out at the sea. The friar continued, "Most importantly, I will be part of the court of England. That can only be helpful for all from the Italian Peninsula."

Giovanni liked this man, his curiosity and willingness to explore and use his new situation to bring knowledge and goods from the Italian Peninsula to England. He hoped this would be a beginning of a strong friendship.

The bustling city of Bristol was situated on the Avon and Frome rivers. The air was damp; a thick fog often rested on the city. Market stalls were set up in grassy fields, not as in Venice on stone squares, or as in Constantinople on hard-baked sand. The rains and cloudy skies were different from Venice's sunny skies. And the English tongue was harsh to Giovanni's ears; he listened to people who were bundled in thick woolen jackets talk constantly of the results of battles between England and the French and the continuing War of the Roses—the civil war for control of the English throne, fought between the Lancaster and York branches, both families with royal lineage.

Giovanni completed his trading in the port city and, before joining Captain Ferra on the ship headed back to Venice, he shared a pint of ale with Fra Carbonariis.

"You have now been in England a few days," Giovanni said. "I hope you have enjoyed a shepherd's pie."

Fra Carbonariis laughed. "The mashing up of potatoes with cow's milk and butter and poured over stewed lamb and peas is quite a gastronomical surprise. I think I shall miss our pasta, but it was delightful."

"Did you know it's believed that Marco Polo brought the knowledge of pasta to Italy? He discovered it on his journey to China."

"Well, then," Fra Carbonariis joked, "We should consider Marco Polo for sainthood."

Giovanni chuckled. "I hope we meet again, Fra Carbonariis. Have a safe journey to the king's court in London."

"And you, back to the idyllic Most Serene Republic of Venice."

Days later, Captain Ferra ordered the docking of the ship in the busy trading port of Lisbon. There Giovanni heard of the country's latest pursuits in finding the southern tip of Africa.

Diogo Cão, a Portuguese explorer, had discovered a river in Africa that was named Kongo. Cão, born in the same year as Giovanni, was an illegitimate son of a noble of the royal household and was awarded an exploratory expedition to head south down Africa's western coast. Sailors talked of how Cão ordered his ship to hug the coast for weeks. They found the mouth of a deep and long river that he decided to explore. Along the Kongo River, he saw dark-skinned natives warily watching as the Europeans entered their homeland. Cão decided to land.

The chief of the natives showed himself. An exchange of gifts was made. Then the natives watched Cão erect a stone pillar, claiming the land for Portugal. Only days later, Cão turned his ship around and sailed the river back to the Ocean Sea. He continued south to a latitude he called the Tropic of Capricorn, naming it after a constellation of stars in the shape of a goat. The heat was intense, provisions were low, and Cão worried that the continent was too massive to ever find its end. Cão ordered his ship to return to Portugal, where he was knighted by the king. Giovanni listened to all the details and realized he felt great envy; Cão, because of his birth and access to the royal court, had been able to gain the Portuguese king's patronage and carry out a successful exploration.

Giovanni later sailed on merchant galleys to Lajazzo and Alexandria. He traded for the fur of Chinese foxes, for lynx and sables, and martens from Siberia and Japan. In Alexandria, a fine and ancient city at the head of the Nile River, he walked among people with skin the color of honey, whose thick, braided hair reached to the ground. He procured spices that could be used for health, such as frankincense for creaking bones, alum that was imported from China, and myrrh from Arabia, used to control bleeding and to clean wounds. There was anise for the winter cough, arak for cleaning teeth, black seeds and cardamom for ailments of the stomach, and the beloved saffron, the most expensive spice of all, for elegant cooking. He bought lutes, mirrors, glassware, swords, and harps in the colorful bazaars. He was taken to hidden caves filled with caches of jewels, gold, and ancient statues from the time of Cleopatra. He visited stables of fine Arabian horses. When he arrived back in Venice, rich citizens sought him out, wanting to lay claim to the most stunning of imported goods.

On the night of Giovanni's return from Alexandria, he and Piero sat at the family dinner, and presented their mother with a necklace of pearls. She exclaimed over its beauty. Signor Caboto was pleased, but cautious. "And you are sure we are not overextending, my sons?"

"We have stayed true to the Chabotto Trading principle, Papà. Fair pricing," Giovanni said.

"But you have brought back horses. Venice does not allow horses," Signor Caboto said. "What were you thinking?"

"I brought back one horse, Papà. It is already in the country, in a lovely vineyard north of the city."

Giovanni had heard that the family Balbi had added a vineyard to its estates. And that Signor Balbi appreciated riding on fine horses while keeping an eye on the yearly harvest. A gift of a young Arabian horse had been sent to the vineyard, compliments of Chabotto Trading.

It was only a few weeks later that Giovanni received a note from Signor Balbi, thanking him. And requesting a meeting at a café in Venice.

"Young Chabotto, I want to thank you for your generous gift. The Arabian horse is especially fine and strong," said the older man.

"Signor." Giovanni bowed.

"You've become successful," Signor Balbi said. "Many of my friends have invested in your businesses, your trading and real estate concerns, and speak well of their returns."

"I am pleased."

Signor Balbi sipped his wine. His leaned back and took a long look at Giovanni. "I have seen my daughter reject suitor after suitor. She is a woman with strong determination. She has frustrated me in arranging a marriage for her."

Giovanni sipped his wine, fearing that Signor Balbi might take him to task and remind him to keep himself separate from the Balbi family.

"Finally," Signor Balbi paused, and then, as if testing tender ground, he continued. "Mattea has told me her heart has been captured."

Giovanni straightened. Could it be that Mattea has chosen another? Or that she had told her father about their conversation?

"If you ever have children, young Chabotto, you will know it is not easy keeping them to your will."

Giovanni wanted to stand up for himself, to share his views of family life. "I do hope to have children one day, Signor Balbi, and hope I'll be able to take care of them in all ways, while allowing them to pursue their dreams."

Signor Balbi took a moment, then finished his wine and stood, signaling the end of the meeting. "Thank you again for your extreme generosity; the horse is now a favorite of mine. And congratulations on your continuing success, young Chabotto."

Giovanni's heart sank. Somehow, he had failed to successfully impress the father of the woman he loved.

Signor Balbi put on his gloves. "I have one more thing to say to you."

Giovanni waited, miserable.

"I feel it is time to give you my blessing. If Mattea wishes to be courted by you, I will not stand in your way."

Giovanni, his heart pounding, quickly stood, causing his chair to nearly topple. He was speechless, emotion constricting his voice. Signor Balbi gave a small, understanding smile, then turned and left the café.

Giovanni quickly paid for the wine and made his way to the Chabotto Trading Company, a new lightness in his step. He began to make plans to call on Mattea. He wanted to arrive with a gift. Should it be a book from England? Or a scarf from Mecca? A necklace from Greece? He saw Piero racing towards him and noticed that his brother had put on more weight. He chuckled to himself, knowing how hard it was for Piero to pass a Venetian bakery without sampling the honeyed sweets. Perhaps, Giovanni thought, he will bring Mattea a simple Venetian jam tart and pine nut cake.

Piero reached Giovanni, his eyes troubled, his voice low. "Gio, it's Papà."

They hurried to Campo San Silvestro. Giovanni entered his parents' bedroom and saw his father in bed, sleeping fitfully. Pale and thin. His mother sat at the bedside, her eyes closed. Her chest moved up and down, signaling she was in deep prayer. Giovanni stifled a cry, realizing with sudden clarity that his parents would not be with him forever. Signora Caboto opened her eyes and saw him. She took his hands. "Gio, God wants your Papà. I must be strong and remember that we've had a very good life. Love makes everything good." Giovanni placed a chair next to the bed and began his vigil.

Only a month later, Giovanni and Piero, wearing black armbands for mourning, sat in a funeral transport boat that was adorned with a carved figurehead of an angel. They were accompanying their parents' coffins to their final resting place on the island of San Michele. The brothers felt the biting air on their faces. It was a week ago that Signor Caboto's heart had failed in early morning, moments after Piero and his mother returned from the church's early mass. Three days later, Signora Caboto had collapsed while working on a lace coverlet to place on her husband's coffin.

Giovanni's face was set. He was now the head of the family, the elder Chabotto. Business and family concerns now rested on his shoulders.

The following week, a messenger arrived at the Chabotto Trading office with a letter. Giovanni recognized Mattea's gold-flecked wax seal. He moved outside to a narrow street, where he could be alone. He opened the letter and read:

Dearest Giovanni,

News of the journeys of your beloved father and mother to heaven has reached me. Please know I think of you in your time of reflection on life and loss, and your parents' love that you always cherished.

—*Mattea Balbi*

Chapter Eleven

"Piero, my boot, it has mud on it." Caboto's voice was tense, his natural easiness was gone.

Piero, dressed in a new tunic of amber velvet, turned to see his brother standing absolutely still, staring down at his feet. He saw a sheen of sweat on his face and looked at his brother's boots. "Gio, I don't see any spots of mud," Piero said.

"There are spots." Caboto collapsed on a hard wood chair. "Your handkerchief, Piero."

"Mine? It is new linen. I spent a good deal on it."

"Don't be selfish."

"Why mine?"

"Because I cannot have a soiled cloth in my pocket when I marry. I will have a wife to think of. Quick, lend me yours."

Piero handed his brother his handkerchief. "Gio, calma. You are head of our family now and today, we are about to become aligned with a very noble family. You cannot crumble."

Caboto rubbed at the toe of his boot, at a spot that, to Piero's eyes, was nonexistent.

The door opened. A servant of the Balbi family motioned the brothers to follow him. Piero moved close to his brother, said under his breath, "But if you want to, Gio, we can run. Leave Venice. Travel the world. I'll be at your side if you don't want to marry today."

Caboto grabbed Piero's arm, as if he needed support. "Piero, my heart is hers. I want to be by Mattea's side for the rest of my life. It is most overwhelming, to feel love."

Caboto straightened and gave Piero back his handkerchief. He strode after the servant and entered the intimate nave of the chapel near the Balbi palazzo. He moved to the altar and Piero took his place at his side. He could see the smiling Sofia in the front pew and Fernando and his pregnant wife beside her. Silvio Balbi sat to the side, his face set, definitely not in favor of welcoming his new brother-in-law.

Mattea entered the chapel. She was dressed in a cream-colored silk empire gown. Its sleeves of fine lace, banded with gold embroidery, flowed into soft ruffles at her wrists. A tiara of pearls held a shimmering veil of silk that flowed down her back and onto the floor. Her face was covered with a nearly transparent lace netting. She walked with her father towards the altar. Caboto took short breaths to calm himself. They faced the priest, who was dressed in a white cassock and a soft brown skullcap, a silk stole around his neck. He blessed their union and, taking their right hands, joined them together and pronounced them, in the sight of God, man and wife. A notary from the doge's palace sat to the side as a witness to the newlyweds' signatures on the marriage papers. This was followed by Signor Balbi, who entered his signature, finalizing his approval of his daughter moving into

Caboto's care. The marriage was now blessed by God, by the Republic of Venice, and by Mattea's beloved father.

After a short celebration, Caboto helped Mattea into the wedding gondola. It was large; two gondoliers were needed to steer the vessel. It was painted deep blue with gold filigree and festooned with flowers. They drifted through the canals of the city; strolling Venetians hailed them with congratulations. Caboto could see Rizo in his rolling chair, Carlo next to him, waving. Caboto stood in the gondola and bowed to his friends as they cheered loudly.

The gondola moved to the new home in the Castello neighborhood that Caboto had purchased for his wife. There, he carried her across the threshold and, as the servants scurried off to prepare the midday meal, Mattea looked at him with great seriousness. "My husband, I want to make this very clear. I see myself as your partner in this adventure of life. I will—forever— share your ambition and curiosity about the world, here and beyond Venice. I believe—together—we will discover and grow and experience great things."

Caboto held her close. It sounded, to him, as if their hearts beat as one.

Caboto's desire to solidify his fortune and station increased when Mattea became pregnant. He nurtured partnerships with heads of the prominent families, with bankers, ship owners, and financiers. Mattea arranged parties in their fine home and the guest list included nobles, sea captains, professors, traders, and merchants. All mixed in their home; class distinctions were not important. Caboto and Mattea's family soon included three sons—Ludovico, Sebastiano, and a newborn boy who was named Sancius. Caboto reveled in his family, his friends, and his business's success. There was little time to consider other things.

One summer day, in 1488, Piero burst into Rizo's chart shop. Caboto was deep in conversation about his next trip to trade goods in Greece. Piero was bursting with news. "The Portuguese have done it! Bartolomeu Dias, a knight of the royal house of Portugal, with two caravels and a supply ship, has rounded the Cape of Storms."

"Cape of Storms?" Caboto asked. "What is that? Where is that?"

"The southernmost point of Africa. The end of the continent has been reached, a new discovery for Portugal. Dias named it that because the winds and rains and waters were reported as most violent, and the ships were blown away from the coast— but it was finally recognized as found—there is now a possible path to the Far East."

Caboto was excited and envious at the same time. "Did he go further? Did he find out how far it is from this Cape of Storms to the shores of the Indies?"

"Not yet. His ship, the *São Cristóvão*, led the expedition. Dias, the sailors say, was convinced that the legend of Prester John—you've heard the stories of the leader of a nation of Christians that two hundred years ago settled somewhere in Africa . . ."

"Yes, I know the story of Prester John . . ."

"Well, Dias—searching the end of Africa, also wanted to find proof that those stories were real. Using the charts of Diogo Cão, he pressed further south on the west coast of Africa than any Portuguese before him. He looked for signs where Prester John's community of Christians might have settled."

"Did he find any proof of them?"

"No. But aren't you listening to the important part of what I'm saying? He did reach Africa's most southern point!"

Rizo pressed. "We need details, Piero."

"Very well. Sailors say Dias and the crew saw whales when they harbored in a bay that Dias named Santa Maria Concepcion. He claimed the area for Portugal and continued south. A massive storm hit. The ships were blown south, and when it became possible, he gave orders to sail back north—on a northeasterly trajectory. They saw land and anchored in a protected area near a river. He named the river Rio de Infante, after one of the captains of the other ships in the expedition. At this point, he did not know he had been blown, literally blown by the wind, around the southern tip, that he was over three hundred miles east of it. The ships had nearly collided with the huge rocks on the shoreline. Then natives appeared, and threw rocks and fired arrows at them, so the crew decided not to venture to land. Dias ordered the ships out of the river's mouth and studied the stars and thought, perhaps—with great luck—he had reached the western part of the Indian Ocean. He wanted to continue the exploration. But by this point, Dias's men were near to mutiny. They didn't want to go on. They were afraid they'd run out of provisions and die in this stormy, unfriendly region. Dias finally ordered the ships to begin their return journey. He followed the rough charts for thirteen days, making calculations that allowed for the storm that had blown them off course. That is when he saw land in the distance and realized that, in going around it, he would be heading north again along Africa's west coast. It struck all—Dias and his crew—that they had, indeed, passed the southern tip of the continent. Treacherous, it is—Dias called it Cape of Storms."

"Quite a feat," Caboto said.

Piero continued. "And the king of Portugal is ecstatic. He has already renamed it the Cape of Good Hope."

Rizo pulled out the maps and charts of the western coast of Africa. "Now explorers will chart more carefully. We'll need information on bays, beaches, obstacles, currents, and tides . . ."

"How long was Dias's return journey to Lisbon?" Caboto asked.

"Almost sixteen months. It is estimated to be more than sixteen thousand miles."

Caboto sat back, thinking. "That means that a ship, traveling from Venice, would have to first round the Italian Peninsula, pass Sicily, sail past Muslim-held lands in northeastern Africa, and sail the rough waters of the Strait of Gibraltar before even getting to the west coast of Africa in order to head toward its southernmost point. Two years, perhaps, to reach it. And who knows how long the journey is across the Indian Ocean to Asia? A voyage from Venice and back would take, perhaps, more than three years. The expense of building strong enough ships and providing provisions would be too much. It would be difficult to attract sailors for this long voyage."

Rizo nodded. "It's not ideal. The chances of losing ships and cargo in storms would be too great."

Caboto sighed. This new possible route, though exciting, was problematic.

A week later, Captain Russo dined with Caboto, Mattea, and Piero at the Castello home. Over a boiled dinner of octopus, Russo shared his news. "A young man from Genoa has gone to Portugal to get King John's ear," Russo said. "He wants to gain patronage for a voyage to sail west to get to the Far East. He wants to cross the Ocean Sea."

"Who is this man from Genoa?" Caboto asked.

"His name is Cristoforo Colombo."

The name sounded familiar to Caboto.

Russo continued, "He's been working on merchant ships sailing on the Mediterranean since he was fifteen. He has a brother, Bartolome, who is a mapmaker. Together they believe they have a strong proposal and hope to convince the Portuguese Royal Court that, by going into the Ocean Sea—going in the opposite direction of the Mediterranean and completing the circle around the globe—they will reach China."

"The Toscanelli theory. Decades old and no one has yet put it to the test." Piero looked at his brother. "Gio, you studied that map for years."

"Piero, we may have met this Colombo. When we were boys." Caboto remembered the brothers he had met briefly in Signor Fallio's shop in Genoa, almost twenty years ago. "Remember the map that I bought from Bartolome Colombo?"

"You still have that map, Gio. It's on the bookcase in your study," Piero said.

Caboto pressed Russo for details. "How was this connection to court managed? The Colombos are not of the noble class."

"The older, Cristoforo, married well," Russo said. "His wife is related to a royal in the court of Portugal."

Caboto felt a surge of yearning to adventure. Colombo was just his age. Bartolomen Dias and Diogo Cão were also in their thirties—all had managed to gain expeditions. What would it be like to sit with a king, he wondered, and ask him to believe in you and your plans—and dreams?

That night, as they prepared for sleep, Mattea nestled close to Caboto. "Why are you so thoughtful, my husband?"

Caboto sighed. "I'm imagining captaining my own ship,

finding a route to shores that could bring great wealth—and add to the knowledge of the world. Having a royal patron."

Mattea sat up, and reached across to her nearby desk for notepaper and a quill. She dipped the quill into a bottle of ink. "Let us list the royal personages who reign in the countries that could back such an endeavor."

"Mattea. Kings and queens are out of my reach."

Her eyes challenged him. "Should we be denied by the absence of trying?"

The next day Caboto talked with Rizo. "It is true, the favor of kings and queens is needed to embark on exploratory expeditions. Italy has no king or queen, the pope does not have an interest in exploration, and many explorers have already gotten the attention of royals in Portugal. The Spanish court is too embroiled in wars with the Moors to consider backing voyages."

"France, perhaps? England?" Rizo suggested.

"They also are distracted with wars. With each other—and internal wars. I don't see a direct path to pursue."

Rizo mused, "You must remember that patronage does not include the financing of the expedition."

"I know. Signor Penzo discussed this in lectures at Scuola Grande. Patronage does not pay for the ship, the food, the navigational tools, and everything an expedition requires. Royals may provide the flag but the funds must be raised."

"Very big funds."

"But think about this, Rizo. Once the expedition is successful and royals see profit, they are usually happy and grant monies—and exclusive rights—to new trading areas to the head of the expedition . . ."

"Yes. The captain of an expedition could become rich . . ."

"And he could get a title," Caboto added.

Rizo guffawed. "Gio, do you see yourself as a duke or a prince or a court jester?"

Caboto chuckled but then became serious. "I like to think of what a title could mean to my family. My sons. A title can be passed on. It assures a place in Venetian society."

"Don't get ahead of yourself, friend. First, you have to get into the same room with a royal and convince him or her that exploration is more important than wars. That will not be easy to do."

Caboto knew Rizo was right. He set about mapping possible routes and drafting letters to foreign kings and queens. He did not know if he would ever get a response.

All he could do was wait.

A few weeks later, when spring blossoms were brightening the trees, Caboto's nemeses from the San Giovanni Evangelista school, paunchy Benito Gravi and greedy Zanobi Trifulo, approached Caboto. They wanted to invest in his trading endeavors, for they had heard of the Chabotto profits. "We are still in the same confraternity, Chabotto," said Gravi. "Loyalty does not end when our lectures ended, as you know."

Caboto did not want to comment on their constant shunning of him in social situations, how they continually blocked invitations and opportunities. And he did not want to count them among his investors, for he always chose carefully, only going into business with men and families he felt he could trust.

"You cannot deny us," Gravi persisted. "And if this venture—

and others—go well, there could be a place at the doge's council next to me for a man of your experience and knowledge of the world."

Trifulo sniffed, "I wouldn't even want to go to Constantinople, but it is good for someone to know it. I have heard sandy dust is everywhere."

"There is sand," Caboto said. "And also great beauty."

Gravi groaned. "Who cares about beauty? We just want to make money. So, will you let us in, Chabotto? If you do, I'll arrange a meeting for you with the doge."

Caboto was seduced by the possibility. If he were close to the doge's circle, his sons would be treated with utmost respect, their futures would be enhanced. He relented. "Let us sit together and make a plan. I have ships heading eastward in the new year, and perhaps I could welcome your investment."

Chapter Twelve

There was loud pounding on the bedchamber door. Caboto groaned. "What is it?"

Mattea opened her eyes, still half asleep. "Who is making such a noise?"

Piero's voice was plaintive. "Gio. The storm—do you hear it? It bodes us no good news."

Caboto listened. January winds were whistling against the windows and rain battered the clay roof tiles. He threw on warm clothing, pulled his hooded cape close to his body, and told Mattea to gather the children to their bedroom.

Caboto hurried with Piero toward the wharf. The rain on the stone streets made the going slick and slippery, and their leather boots were quickly soaked. Even the buildings seemed to scream as they strained to hold upright against the fierce wind. The brothers moved through the packed-dirt alleyways that were already saturated, their boots sinking into mud that was thick and deep. They reached the canal; waters splashed up at them.

No boats were braving the night. The water that surrounded Venice was rising, lashing at the wooden edges on the docks. "*Acqua alta*, brother. The high water is coming."

Caboto had experienced Venice's high waters before. Every few years, an onslaught of torrential rains caused the flooding of the city. Marketplaces and *campi* would be covered with water; many Venetians who had fine homes near the canals and shores moved furniture and goods to the second and third levels for safekeeping. The water was powerful and it showed its strength as it invaded the city.

"Gio, we can't get to the storehouse. Or the wharf," Piero said. "This is the worst I have ever seen. All we can do is wait it out."

Caboto nodded and they made their way back home. "Piero, there are three ships out there, full of our cargo."

"I know, my brother," Piero's voice was tight. "I know."

Caboto thought of the ships carrying the Chabotto goods across the Mediterranean and into the Adriatic Sea. He prayed the ships' captains had found safe harbor. They had invested huge sums in the cargo they carried. Perhaps he had taken too great a risk.

"Gio, the storehouse is in an elevated area," Piero was assuring himself as much as Giovanni. "The rugs and silks have been stored on the top floors. Account books are there too. Our stove and conference tables, on the first floor, will be underwater, perhaps. But might withstand."

Caboto hardly heard him. He was thinking of their investors who were expecting to share in profits. Of Gravi and Trifulo, who had begged to invest large sums. Of the insurance on the cargo that he had arranged with the banks. He also worried that the insurance would not be sufficient.

The winds and rains continued for days and the entire city

became covered with water. Caboto, in his library on the second floor of his home, paced. Piero looked over the books, worried that their future might be at the bottom of the sea.

Mattea kept the children distracted, reading to them in the third floor rooms. But the boys soon felt claustrophobic. They wanted to run, to race through the streets, to see their friends at school. Sebastiano created a game of pirates and soon had Ludovico and Sancius join him—and sounds of a great sea battle were heard throughout the house.

Finally, after a full week had gone by, the rain lessened, though the skies remained gray, and the water was still high. Mattea sat next to Caboto in front of the library's fire. She put her hand on his. "Keep faith, Gio."

"It was the largest cargo we've ever commissioned, Mattea. If we've lost it, we'll lose a fortune."

"Keep faith, Gio," she repeated.

Caboto could only feel fear, remorse, and guilt. "Dear wife, maybe I was too ambitious."

Two of the three ships that carried cargo for Chabotto Trading were lost at sea. Other merchants lamented their losses and all were petitioning the banks to pay on their insurance. There were so many requests that the banks closed their doors, arranging private appointments with only their largest clients. Caboto sent numerous petitions to the banks and was told to be patient. Gravi and Trifulo sent demanding messages, wanting Caboto to make good on their guaranteed profits.

Caboto did not have the personal fortune to cover his losses. In addition, the butcher, the shoemaker, the tailor, and the dressmaker waited impatiently for their bills to be paid.

Caboto could not sleep. Or eat. He paced, trying to find a solution as the waters slowly receded and Venetians ventured out again.

At midnight, a loud pounding on the door of the villa caused Caboto, at his desk in the small library, surrounded by his account books, to look up, startled. Who could it be at this time of night? Caboto heard a servant hurry down the stairs and across the tile floor. Moments later, the servant stood in the doorway to the library.

"It is Signor Gravi and Signor Trifulo."

"Show them in. *Grazie*." Caboto pulled his robes tighter, and poured three glasses of sherry. He did not have a good feeling about this call in the middle of the night, but he must persuade them to be patient.

It was soon clear Gravi and Trifulo were not in a friendly mood. They told Caboto that they expected their investments to be returned, that the demise of the ships and loss of cargo was on him.

Caboto wanted them to be fair. "It is obvious, of course, that the storm is an act of God. I am sick that the gems and antiquities are sunk and likely never to be found. I pray for the souls of the captains and sailors. And I assure you, I'm working late into the night, planning to repay you with profits from voyages to come."

Trifulo snorted. "More guarantees. You think we're gullible."

"Well, we're not," Gravi snarled. He put his thick hands on his protruding stomach. "We want our money back, now."

"I explained that your investment would be used to purchase cargo," said Caboto. "Once goods were back here and sold, then you would make your money back, with profit."

Gravi's eyes narrowed. "You're saying you don't have the funds? If so, we have no choice."

Caboto felt a prickle of fear. "What do you mean?"

"Justice will be called on to force your hand," Trifulo said.

Gravi laid out the plan. "We'll request the doge's finance council to find you unable to pay your promises. You know the punishment for unpaid debts can be severe. Even prison." Gravi puffed out his chest, relishing his threat.

Caboto tried to keep his voice calm. "All I need is time. I'll be able to make up this loss. I just need time. And you must realize that if I'm unable to work, I won't be able to put myself in a position to repay your investment."

They shrugged. Clearly, the monies were not as important to them as making trouble for Caboto. "Venice's Promissione Rule is in place. We cannot adjust it. We are not the doge. Unpaid debts are a serious matter. If you are arrested, it is only the law."

"Would you allow me time?"

"Two days. That is most generous."

"But you know that ships must travel months to pick up cargo, and it takes time to sell the goods!"

The men moved out of the library. The servant, waiting in the hallway in case he was needed, quickly moved to the door to open it for their departure.

Caboto was devastated. All he had worked for, was it to disappear?

The water in the canals was gray, the clouds still thick and promising more rain. The refuse washed into the sides of the canals—the trash, the weeds, the battered fish and drowned rats—filled the city with a foul stench. Venetians walked through the *campi* with scarfs across their noses.

Fernando hurried into the Chabotto storehouse. "Tell me it is not true. Gravi and Trifulo are saying they will see you put in jail."

"They refuse to give me time. The other investors trust that I'll make good. But not Gravi and Trifulo. I walked by the Venetian prison this morning. Imagined myself inside."

"It will not happen, Gio."

"I'm not so sure." He told Fernando of visiting the Venetian branch of a bank owned by the Bardi family of Florence. He'd been told that the losses of many Venetians have stretched their funds and they would not be able to make a loan to Caboto at this time. "I went to the banks owned by the Strozzis and Silviatis. They also regret they could not provide a loan. I headed to the firms of the Gondi and Peruzzi families. Again, I was denied."

"Our family lost ships in the storm, Gio. I don't have funds to help you now, but you know I would if I could."

"*Grazie*, Fernando. I will find a way to gain time. I must."

At the end of the day, Caboto left the premises and moved across the *campo*. He saw Gravi and Trifulo deep in conversation with three red-capped condottieri, former soldiers, now mercenaries, often hired by the city to patrol during festivals and times of unrest. Many were hired privately to use their physical strength to force an issue, or to encourage, with physical violence, an accused to make restitution. Dressed in tunics with shoulder pads made of metal, red caps tight on their heads, they had sticks, helmets, and muskets strung to their backs. Caboto stood in the shadows behind a stone column. He could hear Gravi make his considerations clear. "It is a matter of our investment and Chabotto's assurances. If the city council does not act quickly, it might be seen as a citizen's duty to see crimes are punished."

Trifulo nodded. "The judging council will likely call for whippings of the brothers, perhaps even in public."

Gravi groused, "We're talking a very large sum."

Trifulo added, "Deserving of much more than a whipping. Perhaps the Chabottos will hang."

Caboto hurried home. He huddled with Piero and told him what he'd heard. Piero was stunned. "Gio, surely they will not hang us? You are a member of the San Giovanni Evangelista confraternity. You are married to a Balbi."

"Mattea's father would have protected me. But he is no longer with us."

Caboto hurried to the government house, hoping to arrange matters before an arrest order could be approved and printed in the Venetian news pamphlets. He did not want Mattea to feel disgraced.

"What is it that you desire, Signor Chabboto?" the dry voice of the hunched civil servant queried.

Caboto showed him the order to appear before the Council. "I would request a *gratia*. A waiver. Acknowledging the recent storm and loss of ships were circumstances out of my control. I will happily sign a promissory note that there will be repayment, by me, to Signor Gravi and Signor Trifulo and all investors. In due course."

The civil servant looked at the markings on the paperwork concerning the case. "It looks like no waiver is to be allowed, Signor Chabotto. You are expected to appear in the legal courts the day after the next Sabbath. And face your punishment."

An hour later, Caboto, heartsick, sat across from Mattea. He took her hands. "Dearest wife, you must renounce me. I would not desire you to walk through Venice with all talking about your husband sitting in the Old Prison."

"There is no help?"

"No bank is willing to help. They are stretched too thin."

"We must ask my brother."

Caboto hung his head. "Mattea, I have seen Silvio. He has offered to open the family palazzo to you. And the children. But there will be no financial help for me."

"My father would turn in his grave! Silvio has always been envious of you." Her eyes flashed with anger. "He has not built anything. He has not left the confines of small-minded Venice. He has not excited the wharf with goods from Mecca and Baghdad. He has his entertainments. That's all he cares about."

"Mattea, you must go to him, take the children. I must leave Venice and find a way to repay the debts."

"You will leave Venice? To go where?"

"Perhaps Spain. There are fine ports there. I'll find work. Opportunities."

"To explore into the Ocean Sea." A light of excitement shone in Mattea's eyes. "Yes. It is where we will go."

"We?"

"I'll gather the necessities for the children. I suggest you arrange for transport."

"Mattea. You do not need to flee your home like a criminal. Piero and I will find a way to make this right and come back for you."

"This is an adventure, Gio. I promised you I would always be your partner in adventure."

Chapter Thirteen

Midnight. The March sky was dark, the rain steady and cold. The Caboto family, each carrying a small bag, pulled the hoods of their capes over their heads and slipped out the side door of their home.

Carlo, holding a candle in his *bragagna*, waited for them at a small nearby pier. His new and larger fishing boat was just wide and long enough to carry the entire Caboto family and their bags. Piero helped Mattea into the boat and settled them in low seats in the bow.

Caboto sat near Carlo, and spoke in low tones. "The doge has signed a warrant for my arrest. You must drop us off, quickly. I don't want to put you in danger."

Carlo nodded. "It's good the moon is hidden tonight. And that it's wet and chilly. Even the *condottieri* will be taking cover."

Caboto used the extra set of oars to help Carlo move the *bragagna* through the narrow, deeply shadowed canals. All the homes and shops were dark.

Sancius, the youngest, leaned against Mattea. "Mamma, where are we going in the night? I'm tired."

Sebastiano leaned into him and whispered. "This is an adventure, Sancius, and the rules of the game are that we be very quiet."

"I don't want to play a game. I want to be in my bed," Sancius whined.

Sebastiano's eyes were almost popping with excitement. "How could you choose sleep over adventure?"

Caboto shared a look with Mattea; they had noticed Sebastiano's daring spirit, his attraction to exploits that would task a boy twice his age. Caboto was glad that Sebastiano felt brave, but hoped the young boy would heed his own advice for silence tonight.

Ludovico, ever studious, quietly surveyed the streets that connected the threadlike canals. "Papà, I'll keep an eye out for the *polizia*."

Caboto felt a sudden shame that his oldest son should know that they were escaping to keep his father out of prison. Is this what his son would always remember? Judge him by?

Carlo avoided the Grand Canal until they reached the western edge of the San Polo neighborhood. Daylight teased the horizon as the family transferred to a barge that would take them toward Jesolo. Caboto was reminded of his journey from Genoa to Venice over twenty years ago. Jesolo was the town where Guilio Caboto and his young family spent the night before embarking on a ferry to their new home. His father had taken a chance then, hoping for a better future in Venice. He'd arranged for a home, a share of a business, and a housekeeper for his wife. Now Caboto berated himself for putting his own family in an exceedingly more precarious position, for there was no warm home waiting for them, no business available for him to take over.

It was as if Piero could feel his brother's worry, for he leaned over and whispered, "All will be well, Gio. We are together."

The barge made a steady pace, and at nightfall, the exhausted family reached Jesolo. Their clothes were damp, and the chill of the air had seeped into their bones. Caboto found a small inn and asked Piero to arrange with the innkeeper to bring bread, cheese, and turnip soup to their rooms. Something to warm their bellies and ease them into sleep. Piero nodded, patting his widening girth. "Everything seems better with full stomachs, you know I believe that."

"Piero, I need to find a carriage that will take us to Catalonia. I'll be back as soon as I can."

Piero nodded to his brother. "I'll be on watch here."

Jesolo was quiet and dark. The stars were bright in the sky. Caboto could make out Polaris and the Big Dipper and Orion's Belt; he noticed the light they shone on the ships in the small port. He knew the life of a merchant and a trader, even the life of a sailor. What would he find to do in the mountains, so far away from the sea he loved?

Caboto noticed a stable. There was candlelight in the upstairs living quarters. He knocked on the door.

"Who is it?" A gruff voice came from behind the closed door.

"A traveler. Seeking to hire a driver and carriage for tomorrow. I am traveling with my family."

The door opened. A huge man with a considerable beard, and a thick blanket wrapped around his shoulders, stood before Caboto. The heady smell of roasting meat over a fire pit wafted into the air. Caboto felt his stomach grumble.

"How far?"

"Many days' journey."

The stable owner eyed Caboto suspiciously. "Our carriage can travel about twenty miles a day, if weather holds. Every day costs a good amount."

"I am willing to pay." Caboto showed the man a pouch filled with coins.

The stable owner's greed presented itself. "My son could do it. He knows the roads. Did you say tomorrow?"

"Yes. We will be ready at dawn."

"What's that accent?"

Caboto, hoping the stable owner would not be an expert in Italian dialects, lied. "Rome. I have three young sons, a wife, and a brother."

"Huh." The old man spat, aiming for the ground, but spittle caught on his beard. His voice was suspicious. "I have to be careful. People trying to sneak out of Castile and Leon come this way. Because of the Inquisition. I won't be accused of helping any Jews or infidels trying to flee from the courts of Queen Isabel. I agree with the Catholic royals that everyone should worship the one true God." The stable owner's short speech seemed rehearsed. Just in case Caboto was a spy.

"We are Catholic. Dedicated to the pope," Caboto said. "And we are headed north to the regions of Spain, not away from them." Caboto had heard of the strict edicts of the Inquisition—an investigation to flush out anyone not of the Catholic faith. Many had been put to death for not believing as the Catholic royals of Spain insisted. He, like many people in the more free-thinking Venice, did not agree with these religious dictates for he had met many merchants and traders of many faiths—Muslim, Jewish, Hindu, and others—and respected their beliefs.

But Caboto knew tonight was not the time to discuss this matter with a stable owner.

The man rubbed his hands together, again eyeing Caboto's pouch of coins. "I'll need a deposit."

"Of course. Let us negotiate the price."

The next day the sun promised to shine, despite the low temperatures. After a night of rest and an early breakfast of fresh eggs, pork, and country bread, the family piled into a drafty, aged carriage for the next leg of travel. The driver, the son of the stable owner, was as large as his father and smelled of garlic. He wore a humongous fur coat and hat. Caboto noticed a thick wooden club and musket on the driver's seat, and that the driver's belt held three knives. "You look prepared for trouble. Anything I should know?" Caboto asked.

The driver spoke in a monotone, his eyes simple. "I am called Lorenzo. I am always prepared for the roads. No telling where smugglers and brigands might appear."

Caboto saw Sebastiano's head peek out the carriage window. He knew the boy had heard the driver. Sebastiano's voice rose in excitement. "Papà, smugglers are like pirates on land. Are we going to meet some?"

Caboto hurried to his middle son. "Not on this trip, Sebastiano. And don't mention anything about smugglers to your brothers or your mother. If you do stay quiet on this, I promise we'll hike into the mountains of Catalonia and search for buried treasure when we reach our new home."

Sebastiano put his finger to his lips, signaling his agreement to silence. Caboto nodded to Lorenzo and stepped into the carriage. He closed the doors and covered his family with the furs provided for warmth. They were heading towards an even colder climate.

~

Days later, having stopped only to feed and water the horses, the family arrived in Turin, a large city in the Duchy of Savoy, part of the territory of the Holy Roman Empire. There they rested for a day and then continued over rough country roads to the northwest. Finally, more than a week later, they reached the borders of Aragon and entered lands ruled by the Catholic royals, King Ferdinand and Queen Isabel. Within a day, the Caboto family arrived at a small village called Cerdanya.

Part Three: Catalonia

Chapter Fourteen

Caboto settled his payment with the driver while Piero set off with the boys to find lodging for the evening. Caboto and Mattea made inquiries in the village's shops, hoping to arrange for a permanent home. They inspected a small stone cottage on the edge of the village. It had bedrooms on the second level, and the main floor had a large fireplace in the kitchen. Mattea, used to fine homes, squeezed Caboto's hand and assured him she found it charming. He kissed her. "Your generosity of spirit touches me, my wife. I will make good again. I promise."

They bought simple furnishings from the villagers and quickly set up their home. When signing the necessary papers, Piero watched his brother sign *Johan Caboto Montecalunya*. They had agreed to choose a new name to keep the family's identity secret. They had decided on the name Montecalunya, because it placed the family as one that hailed from the mountains of Catalonia.

After the family was settled, Caboto presented himself to the town council. "I am Johan Caboto Montecalunya, a draftsman, chart-maker, and engineer. My brother, Piero, is an accountant of excellent talent. We have here, under my arm, designs that will prove my competence and ability in design and land management." He held up a leather account book. "And this, to show Piero's expertise with numbers and bookkeeping." Piero rolled out drawings that Caboto had done when they were building their real estate development—plans for the draining of swampland, building strong foundations and bridges to connect land areas. Caboto had learned rudimentary skills of engineering at Scuola Grande di San Giovanni Evangelista, and was able to put them to good use in Venice. And now, hopefully, here.

Cerdanya's town council included three brothers, each with land that needed renovation. They remarked on the serendipity of Johan Caboto Montecalunya arriving. Caboto bowed ingratiatingly, and soon found himself with work.

Months passed. Mattea looked after their sons' education and was soon speaking the Catalan language with the butcher and baker in the village and with the farmers at the weekend markets. She kept up with the political and religious edicts set out by Queen Isabel and King Ferdinand as well as news of the Reconquista battles with the Moors. The goal of these conflicts, which had been ongoing for generations, was to push the Moors off the Iberian Peninsula and take back territories the Moors had conquered centuries ago. Mattea reveled in her new freedom, meeting new people who were different from her Venetian friends, learning how to live more independently in a new place. Caboto ached for news from Venice, from Fernando, Carlo, Rizo, and Signor Penzo. But he could not reach out to them because no one was to know where they were. He knew the *condottieri* had been hired to find him, so it was imperative that he stay out of sight.

One day, Caboto and Piero watched the boys play pirates—imagining the fields as the high seas, the trees as masts, their wooden sticks as swords. Sebastiano ran over to them. "Father, I cannot smell the sea here. It's hard to be a pirate in the mountains."

Caboto agreed. "We'll find our way back to the water, Sebastiano. Seagulls will fly over our heads. You will feel the cold beach under your feet and taste the salt in the air. I promise."

Sebastiano shouted with glee and ran back to Sancius and Ludovico, declaring he was the best pirate known in all the worlds.

Caboto and Piero laughed. And then Piero grew serious. "Gio, why not go to Barcelona? It is the financial center of Catalonia and one of the best ports of Europe. The velvet manufacturers there are highly regarded; we could acquire the best material and garments and send them on trade to England."

"We must stay away from the merchant trade, Piero. That is where the Venetians may be looking. Let's give ourselves more time."

Spring rains had brought flash flooding and cool temperatures to Cerdanya. The Caboto family longed for the sun and Venice's Mediterranean warm air and fragrant flowers. Even in the summer months, the mountains were filled with long shadows and chilly winds. The inclement weather was actually a boost for business because Caboto was hired to oversee the rebuilding and refurbishing of families' homes that were damaged by snows and floods. One day, as he was surveying a wealthy landowner's estate, a small, thin man approached. The man's clothes were perfectly tailored and he was definitely not pleased to be dirtying his boots by plodding through the remains of the spring mud. "Hello, are you Johan Montecalunya?"

Caboto waited for the man to reach him. He noticed the fine leather gloves and shiny brass buttons on his trim coat. Caboto was cautious, for this man was a stranger and he still worried about the long arm of Venice's *condottieri*. "To whom do I have the honor of speaking?"

"Gaspar Rull." The man was out of breath. "Civil engineer. Like you. If you are who they have told me you are." Rull looked around. "My specialty is excavation and design of manor homes, quite grand, closer to the sea." He lifted up a mud-splatted boot and grimaced. "Land gets soaked up here in the mountains and takes a long time to dry."

"And why is it that you are looking for me?" Caboto wanted to get to the point.

"Oh. It's my cousin you are working for now. You are enlarging his pond, correct? For his new livestock? He thinks I can add free advice because that is what relatives are asked to do. We could discuss your plans for a bigger pond, reinforcing its perimeter, and rolling the best boulders into place and such. But I assume you will tell me you don't need any advice." Rull's words were clipped as his breath steadied after his exertion. He wiped a thin film of sweat off his brow.

Caboto relaxed, realizing this man meant no harm. "I'm always receptive to opinions. I do want to think of everything."

"How very open of you. I like that," Rull said.

The two men discussed the Catalan terrain, the depth of the aquifers, and the run-offs of waters from the nearby mountains in relation to ponds and streams in the area. Their conversation continued as they descended to the road and walked their horses towards a nearby inn.

Caboto was interested in Rull's knowledge about the areas near the coast, and Rull was happy to share his opinions. "The Catalan town of Girona, two days' journey from here, where the Rivers Onyar, Ter, and Güell come together. Very fine small city. In need of bridges. The large Jewish population there has recently left, headed to Amsterdam and other places where they can worship as they please. I must say I believe the Inquisition is not doing Catalonia—or any of the lands under the jurisdiction of Queen Isabel and King Ferdinand—any favors. We're losing fine people. But that is my opinion and you must never repeat it for I'll deny saying it." Rull looked at Caboto; his face brightened with an idea. "Wealthy Catalans, all the way to Barcelona, are in need of civil engineering talents. There's even talk of a new harbor for Valencia. Too much work for just me. Perhaps you should come down from the mountains to have a look."

They reached the inn, and tied up their horses. Both were thirsty and hungry. They entered the inn and sat at a rough wooden table. An old man, wearing a torn jacket and a hat of a sailor, sat nearby, looking deep into his beer. He lifted his mug into the air as if in welcome. "Best ale I've had since Naples. You ever had the beer in Naples?" The old sailor looked at them with watery eyes, and beer glistened on his lower lip.

"Naples does have good beer." Caboto was polite. He looked around to get the server's attention and leaned into Rull. "Tell me, Señor Rull. What should you like to eat?"

Rull took his gloves off. "I'm hoping for wild boar. Might get lucky and have a bit of truffle in a mashed potato. It is the season."

The old sailor grimaced. "All they got is pork shoulder soup and nettles. Oh, and sausage. And boiled potato, if they haven't run out." He leaned into them. "You want to hear the latest news? All it costs is a glass of beer. For me."

Rull shrugged. "All right, old man. I'll buy you one. What is the news?"

"There's a new explorer hoping to get the backing of King Ferd and Queen Isa. The crazy man wants to go west into the Ocean Sea to reach the Far East. Name is Cristoforo Colombo. Little guy, they say. Barely reaches the top of the pilot wheel on a ship."

Caboto was interested. "Colombo. I had heard he was in Portugal."

The old sailor continued. "Not anymore. He proposes to go into the mystery sea that's full of monsters and dragons." He burped; the smell of beer and sausage breath wafted towards Caboto.

Caboto waved off the odor and asked, "What else do you know of this Colombo?"

"That the braggart thinks God has chosen him for great things. King Ferd didn't go for the wild idea. But the queen has her own mind. Colombo's been waiting two years for her final answer."

Caboto waved to a server and ordered the old sailor another sausage. "The queen is favorable toward this expedition?"

"I'll take another beer too," the old sailor said. Caboto signaled for another and the old sailor continued. "Word is that the queen's leaning toward yes. Because Spain needs money— have to pay for war somehow—and anywhere there might be gold, Spain wants to get there first." The old sailor warmed to the attention of these fine, generous gentlemen. "The squat, square Colombo, when he was just a deckhand, journeyed on a ship heading to England and back. On the return, the ship was nearing Portugal—Lisbon—when it was attacked by pirates. Both ships were carrying a lot of gunpowder and when his ship was about to explode, Colombo jumped into the sea. Wreckage all around him. He still had wits about him, and grabbed an oar floating nearby, used it to buoy himself up. And then." He stopped to release a loud belch. "This is the story. He was banged up, yes, he was, but the upstart managed to kick his legs in the water—kicked six miles to the shore."

"Six miles?" Caboto was impressed. "I have not heard this story."

"And dragged his bloody body up on the rocks. That's where they found him."

Rull laughed. "If he survived that, he's got to be like a dog. With the skin of a seal. Are you sure this is true?"

"True. Absolutely. Swear on my beer." The sailor shook his head. "Colombo's just a man who doesn't take no for an answer. Getting through that calamity made him think God had chosen him for something great. Had plans for him. They took him into Lisbon, to his brother, the mapmaker. Brothers were reunited; it was all weepy and wet."

"But how did Colombo get from being blown from a ship in Portugal and asking the king there for patronage to Queen Isabel's court?" Caboto asked.

Their soups and sausages were placed on the table.

"Sounds like he's a lucky sailor," Rull said, bending his head to smell the food. "Soup's greasy, but flavorful."

The old sailor lifted his arms to sleepily scratch his head with his bony fingers. Caboto could smell the wool that had been wet and dried too many times and the body odor that was embedded in it. The sailor yawned as he muttered, "So, this Colombo headed to the Castile Court—to Queen Isa. And now he's waiting for her answer."

"Did he travel with his wife?" Caboto asked.

"Naw. The rich wife got sick. Died. He put their young son in a Spanish monastery for upbringing. Probably he's forgotten about him. Used his Portuguese contacts to find his way to Queen Isa's court. He's been waiting for two years now for her answer. Did I tell you that?" The old man's eyes were closing. In a moment, his head met the tabletop and he slipped into a loud, snore-filled nap.

Rull shook his head at Caboto and laughed. "The queen won't give this Genoese the go-ahead. The Catholic royals are too enmeshed in the war against the Moors, the treasury's depleted. Colombo's waited two years and I predict he'll still be waiting two years from now."

That night, Caboto settled into bed next to Mattea. The candle was low and its light flickered in the small room. "Mattea, the family cannot hide forever," he said. "I'm feeling time passing quickly."

"We are mortal, my husband. There is only so much time."

Caboto groaned. "I'm feeling my age. And fearing that I'll never accomplish what I always hoped for. Maybe it's time to take a chance. I met another engineer today. His name is Gaspar Rull. He heard talk that the king's royal council is about to consider plans to rebuild the harbor in Valencia."

"Valencia? That is halfway down the eastern coast of the Spanish lands."

"Yes. And its Turia River is too shallow for large ships and the piers need to be positioned more advantageously. The city wants to have a port like Barcelona's. Only better. Rull and I discussed ideas and how we might put our heads to it. He could use his contacts to get us in front of the Duke of Valencia. The duke has direct contact with King Ferdinand."

Mattea heard the excitement in her husband's voice. "Do you think this opportunity has promise?"

"I do. But I'd have to go to Valencia to prepare charts and drawings. For our proposal." He looked at her, waiting for her reaction.

Mattea took a moment, then blew out the candle. She settled her head on Caboto's shoulder. "Gio. You must go to Valencia. Send for us as soon as you can. The adventure must continue."

Chapter Fifteen

The day after his fortieth birthday, Caboto joined Gaspar Rull in Valencia. The men surveyed the crowded harbor and the city's canals. They measured depths, tides, and currents and designed a system of break walls and piers. Caboto sweated over his drawings, going through dozens of quills and pots of ink. He worked late into the nights, his eyes aching from squinting in the low candlelight. But he wanted to make a good impression for he thought this project could be the beginning of new and important contacts. If he could connect with a duke—and a king—one day, he might be able to propose, like Colombo, his own expedition of exploration. But he didn't want to get ahead of himself; first he had to impress the duke.

The duke's manor house was grand. Caboto arrived, his drawings under his arm. He was shown into a large room lined with chairs upholstered in raw silk imported from China. Mosaic-topped tables from Florence and expensive French Aubusson rugs dotted the space. Heavy Venetian crystal chandeliers hung from the ceiling. Caboto could trace each item to its origins and knew the exorbitant prices the duke paid for his fine things.

The duke wore rings on every finger and carried a lace handkerchief that he frequently pressed to his nose as he spoke. Rull was at ease but Caboto felt the import of the meeting and his breath constricted as he explained their plans. The duke only nodded, not giving away his thoughts. He poured them all a glass of port. As Caboto accepted the rich fortified wine in the heavy crystal goblet, he could not wait any longer. He blurted, "Is there anything else you would like to know, Excellency?"

The duke smiled. "Only if you will make yourself available, at the king's pleasure, to attend the Royal Court and present these drawings again. I am most pleased and I predict the king will be too."

Rull grinned at Caboto; they shared a look of triumph. Their first obstacle had been successfully hurdled.

The duke invited them to a midday meal. As they dined on shellfish, roasted nuts, and stewed beans, the duke described details of the next steps. "As you know, the king and queen rule over separate kingdoms. She has Castile and Leon, and the king has Aragon, which includes Catalonia. Some decisions they make in tandem as rulers, others not."

Rull interjected. "Aren't there those in court who desire a united kingdom—possibly called Spain?"

The duke shrugged. "The king and queen like their autonomy. They rule their own holdings. So, what that means for your project is this: the king has absolute charge of the Valencia harbor plans. All decisions will be his. The queen has her own pet projects." He rolled his eyes disparagingly. "She has finally granted her patronage to the seaman Cristoforo Colombo, after a rather dramatic exchange."

Caboto stopped eating, wanting to hear every detail. "We've heard of the plan Colombo presented to the queen. Sailing west into the Ocean Sea. But I have not heard of a dramatic exchange."

"It seems this Colombo got very tired of waiting for the queen's final approval of the voyage. Years have passed. He sent, in secret, his brother to the French court to investigate the king of France's interest in supporting the expedition. His brother worked his way through the court and found the French king to be amenable. The request to come to Paris arrived and a jubilant Colombo set out. When Queen Isabel heard about it, she sent soldiers to escort him, in an aggressive fashion, back to her court. When he was presented, it was clear Colombo was not happy with her strong-armed tactic—and for having been kept waiting for years. He told her he would now only sail under her flag if he was given the title Admiral of the Ocean Sea, if he be assured of being declared viceroy and governor-general of all lands he might discover and, in addition, be given ten percent of all the riches—gold, silver, gems, spices, and anything else that might be of value. And he insisted that all his privileges would be passed to his heirs."

Rull was astounded. "He dared to make those demands of the queen?"

The duke took another bite of fish and continued. "The king strongly suggested she refuse outright. But Queen Isabel did not want to lose to France. She insisted that Colombo be willing to negotiate his terms. Colombo's anger was too hot and he left the court."

"Turned his back on the king and queen? He's mad," Rull said.

The duke motioned for a servant to refill their wine glasses.

"Colombo headed back towards France. The queen sent soldiers after him again, but this time with a very sweet message that she had decided to agree to all of his demands."

"She agreed? And so, Colombo will make the voyage. Going across the western ocean to reach the East." Caboto felt a familiar conflict. Excitement that the exploration was to be undertaken, but a desire to switch places with Colombo.

"If he's successful, Colombo will be very wealthy," Rull said.

"Yes. Connected to the court of Spain for a lifetime. And beyond." The duke sniffed his lace handkerchief.

Rull and the duke continued to discuss the possible windfall of position and riches ahead for Colombo. Caboto could only think of Colombo's great fortune—to be able to outfit ships for a journey into the unknown, his opportunity to chart new waters, and to be in charge of one of the greatest adventures of the time.

Several months later, Caboto was in Valencia, still waiting for the king's summons to discuss the harbor project. He concentrated on drawing more detailed plans. Rull had gone back to work for his rich private clients. Finally, a messenger arrived. They were to go to Barcelona, where King Ferdinand was holding court. In the carriage that carried them north to the largest city in Catalonia, Rull grumbled. "It is always a waiting game with the royals. And then, when called, we are to drop everything and hightail it to them. I'm in the middle of a project that is worth a great amount. I don't want to lose my client. What if, when we get to Barcelona, we are asked to wait more months?"

Caboto understood his frustration. He hadn't dared send for his family without assurances there would be money to find a place to live, to afford good schooling for the boys. "We must remain positive, Rull. The duke is a guest of the king in Barcelona and he is our champion. Confidence is the only path that I can choose for us."

When they reached Barcelona, Caboto and Rull sent word to the Duke of Valencia that they had arrived and were available to meet the king at any time. They spent days walking through its busy harbor on the Balearic Sea, taking in the circular walled city and studying Barcelona's grand harbor. Caboto watched the loading and unloading of goods from around the world, remembering his best days in Venice. He sighed. How he longed to be on one of those ships. He put it out of his mind and turned to Rull. "Surely the king would not be so insensitive to ask for our presence only to tell us no? Why would he invite us to court to give us bad news?"

"King Ferdinand is known to be congenial. But also ruthless," Rull said as he sidestepped a puddle of water, always keen to keep his boots pristine. "He might hope to impress and charm and then tell us to re-budget our proposal for a lesser sum. To trim and find savings. All the while impressing us with his grand court and presence."

"You mean to soften us up to do more work for free," Caboto said.

"Yes, dear Montecalunya. But, as you say, let us hope for good news."

The day at the king's court was finally set and their carriage entered the gates of the palace. Passing soldiers who stood at attention, ready to take on any enemy of the king, Caboto was reminded that the wars with the Moors were still ongoing. Some of the king's governing decisions were unpopular and the royals, in general, were often targets of nefarious attacks.

Getting out of the carriage, they walked to the massive oak

doors, studded with iron. These, too, were flanked by soldiers. They were ushered inside by guards in leather jerkins and spurred boots. Caboto noticed the magnificent floors were covered in clay tiles, each of them painted and glazed in warm colors. The ceilings were also painted; they depicted scenes of lords and ladies frolicking with gods in gardens, tossing flowers trimmed in gold leaf into the air.

They waited outside the king's Royal Hall. The talk of the other petitioners and guests in the waiting area centered on the request of England's Henry VII to forge an alliance through a marriage of Henry's eldest son to the king and queen's youngest daughter, Catherine of Aragon. The consensus was that Queen Isabel and King Ferdinand had no need to curry favor with England for they were feeling strong after winning the latest skirmishes against the Moors and increasing the territories of Castile and Aragon. And now, with an expedition heading through western waters to the Far East and the queen's confidence that Colombo would find gold that would soon be in their coffers, the Catholic royals felt they could put Henry VII's request aside. Caboto listened to the chatter, realizing again that every bit of political maneuvering affected royal decisions.

"Johan Caboto Montecalunya and Gaspar Rull," a kingsman called.

Caboto's heart was in his throat. He was about to meet King Ferdinand V, ruler of Aragon and Catalonia, one of the most powerful royals in Europe. They entered the Royal Hall. King Ferdinand was a large man and full of energy, his dark eyes lively in a long face, his full lips prominent. He wore a black velvet cap and a richly embroidered surcoat of gold cloth, open at the neck, with a white shirt beneath it. Gold chains hung heavily on his chest. He sat at a massive raised table and Caboto and Rull stood before him, their hats in their hands.

"You have had to wait months for this meeting. I know that. But rejoice with me. Our soldiers in Granada have been successful and we've taken that territory back from the Moors."

Rull bowed. "Congratulations, Your Highness."

Caboto realized he should give another bow, quickly did so, and mumbled his congratulations. The king motioned with his long fingers for an advisor to unroll Caboto's renderings onto the table. Weights were put in the corners of the large pieces of vellum. King Ferdinand motioned for an olive-skinned man in a dark, full-sleeved robe and brimmed hat to join him. The man carried a small pair of spectacles in his hand and brought them to his eyes as he gazed down at the drawings.

The king clapped his hands together and looked at Caboto and Rull. "I am pleased with your plan."

Cabot's spirits soared.

Then the king turned his thick lips downwards in an exaggerated frown. "But my council has advised against it."

Caboto's heart sank.

The king stood up and nearly shouted, "But I have decided they are wrong. Your new harbor design will be significant and a great benefit to our kingdom. It will show our strength and might. I approve these plans. Congratulations, you have pleased your king."

Caboto let out a long-held breath and felt strength return to his body.

The king continued, "I introduce you now to my financier, Señor Luis de Santángel." He waved towards the man in the brimmed hat and dark robes. "He will be in charge of gathering the monies for the new harbor. He has secured financing for the queen's latest passion, three ships heading west into the Ocean Sea to get lost. Most assuredly." The king grimaced, clearly thinking the expedition would be a folly.

Caboto spoke quickly, not taking time to consider his words. "Your Highness, I have participated in a good amount of sailing expeditions. I'm knowledgeable in map- and chart-making. And I have studied the possibilities of success of sailing west into the Ocean Sea. To reach the East. There are others who believe, as I do, that this is a viable plan. A good journey. I have studied the maps of Toscanelli, as Colombo has, and I know winds and celestial navigation. With those tools, a fine sea captain will not be lost. I must say, I feel great excitement about the queen's passion."

King Ferdinand looked over his long nose to Caboto. He had not given Caboto permission to speak.

Rull elbowed Caboto, signaling him not to displease the king. To keep the focus on their harbor plans.

Caboto swallowed hard. "Pardon my impertinence. However, I would like to say, if any kingdom was to prosper, it should be yours and Queen Isabel's, Your Highness. The most deserving and the most forward thinking. And, in that, building a new harbor in Valencia, in your honor, King Ferdinand, will be a tribute also."

The king took a moment and then decided to accept the flattery. He nodded. "So, let it be." He eyed Caboto. "You are a sea captain? I thought you were an engineer."

"I have sailed to ports in the Ottoman Empire, Africa, Sicily, and many other harbors. I have the knowledge of a sea captain, although I have yet to hold that position. But I am a capable leader, I know it. I could lead an expedition to add riches and knowledge to Spain."

Rull jumped in. "But his business now is as an engineer, who understands how to make a harbor most efficacious. His knowledge of seafaring is only a plus for you, Your Highness, in regards to your harbor."

King Ferdinand clapped his hands again, signaling the end of the meeting. "All right. Well, Santángel will keep me informed. You are now expected to progress. And of course, see grand completion to my satisfaction."

Caboto and Rull bowed and walked backward out of the Royal Hall—for one was not to turn a back on a king.

Back in the waiting room, Rull turned on Caboto. "What were you talking about in there? It was like you were angling for ships and patronage. As if you wanted your own expedition to explore uncharted horizons. We are here to get paid to build a harbor." Rull, now quite angry, headed out of the palace.

Caboto followed, thinking he should apologize. But the truth was more important. "It is my deepest dream, Rull, to make a journey like Colombo's. I admit it."

Rull shook his head, his voice hard. "Well, this Colombo beat you to it. You are a harbor designer. Concentrate on that."

A week later, in a meeting with Santángel, Caboto and Rull were instructed to go back to Valencia to continue plans and preparation. Santangel said, "The financing of the queen's project is completed. I have reached out to Italian banks owned by the Bardi and Strozzi families, to banks in Austria and Germany, to wealthy speculators, and to noble Spaniards who wish to please the queen for their own reasons. The wealthy navigator and cartographer Juan de la Cosa has also contributed. I would say Colombo's expedition will be ready to depart in the spring."

"Very interesting how you put together financing from different persons and republics and empires," Caboto said. "May I ask, did the Catholic royals contribute any monies?"

Rull coughed, amazed that Caboto would be so bold. He quickly said, "Of course, it is of no concern of ours. We only care about the harbor."

But Santángel answered Caboto's question. "The Catholic royals' participation is to provide the flag, which is of the utmost importance."

Caboto nodded. "I understand it signals protection and will keep away pirates and unfriendly ships."

"That is what we hope," Santángel agreed. "And it should suffice because it is known Spain has a strong navy. And that Spain is not afraid to avenge any attacks."

"Yes, of course, as they've been aggressive against the Moors. And very vigilant in the Inquisition," Caboto said.

"The Catholic royals rule as they see fit. It is their duty and right." Santángel put his eyeglasses into a small case, slipped them into his pocket, and eyed Caboto. It was clear he wondered why this engineer was asking such questions. "Perhaps you have heard that I was born and raised a devout Jew. And that I am a converso."

"That you were baptized into Catholicism," Caboto said.

"In order to live in this kingdom and continue to serve my king and queen. I have been given the privilege of baptism because they value my advice and because I value my station with them."

Caboto nodded. He thought he heard resentment in Santángel's voice.

But the man quickly changed the subject. "The difficulty for Colombo was attracting a crew. There were, at first, no volunteers. The fear of what the Ocean Sea might hold was too great. But Martin Pinzón has recently signed on, so that has changed the situation."

"The navigator?"

"Pinzón's the best in Spain. Many sailors from Andalusia have journeyed with Pinzón, and have complete trust in him. He will be given the command of a caravel that has been named the *Pinta* and his brother, Vicente, will captain a caravel that has been named the *Niña*. Both are near sixty-two feet in length. Juan de la Cosa will serve as navigator on the wide carrack, the flagship *Santa María*. It will, perhaps, be the slowest but the strongest ship, with three sails. Colombo will be admiral of the entire fleet. The queen has promised amnesty to convicted criminals if they sign on. Four have accepted her offer. The departure is scheduled for April, six months from now."

Santángel paid Caboto and Rull the initial fee for their services as engineers and bid them good day.

Caboto was pleased. The payment allowed him to find a small villa on the water in Valencia and send for Mattea and the family.

"Papà!" Sebastiano ran into his father's arms. "We are by the sea again. Just as you promised." Sebastiano disengaged and called to his younger brother. "Come on, Sancius!" The boys ran on the beach, chasing seagulls.

Ludovico helped Piero unload their belongings from the carriage. "Did you really meet the king, Papà?"

"I did. And our family is now connected, in a small way, to the court."

"Uncle Piero has been teaching me accounting. I want to help on the harbor project."

Caboto realized that Ludovico, now age fifteen, was very much like Piero. Steady, good-natured, and realistic. And not afraid of hard, meticulous work. "I would be proud to have you as Piero's assistant."

Ludovico grinned. Piero put his arm around his nephew's shoulder and said, "First things first. Let us see what is in the larder, for I'm hungry."

Ludovico laughed and followed Piero inside. "You are always hungry, Uncle."

Mattea breathed in the sea air, and eyed the small, elegant villa. "I may miss our stone cottage in the mountains, Gio, but I'm glad for this fine place."

A housekeeper moved out onto the terrace to greet her new mistress. Mattea's smile grew wider. "And does she cook too?" She kissed Caboto warmly and happily moved into her new home.

As Caboto waited impatiently for the harbor project to begin in earnest, he kept up with the news of Admiral Colombo's expedition. The spring season came and went and no ships sailed west into the Ocean Sea. The early months of summer passed. Santángel was not communicating with Rull and Caboto; their project, too, seemed to be on hold. But news finally found its way to Caboto; on August 3, 1492, the *Santa María*, *Niña*, and *Pinta* set sail from the port of Palos de la Frontera, flying the flags of Spain's unique kingdoms, Castile, Leon, Granada, Catalonia, and Aragon.

October leaves were falling from the trees and all of Spain—indeed, all of Europe—waited for news of Colombo's voyage. Many wondered if Colombo and the crews of the *Niña*, *Pinta*, and *Santa María* would ever be seen again. Caboto spent his days in the small workshop he and Rull had rented near the harbor. They were still waiting for the financing to begin construction. One day, Piero and Ludovico burst in. "Terrible news, Gio," Piero wheezed, winded from his run to the workshop. "There has been an assassination attempt in Barcelona."

Ludovico shouted, "Papà, King Ferdinand has been stabbed."

Caboto dropped his quill onto the desk, spilling ink on his latest drawings. They headed to the cafés, where news could be heard. The details of the violence were not clearly understood, but King Ferdinand's stand on the Inquisition as well as his harsh taxes in Catalonia and the battles with the Moors, made enemies. Rumors flew and Caboto tried to discern fact from fiction. Doctors were at the king's bedside, and all kingdoms in Spain were asked to pray for the king.

The Valencia harbor plans were put on hold. Santángel sent a note stating that financing of the harbor was not his priority at this point, but to await instructions. Caboto packed up his charts and renderings and retreated from the workshop to the villa. Frustrated, feeling his life was always on hold, Caboto idled at nearby cafés, awaiting news.

Finally, in early March 1493, information on the *Niña*, *Pinta*, and *Santa María* arrived. After facing storms and rough passage on the return voyage from newly discovered islands off the coast of India, winds had blown the ships off course and they had landed not in Spain, but in Portugal. King John II was not welcoming—after all, he had missed his chance to sponsor this voyage and he had no desire to aid a rival kingdom. Bad blood festered and as soon as weather permitted, Colombo's ships quickly sailed away and finally landed in Barcelona on the fifteenth of March.

Colombo received a hero's welcome. He reveled in the attention and wrote a four-page letter that the king and queen sent to a printer and distributed throughout their kingdoms. Caboto quickly bought several copies. The pamphlet detailed discoveries of sleeping nets called hammocks, chilis, dried leaves that were rolled and smoked, pineapple fruit, and a squawking bird called a turkey that was considered good for eating. The pamphlet told of Colombo's interaction with native peoples called Indians— named thus because Colombo was sure he had reached islands off India. The natives were of "handsome stature," with skin the color of copper. They carried bone-tipped spears and wore gold rings in their noses. Colombo also noted the many small colorful birds that actually spoke and sat on sailors' shoulders, and of light and narrow boats that glided over the top of the waters.

The pamphlet, quickly printed in many languages, became a much sought-after item. Caboto and his sons, especially Sebastiano, drank in every detail of Colombo's celebrations. They heard of the processions that were taking place in villages and towns throughout Spain, with Colombo leading the parades astride a fine horse, followed by six Indians who carried cages of birds and baskets of shells. The queen and king provided Colombo with the best lodgings and assigned him a food taster—for he was considered too valuable to be poisoned. He was also awarded a coat of arms and a footman to open doors for him and serve him at table.

Caboto wondered, now that he and the famous Colombo were both working for the Catholic royals, would their paths cross? He had questions to ask of the explorer. He wondered why Colombo had not brought back spices of the Far East—the black pepper, ginger, and cloves that were so coveted. Where were the silks, ceramics, swords, antiquities? He wanted to know if the crew had taken depth measurements of the seas and if they had kept notes on currents and tides.

Caboto shared his questions when he and Rull met at a café. Rull said, "You do know about all this, don't you, Montecalunya? Charts and winds and navigation." Rull studied Caboto, realizing, perhaps for the first time, that the harbor design was only a job to Caboto; it was not what he desired for his life's work. "Perhaps after this harbor project, you'll sail with Colombo on his next expedition."

"That would be a dream, Rull. Has a second expedition for Colombo been planned?"

"That's what I have heard. The chief of the island called Hispaniola—the one called Guacanagari, who gave Colombo the gift of a gold necklace—according to Queen Isabel, is to be visited again. As soon as possible. To find the location of the gold mine. Colombo left forty men on Hispaniola to build a fort called La Navidad—and to search for gold."

A few days later, Caboto received a message asking him to meet with Luis de Santángel. The two men met at the Duke of Valencia's home.

"Johan Caboto Montecalunya, it is good to see you again."

Santángel looked thinner, his eyes weaker. He placed his glasses on his nose and smiled at Caboto.

"Señor Santangel." Caboto nodded his head deeply. "I trust the king has healed."

"He is still a bit weak, but every day grows stronger." Santángel motioned for Caboto to sit. "The king would like you to do him a service while the Valencia harbor project is delayed."

"I am at the king's service." Caboto said.

"The city of Seville, in the southwest Andalusia region, has been won back from the Moors. It is in need of a bridge over its river. King Ferdinand was impressed with your engineering skills, your knowledge of tides and currents and all things concerning sea navigation. He asks that you undertake this task. He would like the bridge to be made of bricks." Santángel put a pouch of coins on the table. "This is to pay for you to go to Seville and design the king a bridge of bricks."

Caboto nodded, hiding his true feelings of frustration. The family's accounts were near empty and he was worried about his debts. The appointment was appreciated, but he knew this project would keep him on land for the next few years.

Caboto moved his family to Seville, on the eastern shore of the Guadalquivir River. The Muslims had made this city one of their centers and ruled over it for three hundred years. When the Catholic royals took the city back, many mosques were torn down and cathedrals were planned as replacements. Surprisingly, the royals retained the Muslim fortress of Alcazar; it had been turned into a royal palace to be used by the king and queen when they visited the city. Caboto's workshop was set up near its carriage house.

Caboto began surveying and designing a bridge that would

traverse the Guadalquivir River. The river was large and could handle ships as large as 150 tons. There was healthy trading in the city where English traders brought wool. Sugar arrived from the Canaries and jewels, antiquities, spices, and silks from the East.

Caboto was just about to start construction when another visit from Luis de Santángel changed his life once again. The two men stood at the bridge site. Caboto provided Santángel with drawings and let the king's representative know that everything was going as scheduled.

"That is good to hear, Montecalunya," Santángel said. "For the king has another request of you."

Caboto waited. Would the king be sending him to another part of the kingdom? Would he ever be able to complete a project?

Santángel continued, "You may have heard that Admiral Colombo's second voyage is to be undertaken. Seventeen ships have been commissioned."

Caboto had not heard the size of the expedition. "Seventeen. That is a large."

"Yes. And sites of harbors on the newly discovered islands, now claimed by the kingdoms of Spain, will have to be determined. An engineer of your caliber is needed. The king would like you to sail on this second voyage with Colombo, and design harbors for this New World."

Caboto could not believe his ears. He stood absolutely still. Could this be a dream?

"Montecalunya? What should I tell the king?" Santángel asked. "The expedition is scheduled to depart in a month."

Caboto could hardly speak. His voice was low, raspy, emotional. "Please tell His Highness that I will prepare immediately for the voyage."

Chapter Sixteen

In mid-September 1493, Caboto and Piero traveled south to the port of Sanlucar de Barrameda, just north of the city of Cádiz. They moved through the large crowds that had gathered to glimpse the famous explorer Colombo. As they approached the wharf, Caboto saw two carracks, the *Gallega* and the flagship *Marigalante*; he knew them to be part of Colombo's expedition. Workers and crew led horses, cattle, and pigs as well as crates filled with grapevines and casks of beer and water into the lower decks. Barrels of rice and oilskin bags of dried beef and dried fish for the long journey were also loaded. They noticed carriers of cats being brought onto the ship; the felines would be released days into the voyage to combat a constantly growing rat population.

Caboto looked to the next pier and out to the moorings, and there he saw a flotilla of the lighter and faster caravels destined for the voyage. He could make out some of the christened names, the *Fraila*, *Prieta*, *Gorda*, *Quintera*, and *Rodriga*. Sailors were busy preparing their decks and riggings.

Caboto knew that two of the seventeen ships were designated to sail from Cádiz to the newly discovered lands and discharge cargo and settlers, then quickly be loaded with the gold and exotic treasures gathered over the last nine months by the sailors who had been left on Hispaniola, and, in a short turnaround, return to Queen Isabel. The fifteen other ships were scheduled to stay in the uncharted regions for a longer time—to explore and claim new territories for the Catholic royals.

Caboto found his name on the list for one of the caravels, the *Rodriga*. Piero pointed to the cargo being loaded. "Look, Gio. Cannons. Muskets. Crossbows." He half joked, "Your ship will have enough armaments to fend off any inhospitable natives."

Piero was worried. Caboto knew this and calmed him. "Colombo's crews returned in fine fashion from the initial voyage. No cause for dire thoughts."

A pimply young sailor, barely into his teenage years, pushed forward and stood in front of them. He wore a new wool sailor's coat and hat. "Are you Señor Johan Caboto Montecalunya, the engineer? Set to sail on the *Rodriga*?"

"Yes, I am," Caboto smiled. The youth reminded him of his sons, when they would dress up to play explorers.

"The admiral, Señor. He wants to see you in his quarters and says now is a good time."

"Very well. Lead the way." Caboto and Piero followed the boy and boarded the *Marigalante*.

Piero muttered under his breath, a spark of humor in his eyes. "Will the admiral recognize us as two boys hailing from Genoa?"

Caboto laughed. "I hope we look different, thirty years later."

As they were ushered into the admiral's spacious quarters, both had to duck their heads to move through the doorway. The young sailor hurriedly left without making introductions. Colombo's broad head and shoulders were bent over a large chart spread out on a heavy desk. Caboto recognized him from his likeness that had been stamped on the celebration pamphlets and saw that the admiral's short, sturdy, muscular frame was a perfect fit for the compact quarters. Beside him, moving weights to various parts of the map as they discussed routes, was a man of a similar stature, with a freckled face. He wore a long leather jacket over a woolen shirt, and thick leggings and boots. Both men wore worn velvet caps over their shoulder-length hair.

The men did not look up or acknowledge the arrival of the guests, so Caboto was able to take in the room: maps tacked to the wooden paneling, navigation instruments organized on a velvet cloth next to a large leather-bound Bible, a narrow bed and desk bolted to the floor, a crucifix hanging above the bed's headboard. A storage trunk, covered with animal fur, sat next to the desk, and was secured to the floor so it would not move as the ship rolled in the ocean waves.

Servants in gray jackets, ankle-length trousers, and black and white striped leggings entered and made themselves busy. They outfitted the shelves near the admiral's bed with private stores of salted meats, nuts, and wine.

Piero coughed. Caboto gave him a quick look as if to say, *Was that necessary? Was it a plea for attention?* Piero's face did not give away his intention but his eyes sparked with mischief.

"So, you are Señor Montecalunya, my harbor engineer

and designer?" Piero had succeeded in getting the attention; Colombo acknowledged them, but still did not look up.

"Honored to be included in this voyage, Admiral." Caboto bowed. "This is my brother, Piero. He has come to see me off."

Colombo waved towards the man beside him. "I, too, have my brother with me. Bartolome. But he is joining the expedition."

Caboto took a folded map from his pocket, a small child's drawing of the Ocean Sea. "I believe we have met, Admiral. I purchased Bartolome's first map in Signor Fallio's shop in Genoa."

This stopped both Colombo brothers. Their eyes were now riveted on the Cabotos. Bartolome reached for the map. "May I?"

Caboto handed it over and watched the Colombo brothers look at the childlike drawings of ships in Genoa's harbor, the cartoons of sea serpents, mermaids, and underwater castles that dotted the sea. They dissolved in laughter and talk, one on top of another, in a combination of Italian, Portuguese, and Spanish of their past beliefs in monsters and dragons in a mysterious ocean.

Bartolome chortled, "I drew many maps Signor Fallio promised to sell. This might be the only one that was purchased."

Colombo looked at Caboto, curious. "Johan Montecalunya is not a Genoese name."

"I was born Giovanni Caboto, son of Guilio, the Genoese merchant."

"*Bravo*. Then you know, firsthand, the superiority of Italian wines. But today, we will drink to Signor Fallio with Spain's bounty." Colombo signaled a servant to prepare glasses of wine. "What would Fallio of Genoa think of us now, Caboto? No longer boys in his map shop, but men making new maps." Colombo raised his glass for a toast. "He would be proud of me. I've made good." Colombo headed to his desk, moving sandglasses into a line according to their size. "Remember when Signor Fallio was excited about the Toscanelli map? I've been in correspondence with the mapmaker. Look." Colombo opened a drawer in the desk and took out at letter with a red ribbon tied around it. "He sent me a copy of the letter he wrote in 1474 to King Alfonso of Portugal. It details his ideas about sailing west to the Spice Islands and Asia." He pointed to a passage in the letter. "See, here Toscanelli writes, 'The voyage across the Ocean Sea is not only possible, but certain to yield profits of greatness and to bring fame to all Catholics.'"

Colombo tapped the letter to his chest, close to his heart. "I carried it with me on my first voyage and it brought me luck. I have proven him right. I will be in the history books."

Caboto was taken by Colombo's ego, his high energy, how he moved quickly and talked at a fast clip, how he was able to do multiple tasks while holding a conversation. "Your success is known by all," said Caboto, flattering the navigator.

Colombo moved to one of the maps on the wall. "Let's talk of the voyage and the harbors you will design for me. I shall need quite a few, for I have discovered many primitive islands off India. The aim of this expedition concerns colonization and, most important, exploration to unearth precious resources. First, colonization. I left forty men on the island of Hispaniola to build a fort—I named it La Navidad. They were left to begin working the land and to befriend the natives. As you know, it's been nine months and I expect them to tell me of a gold mine." He licked his lips and rubbed his hands together. "The farmers, fishermen, and traders sailing with us will join La Navidad. They have committed to building island communities to bring honor to our queen. As you know, without colonization, it would be difficult for the royals to continue the claim."

"Of course. Settlements protect the crown's stake of ownership."

Piero interjected, "But I have always wondered, if there have been discussions of the rights of the more advanced country . . ."

"What do you mean, rights?" Colombo's eyes narrowed.

"The belief that an advanced country takes it as their right to claim land that is already inhabited."

Colombo waved off the question as not important. "First, these people are primitive. No proper religion. They can't read or write. We bring them opportunity. They will be grateful to be included under the Catholic royals' reign." He stared at Piero. "Surely, you see that."

Caboto put his hand on Piero's arm, knowing that Piero liked to debate the values of colonization and peoples' rights, and that his questions were, at times, not appreciated. Caboto steered the conversation to a new topic, moving to the map on the wall. "Will our first landfall be at Hispaniola?"

Colombo joined him. "I'll determine that as we travel. But Hispaniola remains a priority. It seems to be a large island. There are many bays for you to explore; one or two might make good harbors. You'll take measurements to ascertain that. I don't want a repeat of the last journey where the *Santa María* ran aground."

Bartolome sipped his wine and defended his brother. "That was due to a faulty watch and faulty navigation, Cristoforo. You gave orders. They were not followed properly. Not your fault."

Colombo held up his hands as if to contradict. "The admiral must take ultimate responsibility," he said, but clearly was not accepting any blame.

Caboto said, "With charts, you should be able to avoid those problems. And charts, as you know, are best made through experience. On site."

"I've heard you are an excellent chart-maker," Colombo said, as if wary of noting praise given to another.

"I trained for many years in Venice." Caboto remembered the wonderful days around Rizo's iron stove, eating fish with their friends, talking about charting the entire world. He wished he could share the news of this adventure with Rizo, Carlo, and Fernando.

Piero, as if feeling Caboto's longing for those days, put his hand on his brother's shoulder. "Gio's charts of the Baltic and the Aegean Seas were used by many captains."

Colombo pursed his lips. "Well. Good."

Caboto felt Colombo's interest wane. It seemed as if when he was not the center of attention, Colombo would drift to his own concerns. Caboto returned the conversation to a topic where Colombo could shine. "We've read how the natives were friendly and helped repair your flagship."

Colombo smiled, engaged again. "Perhaps it was fortuitous. Hispaniola is rich and warm, and the Taino tribe friendly. The Tainos inhabit many of the nearby islands. We'll have to see how far their good will extends. See if there grows any discontent with our presence."

"You expect resistance, Admiral?"

Colombo shrugged. "The master gunner has assured me all will be ready, when and if needed. The cacique—that is what the Taino tribe calls their chief—and his people have been content, thus far, with our gifts of hats and coins and glass beads."

"And knives, mirrors, and scissors," Bartolome added.

Colombo nodded. "We traded these things for the gold rings

they had in their noses." He frowned. "We didn't find the source of the gold, but it must be there. The nose rings tell me that. The chief spoke of a land he called Cuba." Colombo pointed to an X on the map. "I think it will be there. We were close to finding out but, well, things happened."

Colombo pursed his lips, shared a look with Bartolome. Caboto felt the import of the moment, but did not understand what lay behind it.

Colombo continued, a dark look on his face. "I had hoped to stop there on the first expedition, but then it became necessary to sail back, quickly, to the queen. I will claim Cuba on this voyage. The name Cuba, in the Taino language, means a rich and bountiful land. I feel certain the gold is there." He rolled his shoulders as if feeling the pressure.

"Do the Tainos understand the worth of a resource like gold?" Caboto asked.

Colombo frowned. "It doesn't seem to be of primary importance to them. So, they shall not miss it if we take it."

Caboto felt a twinge of repugnance at Colombo's cavalier attitude. He saw, out of the corner of his eye, Piero stiffen.

"What is of primary importance to them?" Piero asked, his voice cool.

Bartolome answered. "They're simple. They have their chief and a few other important men. The rest are workers, happy to labor. The women farm, the men fish and hunt."

"And what of religion?" Caboto asked.

"The chief has a holy man who is a respected advisor. He is called a *bohique*. He claims to have direct conversations with their gods."

"Gods?" Caboto said. "As in multiple gods?"

"They believe that different gods look over them in different ways. One for fertility, one for good health, one for rain, one for wind, one for sun—seems to be one for almost everything. Clearly, these heathens must be instructed. To that end, the queen has sent six Catholic missionaries on this expedition. The queen insists on conversion of the natives."

Piero bristled. "That is assuming our beliefs are the right ones."

Colombo's retort was quick. "When we are sailing for the king and queen who represent the Catholic Church, we do not question our task." He puffed out his chest, challenging Piero. "Are you?"

Piero gave a supplicant's nod of his head. "You have the experience here, Admiral. Noted." Piero did not want to cause his brother problems.

Bartolome settled, cross-legged, on the trunk, and looked at his fingernails. "It is a different world. For example, both men and women in the Taino tribe take multiple marital partners."

Caboto was surprised. "Not like our society. As for me, I am happy with one wife."

Bartolome added, "The unmarried women are naked. If she is a wife, she wears only a small apron that hides her most feminine anatomy. Will you be offended, Caboto?"

Caboto knew he was being tested. "In the Ottoman Empire, I saw many women covered from head to toe. Only a peek at the women's eyes was possible. It is interesting to know that in the New Indies it is the opposite. One advantage of exploration is to observe how others live."

Bartolome grinned. "Then you'll enjoy a feast with the chief of the tribe—of lizard, suckerfish, earthworms, and turtles."

Piero grimaced and laughed. "Perhaps, Gio, it is wise that I'm staying on European soil with the family."

Caboto spied a familiar book on Colombo's shelves. "Ah. You have *The Travels of Marco Polo*."

Colombo nodded. "It's quite worn. Whenever I think of the obstacles ahead and wonder if they can be managed, I look to his memoirs. Polo was never satisfied and never gave up. I shall follow his example."

Caboto knew that his ambitions were similar to Colombo's and that Marco Polo served as his own inspiration. But he felt it was not the time to share this information. Colombo would not appreciate what he might see as competition.

A short while later, Caboto and Piero made their way to the *Rodriga*. "It is expected that we will be thirty days on the voyage to the New Indies. I'm scheduled to be in the early return with the first cargo. All told, no more than three months. I should arrive home for Christmas."

"I am happy for you, Gio. Finally, west into the Ocean Sea." He motioned for his brother to take his leave, not trusting his rising emotion. "The ship awaits."

Caboto could feel his brother's eyes on his back as he walked onto the gangplank—and onto the main deck. When he turned around for a final wave, Piero was gone.

Caboto had to lower his head to enter his cramped cabin near the *Rodriga*'s gun room. He eyed the shallow bookshelf and small table. He sat on the thin berth, felt the sway of the waters below, and listened to the sound of gulls and sailors preparing the voyage. Anticipation welled in him. He quickly unpacked his few pieces of clothing and instruments used for navigation. The tools of the engineer he left in his leather bag, for they would not be needed for weeks.

Captain Pablo Torres, a wide-chested, toughened man with a dark beard streaked with silver, stopped in the open door of Caboto's cabin and introduced himself. "I have copies of the charts and rutters from the first voyage. If you would like to study them, you may. I have the permission of Admiral Colombo."

Caboto's exhilaration doubled. Here was a chance to learn firsthand with the captain. "Captain Torres, that would be of great interest to me."

"Then we'll meet in my quarters, as soon as we are into the Ocean Sea." Captain Torres patted his beard and took his leave. A moment later, after placing a locket that contained a cut of Mattea's hair next to his berth, Caboto headed to the deck. He wanted to be in the thick of the final preparations for the voyage.

On the morning of September 24, 1493, Caboto noted in his rutter that the seventeen ships under Colombo's command were considered ready. The winds were favorable. The crews were in place. From the deck of the flagship *Marigalante*, the sound of a cannon-fire struck through the crisp air. Sails billowed in the strong breeze. The ruddy-faced quartermaster of the *Rodriga*, second in command to the captain, blew his whistle and shouted in a deep and gravelly voice, "Hoist anchors!"

Caboto's heart pounded. He was off on the voyage he had dreamed of as a young boy.

Chapter Seventeen

Days later, Caboto stood next to Captain Torres as the pilot docked at the largest of the Canary Islands. Caboto stood in the same place not long after that, on October 13, as the *Rodriga* fell in line with the other ships, sailing away from the Canaries and into the vast ocean. Captain Torres told Caboto that Colombo had announced a slight change in course. "We'll adjust to a more southerly route from the first voyage, seven degrees. The admiral believes he'll trim the number of days at sea. Let us hope he's correct," Captain Torres said.

By the end of the second day, all sight of land was gone. Only ocean, thin clouds in gray-blue skies, and, at a distance, the sails of the other ships. Caboto's throat tightened, thinking of his deep desire to see his family again. He had to remind himself of what he had told Piero, that Colombo had already made one successful voyage on the Ocean Sea, that this second expedition was not a journey into total mystery.

But a niggling worry persisted. What if it had been only luck that the *Niña*, *Pinta*, and *Santa María* had not crossed paths with the ocean's treacherous elements? What terrible and frightening dangers might they encounter on this second voyage?

On the fifth day on open water, Caboto sat with Captain Torres and the navigator, Juan de la Cosa, in the captain's quarters. They cut through dried sausage and a hunk of cheese and talked over the notations on currents in their copy of Colombo's rutter. "I have only praise to add to the admiral's reputation," Cosa said. "Colombo has a God-given gift—he not only measures the currents and winds, but feels them. His notes are meticulous. The currents are, indeed, strong but Colombo has excellent notes to combat them with positions of rudders and sails. I'm happy to report we are keeping on course." Cosa showed them his own assessments in a new ship's logbook. "Now, with our recent dead reckoning marks, I'm able to add new calculations, taking into account that we are traveling in the near winter. The variations from the first voyage are, I believe, a result of the difference in the calendar months chosen for travel. The first voyage was August; this is nearly November."

Torres nodded. "The admiral expects to need yearly charts— for all future voyages. Put down every detail."

Cosa stood and took his leave. "You shall have it, Captain Torres."

Caboto and Torres continued their midday meal. "Admiral Colombo is known as one with the talent to feel the wind and the water," Torres said. "But perhaps not the temperature of the men. It is something I hold as important as charts."

"I heard there was unrest on the first voyage." Caboto said. "But surely that was because of the men's fear, wondering if land would be sighted. Ever."

Torres chewed on another slice of sausage. "And that is why

Admiral Colombo kept two sets of diaries during his first journey. One true, one not."

"Two sets? I did not know that. Why?"

"The false log was adjusted because the journey was taking many more days than anticipated. He wanted to calm the crew's fears and let them think they were much closer to home than they were. The true log was kept under lock and key in Colombo's quarters and showed the actual number of days and distances. Even with this lie, there was one point when his quartermaster alerted the admiral that men were talking of mutiny. Meals had not been generous. Shifts were long. Colombo stayed in his cabin, did not mix. Tensions grew and the crew wanted to turn the ship around and head home. To appease them, Colombo finally promised if land was not sighted in two days' time, he would order the ships to turn back himself."

"Was land sighted in that time?"

"On the morning of the second day, sandpipers were seen flying overhead. Then a sailor spotted a piece of floating wood that looked hand-hewn. And then a branch, with berries still attached. Spirits rose. Sailors began to think of the bounty that they anticipated, lining their pockets with gold. The ships traveled another twenty-seven leagues, with the *Pinta* as the lead, helmed by navigator Martín Pinzón."

Caboto reached for a large crumb of cheese. "I know of Pinzón's excellent reputation."

Torres was about to say more, but held his tongue.

"What is it?" Caboto queried.

"Let us say Captain Pinzón turned out not to be a trustworthy comrade of the admiral's."

"How so?"

Torres settled back and patted his thick beard. "Let me say

this for now. Pinzón's death came at a very opportune time for Admiral Colombo."

"Now I'm more intrigued." Caboto leaned forward.

But Torres enjoyed stretching out the story, weaving his tale slowly. "We'll be sailing for weeks. We'll build up to that. Shall I tell you now of Colombo's first landing?"

Caboto realized he would have to be patient. He chuckled, "Yes, tell me all."

Torres unbuttoned his jacket, giving his stomach more room for the digestion of the sausage. "The admiral promised a silk doublet and coins to the sailor who first spotted land. Two hours after midnight, on that day in October, a sailor on board the *Pinta* called out that he had sighted land at a distance of two leagues. Pinzón, the captain of the *Pinta*, fired a cannon, alerting the other ships. The crews on the decks of all three vessels erupted in cheers. The admiral led a hymn, *Salve Regina*. Then, as Colombo has told me, he went back to the admiral's quarters, sank to his knees, and thanked God."

"Hispaniola, if I remember correctly from my readings, was not the first island sighted."

"Good memory." He tapped the copy of Colombo's rutter. "Details are in here. The first island, populated with naked natives, was called Guanahani. The admiral brought the royal standard and two banners to plant in the soil and called to the secretary of the fleet, Rodrigo Sánchez of Segovia, to bear witness to the claiming of the island for Isabel and Ferdinand."

"The natives didn't question his actions?"

"How could they know what was happening? They simply watched, curious about these men in strange clothing. The admiral gave each native a gift—a red hat and a string of beads. The chief of the Guanahani then showed himself and signaled the natives to give gifts of parrots and fruit to the sailors. For the moment, all were pleased."

"For the moment?"

The quartermaster knocked on the door, interrupting them. "Captain Torres, you wanted to oversee the change of crew. The eight-hour shift is complete."

"I'll be there." Captain Torres stood up.

Caboto stood and bowed. He had to accept the day's story-telling was at an end.

Days passed. The *Rodriga* moved at a good pace, but always behind the *Marigalante*, staying part of the group of caravels. Caboto grew accustomed to the ship's rise and fall in the waves and his movements on the deck became increasingly steadier. Every night he viewed the stars. He found Polaris, and noted in his rutter the movements of constellations in the night sky. During the day, Caboto watched the quartermaster review the articles of the ship with the crew. The articles itemized respon-sibilities, and Torres believed the repetition of expected duties was good for discipline. The boatswain, the sailor in charge of keeping the ship in shape for travel and battle, organized groups to look after the decks, canvasses, ropes, lines, and masts.

Caboto knew the quartermaster and boatswain were motivated to excel at their jobs by the fact that their share of any treasure found on the expedition depended on their performance. Caboto also became friendly with the ship's cooper, the muscled and bowlegged sailor in charge of repairs. The cooper's duties included being the surgeon's assistant, for his tools and his talent with the saw were expected to be put to use if a sailor injured a limb so badly that it needed to be cut from the body.

As the journey continued, Caboto's admiration of Torres's sailing skills increased. One day, Caboto, knowing that the *Rodriga* was a nimble ship, wondered aloud why Captain Torres did not fill the sails to full advantage. "Captain Torres, you're purposely staying twenty leagues behind the flagship. This caravel is obviously faster than many of the ships, including the admiral's carrack."

Captain Torres nodded. "I am happy to stay behind. The admiral will not tolerate even a hint of what he experienced with Pinzón."

"Ah. The story of ruined trust you still have to tell me."

"It is a story of betrayal. We shall get to it tonight." Captain Torres's eyes twinkled.

That night, as a fine fortified wine—a Spanish port—was poured, Torres told Caboto of Pinzón's deception. "It was determined that the three ships on the first expedition would cruise near the coast of Cuba. The vessels were already loaded with bounty—plants, birds, lizards, cotton, wooden carvings, and natives—things and persons Colombo hoped would impress Queen Isabel. But still, he wanted to find the source of gold. One early morning before dawn broke, Pinzón, in a surprise move, disobeyed the admiral's orders and separated from the other two ships and sailed off, determined for the *Pinta* to make landfall in Spain before Colombo. Pinzón wanted to deliver the first cargo to the queen, take credit for his ship being the first to sight land—to take credit for the entire expedition."

Caboto was stunned. "I have not heard of this betrayal."

"There was a reason for that. Pinzón did reach Spain first. But, unfortunately for him, God did not choose him to be the hero. He'd fallen ill on his villainous return voyage and died before he could leave his ship." Torres swept a droplet of port off his beard, and licked his finger, not wanting to miss one taste of the fine liquor. "Men who make decisions to pursue personal glory, and disregard their honor, gain little respect from me."

"I agree, Captain." Caboto nodded. He added, "This story was not part of the celebration pamphlets."

"The admiral and the queen decided the betrayal diffused the expedition's greatness. Pinzón's crew was disgraced and did not share in the promised bonuses." Torres burped, happily content with his port. "The captains on this second voyage cannot take this history too lightly, for it preys on Colombo's mind. He now has seventeen ships to watch. Very carefully."

Another week of steady progress was registered in Caboto's rutter. And then, the favorable winds suddenly ebbed and the sails languished. An overpowering heat poured from the sun and the cool waters could not combat its power. Sailors stripped to the waist. The stores of water and beer were in demand, but Captain Torres kept an eye on the rationing. At the same time, he lifted the men's spirits by presenting musical events at sunset. Sailors on guitars, fiddles, and flutes played up-tempo tunes and some of the sailors doffed their caps and danced, while others sang at the top of their lungs. The quartermaster, following the Captain's orders, dipped into crates of thick and chewy beef jerky and went from sailor to sailor, slapping them on their backs, offering pieces of jerky, and encouraging them to believe that they had not sailed into a permanent zone of heat and ruin. That the weather would change and riches surely lay ahead.

One morning, Caboto woke and realized the sweat that

had covered his body for a week had cooled. His mouth was no longer dry and parched. A promise of fresh, moist air had slipped into his small cabin. He moved onto the deck and saw that rain had fallen in the early hours and a new wind whipped the sails. The sky was streaked deep red behind a climbing sun. The quartermaster, his skin peeling from the days of heat, saw Caboto and called out, "The color of the sky is warning us. Red in the morning could mean bad weather." Caboto looked at the flags now responding to the wind. *What is worse*, he wondered, *no wind, heat and slow seas, or a gale that could push the ships off course and cause them to be lost forever?*

He heard the squeak of rats, peeking their noses out of the cracks in the floorboards. They were sniffing, intuiting the changing weather. Two cats streaked across the deck, ready to attack the rodents. But the rats were too quick, and slipped back into their small spaces, leaving the cats mewing with frustration and hunger.

And then that evening the storm hit, hard. The winds raged, the ocean swells mounted, white caps rose and fell and rose again, at times higher than the ship's rails, sending saltwater onto the decks and onto the backs of the men. Sailors, on shift, tied themselves to railings. The pilot tied down the ship's wheel; it was all he could do to keep the rudder in its proper place, and the ship upright. The stars were buried behind angry dark clouds; visibility was minimal. Caboto could no longer make out any other ship in the flotilla. They seemed alone in the vast ocean. Caboto did not believe in sea monsters, but what if they had been drawn into a natural phenomenon that, until this voyage, was uncharted by man? A swirling mass of wind and water that destroyed anything that came into its vicinity?

That night, a great homesickness swept over him. He longed

to see Mattea's face, hold her, discuss the day. He wanted to watch his boys grow closer to manhood. Finally, on the storm's second day, exhaustion pulled him into a troubled sleep and he dreamed of them, reaching out to his family, but never gaining ground, never able to touch them.

Finally, the storm subsided, the winds slowed, but the rains continued. A distrust of the universe, and of God, was etched on every sailor's face. Was this only a respite or was it a reprieve? The ocean's current was moving fast and the sails strained. The course had to be aligned with the stars. How far had they been blown off course?

And then the rain became a drizzle. The sun appeared and a rainbow spread across the sky. The decks glistened. In the distance, the sails of the other ships could be spotted, their flags waving. The sailors cheered in relief.

The quartermaster moved over to Caboto. "Did you think it would never end?"

Caboto, his skin still sporting a green tinge from seasickness, sounded weak. But he forced a cheerful comeback. "I never doubted we would weather the storm."

The quartermaster laughed. "It always seems better once we can stand on our legs again without holding on to the rails."

That night, Caboto joined the pilot in watching the shades of violet fill the sky. A half-moon and the stars shone brightly. He watched a sailor yawn and rub his ball-shaped stomach. Caboto imagined he was thinking of a roasted pig on a fire pit almost ready to tear his teeth into, of a paella of sausage and shrimp, a deep red wine from Andalusia, and peaches slathered with cream to end this grand meal. He imagined the sailor was doing all he could to avoid thinking about the strips of salted beef and the barrels of rice where the weevils had nested.

~

It was just dawn on the third of November, twenty-one days into the voyage, and Caboto, deep into sleep, was startled awake. Was that the sound of a cannon firing? Was danger afoot? Had pirates ignored the flag of Spain and attacked? He pulled on his cloak and hat and quickly headed to the deck. The wind was blowing westerly at a steady pace, the scent of sweet vegetation filled the air. Sailors, miserable only a day ago, were now full of great expectation.

"The flagship has sighted land!" a rigger, high on the mast, called down. "I'll see what I can see."

Torres joined Caboto. "On the first voyage to these West Indies, ships sailed thirty-five days before seeing land. We've taken two weeks off that time. Even with the storm, here we are. The seven degrees difference the admiral called for, that might have made it possible. What a few degrees will do, eh?"

Caboto felt anticipation fill his body. Soon he'd be on solid earth, walking on a stretch of land that no European had walked before. He watched as sailors lowered a small boat from the deck of the *Marigalante*. Colombo sat prominently at the bow, the flags of the queen and king on iron standards waved in the stern.

The landing crew was rowed to shore.

The sailors of the *Rodriga* waited, hoping to be ordered to the beach. They wanted to find fresh fruit on trees, birds that could be roasted, roots to be boiled and chewed. But it was barely an hour later that Colombo was seen, quickly getting back into the landing craft. The boat was rowed back to the *Marigalante*. Messengers, in smaller boats, rowed to the other ships, yelling, "*Avast! Avast!*" They announced that the admiral had named the island Domenico, Day of Discovery, and claimed it for the queen, but after a short exploration, the landing party had come across mounds of skulls, femurs, ribcages, and other bones stripped of their flesh.

"The admiral fears it is cannibals who inhabit the place," the messengers shouted. "We are to move on."

Caboto was stunned. In all his journeys, he had not encountered peoples who feasted on human skin, organs, muscle, and fat. That night, he made a note in his rutter: Domenico was an island to be avoided—until civilization could take hold.

The flotilla sailed on to another series of islands. Colombo claimed each for Queen Isabel, naming them Guadaloupe, Santa María la Antigua, San Jorge, San Cristóbal, Santa Cruz, and San Juan Bautista. At each island, he appointed a ship and crew to anchor and explore. After three days, they were to rejoin the flagship in Hispaniola to report their findings. The *Rodriga* was not assigned an island; it was ordered to follow the *Marigalante* to Hispaniola.

The ships approached the green island of Hispaniola. Palm trees swayed in the soft wind. The beach was white, sparkling under a strong sun. The high-pitched chirping of birds was the only sound to be heard. All had expected a grand welcome, a racing out of the community of sailors that had settled there nine months previously. Why were they not there, waving and shouting in welcome? Where were the huts, the fishing boats, the signs of activity?

The cannon on the *Marigalante* fired. But there was no answer. All was eerily quiet.

The quartermaster on the *Rodriga* shouted, "Drop anchor!" The anchor hit the sea with a great splash, descending into the water to grab on to the heavy sand and shell bottom.

Again, the flagship fired a cannon. Nothing.

Caboto watched as a small party from the flagship went ashore. Caboto waited; the air was warm, thick. The sailors on board the *Rodriga* chafed; they wanted to get on land but they also knew that something did not feel right. Caboto saw Captain Torres nod to the master gunner. With keys in hand, the master gunner headed to the gun room.

And then the mosquitoes found them. Caboto heard their despotic buzz near his ears. He swatted at the insects, but they were persistent. While he slapped at one, another pierced his skin and feasted on his blood.

"This is nothing like it was on the first voyage, in the hotter weather." A sailor stood near him, swatting at the insistent predators. "Then they came is such large groups, it was like a deadly, black blanket wrapping itself around you."

Caboto slapped at another enemy insect that had settled on his neck. He moved to the stern, found a bit of wind, and continued to wave his arms to keep the insects at bay.

Another sailor called up to Caboto, "Find the eucalyptus trees on the island, and rub your skin with the leaves. Helps keep the little monsters away."

Hours later, a messenger rowed out to the *Rodriga* and told the story. The group had found the fort, La Navidad, burned to the ground. There were burned bodies of both settlers and natives. No sign of human life. Colombo had hiked inland, guards with muskets at his side. He made his way to King Guacanagari, the chief who had given Colombo the golden nose rings and helped repair the *Santa María* when it ran aground.

The reception was cool. The king told Colombo that the settlers had been killed for they fought and stole from the natives and were disrespectful to the women of the island, kidnapping them and holding them as captives. King Guacanagari said he tried to reason with the settlers, but he could not contain the problem. Colombo had asked if the relationship could be repaired but the king did not offer him presents or kindness—or hope.

Captain Torres looked at the written order that was given to him. "Admiral Colombo wants us to sail northwest to another part of the island. We'll need a place to drop anchor."

The ships sailed on for another day and anchored in a bay. Colombo went ashore with a landing crew, planted a flag, named the new site La Isabella, and ordered sailors to set up camps.

In the next days, Caboto, with a small assigned crew in a small landing boat, explored the shorelines. They checked depths of the water, recorded notes on currents and tides and treacherous shoals. They hiked various sites, tested the strength of the grounds along the shores, and identified trees that might be used to build piers. Caboto spent days on his charts, often continuing by candlelight into the night. He wanted to make sure his work would be useful—and also well received—for he wanted to impress the king.

During the weeks in Hispaniola, a small tribe of Tainos made their way to the La Isabella site; most were content to watch the foreign men take what they wanted from the land. Caboto, too, watched as fruit plants, palms, thin boats lined with tree bark, headdresses made of feather and animal bone, shells, and baskets were loaded onto the *Rodriga* and the *Gorda*, two of the swiftest caravels.

A large hut had been built in a breezy spot on a beach for the admiral's use. Its sides were made of thin wood and its roof of palm leaves. A table, brought from the flagship, was set up, a chair placed next to it. A few days after Caboto had delivered rough drawings to Colombo, he was ushered inside. Caboto could see that the stress of the journey had taken a toll for Colombo looked smaller, his shoulders more hunched. He knew that Colombo was dealing with many details: appeasing the natives, calming the fears and concerns of the new settlers, and the disappointment of the sailors who had expected to find, and share, precious resources.

Colombo motioned for Caboto to sit. He unrolled Caboto's charts. "You have identified places for harbors."

"Excellent possibilities, Admiral. If I may suggest, your next expedition could include the necessary iron works and timbers and trained workers, everything needed to build a harbor worthy of large galleys and smaller caravels. I'm working on more exact plans now, so that on your return, you can present finalized drawings to the queen and king."

"That I will do," Colombo nodded. "The *Rodriga* and *Gorda* will return to Europe early next week. The other ships will follow me to explore the island of Cuba. I have decided to leave Bartolome here to be in charge of this settlement. He seems to have a way with the chief. I want to avoid the problems of the last settlement." Colombo sighed. His energy, usually so high, had dissipated. He looked tired.

"Any sign of the gold mine you're hoping for?"

"The source has eluded us." Colombo said. "But I will find it." Colombo strove to be positive. But both knew that Queen Isabel did not like disappointment and it was clear this knowledge was paramount in Colombo's mind.

≈

Strong winds assured the swift returns of the *Rodriga* and *Gorda* to Cádiz. Captain Torres was busy finalizing his logbook of the voyage. Cosa recorded every variant, every wind change and current. The quartermaster and boatswain kept the excited crew busy; all wanted the ship to gleam as it entered the Spanish harbor.

Caboto stood on the deck, searching the wharf. His eyes finally found Mattea. She stood tall, wearing a velvet cape and a hat with a peacock feather. He saw Piero and his sons next to her. Ludovico seemed to have grown a foot taller and now, at age eighteen, was clearly working on a beard. Sebastiano, sixteen, and Sancius, two years younger, waved wildly. Caboto quickly wiped unexpected tears from his eyes and impatiently waited for the ship to gain proper position at the pier.

The gangplank was put in place. He hurried to his family, and pulled each to him with such vehemence that Piero was worried. "Are you all right, my brother?"

"Yes, yes," Caboto said. "Perfect now."

He pulled Mattea to him and kissed her on the lips.

"Gio," she whispered, embarrassed. "Such a public display of affection."

"Forgive me, my darling. I missed you."

She smiled at him and blinked the tears from her eyes.

Piero announced it was time to eat, that he had arranged a supper for them at the inn. As the family headed away from the ship, Sebastiano walked alongside his father, listening to every detail of the voyage. Finally, he said, very seriously, "Someday, Papà, when you lead your own exploration, I'll be at your side. We'll plant a flag together."

Caboto smiled. He realized Sebastiano, his most adventurous son, sounded so much like his younger self.

But Caboto no longer wanted to wait for someday. He knew

it was time to set up his own expedition that would sail west to reach the shores of Asia.

Chapter Eighteen

A month later, the family was back in Valencia. Caboto walked with Luis de Santángel and pleaded his case. "Admiral Colombo has yet to reach the mainland of India. Or China. Or Cipango. And the outlying regions of the Indies that Colombo has claimed—they have not contained the resources Spain desires. I have another plan, a new direction—more northerly—in mind. As Portugal has proven with their multiple expeditions helmed by Vasco da Gama, Fernão Gomes, Pêro Escobar, Bartolomeu Dias, Diogo Cão, and others—there is much to be gained in sending out more than one explorer to find the bounty of new lands."

Santángel shook his head. "Queen Isabel and King Ferdinand are stretched too thin with the country's politics—and with their patronage of Colombo."

Caboto pressed, "Señor Santángel, the Muslim Turks have created an even stronger stranglehold on the Silk Road. There is no relief in sight; European trade with Asia has become treacherous. Expensive. The Catholic royals could change that."

"I hear your passion," Santángel told Caboto. "But it is not a good time."

Caboto did not want to give up. "Señor de Santángel, perhaps if I could talk to the king."

Santángel was adamant. "The king is in a dark mood. Very frustrated. For financial reasons, his plans for a grander Valencia harbor were put on hold. And the Seville bridge, also unfinished. There is no money and no desire to commit to new projects. A meeting with the king to gain support for an unproven plan will only remind him of recent failures and he will not be happy." Santángel stopped, and adjusted his brimmed hat. His eyes were hard. "I cannot recommend your proposal. You know very well that, in these new lands, the immediate rewards—such as gold—have not shown themselves."

Caboto still argued, "That is why it would benefit exploring a northerly route to a different part of the coast of Asia. To find a more civilized kingdom."

"You've been paid for your work in Valencia and Seville. And for your harbor designs for Hispaniola," Santángel said. "Be content."

Caboto swallowed hard. He did not want to be content.

That night, the Caboto family looked at other possibilities. Sebastiano held up a list he'd made. "Look, Papà, in Europe, only Portugal, Spain, France, and England are committed to supporting daring explorations to find passages to Asia. Henry VII of England—like France—was very interested in funding Colombo's first expedition heading west. He was not happy when Queen Isabel exercised her option on Colombo's services."

Caboto nodded. "I've been to Bristol as a merchant trader in years past. I know the English have gone as far as Iceland."

"But no further," said Sebastiano.

Piero looked at his own notes. "The English have always been frustrated at paying some of the highest prices in trade from the East."

"Why do they pay more?" Sancius asked.

Ludovico explained, "Because their country is near the end of the trade route from Asia. Ships leave the shores of the Ottoman Empire, head toward the Italian Peninsula, and sell there. What is left is sent on to Spain, France, and Portugal, the closer ports. Finally, the spices, antiquities, silks, and other goods head to England's ports. Each leg of the journey adds to the cost." Ludovico, much like his uncle Piero, had his eye on the accounts. "Papà, an important selling point to King Henry could be bringing down the cost of goods. That might appeal."

Sebastiano, always attracted to competition, added, "And to outshine Spain. England wants to dominate. That will be an incentive also."

Caboto remembered Fra Carbonariis, the Italian friar he had befriended on one of his first journeys as a trader to Bristol. That was years ago, when he'd lived in Venice. Fra Carbonariis was part of Henry VII's court. Would the friar remember him?

Caboto determined to send a letter to Fra Carbonariis and get it on the next boat heading to England. He looked at his family. "We shall see—perhaps I have a friend in court."

Chapter Nineteen

Caboto's 1495 letter to Friar Carbonariis left Valencia on the next ship heading to London. Caboto hoped for a response, but he did not want to rely on only one possibility. He asked the family to learn all they could about Henry VII. Every evening, when the family sat down for a meal, they shared information. The studious Ludovico reported on accounts of Henry VII's battles against King Richard III, the older and more experienced king of England who, in some people's opinions, had wrongfully seized the throne from the mad, unpredictable King Henry VI and his rightful heirs. Against all odds, young Henry had defeated the powerful Richard of York at the Battle of Bosworth Field, and ended the War of the Roses. Henry VII, of the House of Lancaster, became the first Tudor king.

"Why is he called a Tudor?" Sancius asked.

Ludovico had the answer. "His grandfather married the widow of Henry V, Queen Catherine. His name was Owen Tudor, so it's really the king's last name."

"But what is the House of Lancaster?" Sancius was confused.

"Here the word house refers to a family. But there are many generations and marriages in a house, so people won't all have the same last name." Ludovico looked to his father. "I'm trying to figure out the lineages, Father. It's complicated, but might be important to know. I'll draw you a chart."

Caboto smiled and nodded.

Sebastiano talked to traders and sea captains at the piers in Valencia. "Papà, I heard that King Henry VII is only a few years younger than you are."

Mattea added, "The king and his queen have three children. Gio, you will have this in common with him."

Sebastiano nodded. "And Papà, like you, he is tall. And he is popular with his subjects for he favors the merchant and manufacturing classes."

"Why does he favor them?" Sancius asked.

Ludovico, knowledgeable now about trade and profit, said, "Because one of the king's goals is to save his kingdom's economy. Before the War of the Roses, there was a Hundred Years War—a long struggle over who would rule England, including wars with France. So much money is spent in war that a kingdom can be crippled. Now, finally, there seems to be some peace and King Henry wants to put food back on citizens' tables, and raise the standards of education. He's interested in architecture, literature, and the theater."

Sebastiano added, "He also supports the building up of his navy. That means there is a good amount of shipbuilding."

Mattea leaned in. "There may be ships already built that could make the voyage across the Ocean Sea."

Sebastiano was excited. "Just what I was thinking, Mamma."

"Most important to us is that Henry VII has made it known

he's willing to defy Pope Alexander VI's Treaty of Tordesillas," said Piero. "The one set forth in 1493."

Sancius sighed. "There is so much I don't know. What is in the treaty?"

Piero cut his meat, and dipped it in the sauce of lamb juices and turnips. "The treaty divides all newly discovered, uncharted territories between two countries, Spain and Portugal. The rights to all lands and seas lying west of a rather arbitrary meridian, chosen by a pope who has never sailed or explored, are given to Spain, and lands and seas to the east of the line are given to Portugal."

Sebastiano guffawed. "The pope is trying to stave off wars between the two countries. They're the only ones mentioned because they're the only ones daring the explorations. But if other kingdoms or empires become more daring, I predict the treaty cannot be enforced. Uncharted lands should go to those who have the courage to look for and find them."

Caboto laughed at Sebastiano's vehemence. "Perhaps you should become a cardinal and advisor to the pope."

Sebastiano raised his chin, defiant. "I will be a great explorer one day."

Sancius clapped, enthralled with his brave brother's confidence. "I know you will, Sebastiano. Papà first, and then you!"

Piero broke a piece of bread, put it in his mouth, and chewed. "Henry VII is not happy with the pope making this proclamation—or even for the pope thinking he has the right to do so. Henry VII had great ambitions to expand England's kingdom. Perhaps the scene has been set for a proposal to England."

Two months later, as the family served themselves from platters filled with fish sausage, sardines, sea bream, and rice steeped in fish stock, a servant entered and bowed to Caboto. "Señor, the parish priest is at the door. He says he has a letter for you from England."

Caboto felt a prickle of excitement on his neck. He stood. "Please ask the priest to join us. I happen to know sardines are his favorite supper."

Their parish priest joined them and was soon happy popping the fried sardines into his mouth. He was oblivious to the family who was no longer interested in their food.

Caboto opened the letter and read it.

Sebastiano was impatient. "Papà. Tell us what's in the letter! Is it from Fra Carbonariis?"

Caboto put the letter down onto the table and was very still.

Piero studied his brother. "I cannot tell if you are happy or disappointed, Gio. Your face has lost its color."

Caboto wanted to keep his voice calm. Finally, he spoke. "The letter is, indeed, from Fra Carbonariis. He's assured me he'll get me an audience with King Henry VII. And that he'll try to pave the way for the king's favor of my planned expedition."

There was silence around the dinner table. Except for the priest, who was busy reaching for the bowl of rice. "Very good supper, Señora. Tasty. Very tasty," he said and wiped dripping oil off his chin. He looked up, feeling the tension in the room. "What has happened?"

Sebastiano turned to Mattea. "Mamma, what do you think?"

Caboto looked to Mattea, waiting for her reaction.

She raised her eyebrows, a soft smile of her face. "I think I shall begin to pack."

Part Four: England

Chapter Twenty

Caboto walked with Mattea along the Bristol wharf in early January 1496. He appreciated the touch of her arm in the crook of his elbow. She said, "I had heard that England was stuffy and cold and rainy and that its poetry reflected that. But I am finding the opposite." She laughed. "All is good here, except for the food."

Caboto knew Mattea was determined to make the best of their new home. The family had arrived in the port city only a month before. It seemed as if rain, fog, and cold air were their constant companions. Caboto had insisted they arrive dressed in the fashion of well-born Englishmen and women. Stretching their dwindling funds, he had found them a stone manor home in a refined area of Bristol; it let in drafts around the windows and there was a leaky roof in the kitchen, but it had a painted fence and fine trees in its front yard.

And, most important, Caboto announced the family name would now be Cabot, so they would appear more English. He had sent a letter to Fra Carbonariis, alerting him to their new chosen name, and that he had arrived and hoped that a meeting with the king could be arranged at an early convenience.

And then they waited.

The English were not as open and friendly as the Italians or Spanish people, for decades of wars had made day-to-day living difficult. The wars had depleted villages of young and older men, and many widowed women struggled to feed their children. As bustling and international as Bristol was at its harbor, the outlying neighborhoods were poor and their residents could only covet fine clothes made of silk, jewels, furs, and spices. Mattea visited market stalls and, slowly, was able to find friendly conversation as she chose turnips, onions, cabbage, and carrots, veal and lamb and milk to be delivered to their home. She longed to find fine olive oil but had to be content with animal fats, butter, and cream. She learned to distinguish the most flavorful mushrooms to serve with potatoes. She learned to mix a rich porridge that laid heavy in their stomachs but helped warm them on cold mornings.

Finally, in late summer, a letter from Fra Carbonariis arrived. He wrote that Henry VII would be holding court in Bristol in a month's time. And that Caboto was to be listed on the king's calendar.

Fra Carbonariis arrived in Bristol before the king. Caboto met him at Saint James Priory, a church built by the Benedictines. Caboto and Father Carbonariis settled into the church's refectory by a warm fire. "This first meeting with the king must go well, Fra Carbonariis," Caboto said. "I know I may never get a second chance."

Fra Carbonariis, a head cold making his voice sound nasal and pained, filled Caboto in on King Henry VII's particular interests. "He wants to find a route going west to Asia; specifically, he desires more trade in alum and other goods from China. He also wants to expand his kingdom with new territories—sooner rather than later—because he does not want to fall behind Spain and Portugal."

"Do you have advice on my approach? Who is the king's closest council?"

The friar used a poker to move a log in an attempt to encourage the flames. "King Henry VII believes in the divine right of kings. Royal absolutism. That he and God are in direct conversation and therefore his decisions are God's decisions. The king will listen to advisors—but to his own voice, most of all. He is also tight-fisted with England's monies. He will expect other funds to be accessed if your plan is to go forward."

"Could I expect investments from some of England's noble houses?"

"Many are in debt from the wars. Others profited from the wars. We must approach the latter. Also, the banks of London. And, I think, we will be able to involve Italian bankers and financiers." He blew his nose. "We are Italians, are we not? I am from the Republic of Milan; you have Genoese and Venetian sensibilities." He smiled at Caboto. "Italian bankers may be generous."

Caboto did not respond. His reputation in Venice could still be a problem.

The months slipped by. Autumn rains came and went and Caboto waited to hear from the king. He and Sebastiano spent time at the wharf talking to sailors who had sailed as far north as

Iceland and to the northern coasts of Ireland. Information about the waters, winds, and currents were soon reflected in Caboto's charts. To earn money, he made contact with traders and represented goods from Sicily and Constantinople to merchants in Bristol. He soon gained their respect for his acuity and fair pricing. Many became interested in his ideas and plans for an expedition into the Ocean Sea.

But time was passing, and Caboto's frustration grew.

Mattea joined the impatient Caboto in his nightly stargazing. One night, she reached for his hand and stroked it, trying to calm him. "The king will meet with you soon, my husband. This will be our time, I know it."

Finally, the request for Caboto's presence at King Henry VII's royal court arrived.

A rumble of boots sounded on the stone floor, and the king's royal council swept by the waiting Caboto and Fra Carbonariis, wafts of prized cinnamon and cardamom spices emanating from the council's furs. Doors to the royal chambers closed behind them. A moment later, an aged royal page appeared and announced, "His Royal Highness will now see Friar Carbonariis and John Cabot."

Nervous, but determined, Caboto followed Fra Carbonariis into the royal chamber. He was armed with copies of his charts and maps. He bowed to the king. "I'm honored to be in your presence, Your Highness."

King Henry VII's mouth was wide—a thin line that stretched across his face. His dark hair descended to his shoulders, and a gold chain held his fur-lined, cranberry-colored cloak in place. His boots were polished leather and he carried leather gloves. He took his time in responding. He leaned back, looking up to the stained glass windows that lent streaks of color into the room.

Caboto glanced at Fra Carbonariis. Was there a problem? Fra Carbonariis shrugged, also confused.

Then, the king sighed and looked down his prominent nose at Caboto. "Oh dear, you have an accent. But it is not of the Castile. Or Catalan area." Henry VII leaned forward, looking at him closely. Measuring him. "I have heard your name was, only months ago, Johan Caboto Montecalunya. Your accent does not match your name."

Caboto's heart pounded. What if King Henry was disposed against him because of his birthright?

Caboto chose honesty. "Your Highness, I was born Giovanni Caboto, in Genoa. I then lived in Venice. And then Catalonia. There I designed harbors and bridges and oversaw construction for King Ferdinand. But my family now resides in England. Most happily. I have a wife, a brother, and three sons."

The king took another long moment, then said, "I have three children."

Caboto remembered the research his family had done. He nodded. "They are always in our prayers at church, Your Highness. As you and your queen are too."

Fra Carbonariis bowed to the king. "Your Highness, as I have mentioned to you previously, this man is of great experience. He has recently completed sailing with Colombo to New Lands, as harbor designer. He is an expert navigator, linguist, chart-maker, and a brave and reliable subject to your fine kingdom."

Caboto pressed on, "We have taken the name of Cabot to show honor to the English tongue. And the English throne."

The king slapped his leather gloves against his hand in a

steady rhythm. "So, if we are to embark on business dealings together, we will be doing it with a man named John Cabot. A man who lives and thrives as I see fit, in my England?"

"Yes, Your Highness." Caboto, his mouth dry, felt a drop of sweat fall from his forehead to his jaw.

The king seemed to weigh his appraisal. "You actually can speak our fine language. Not badly."

Caboto bowed at the faint praise. "Every day I master more, Your Highness."

The king looked back up to the stained glass windows, as if asking the saints and soldiers depicted there to give him advice. He mused, "Colombo was born in Genoa."

"That is true, Your Highness," Caboto said. "Many in Genoa are fearless sea captains."

The king pulled at the corners of his thin lips. "Cabot. I will tell you this. We have studied your plan for an expedition. We deem it very thorough. Father Carbonariis tells me you have worked with him to secure interest of many lords of England. They are open to consider financing—if our patronage is secured?"

Caboto handed the king a letter that had been written and signed by a group of investors, mostly merchants he had befriended at the wharf. King Henry handed the letter to an advisor to be read aloud. The advisor spoke in a clear voice, "We are in support of John Cabot receiving the royal grant of right under the king's banner, to discover and find whatever islands, countries, regions, and provinces, in whatever part of the world they be, which before this time have been unknown to all Christians . . ."

King Henry waved for the advisor to stop reading. "These investors will, of course, expect a profit from the expedition."

Caboto nodded. "Asia is full of riches, as we all know . . ."

The king interrupted, his voice commanding. "It is necessary, John Cabot, if we were to pursue this support of your expedition, that the royal purse not be touched. I would insist, however, that the court receive one fifth of all treasures and goods."

"Only fair, Your Highness," said Caboto.

"And that the expedition avoids the southern route chosen by Colombo. Pope Alexander has stuck his nose into the affairs of kingdoms and their acquisitions of new territories. We do not agree with the Vatican on this, but for now, we would like to avoid direct conflict. Spain must not feel encroachment. They like war, as you know."

Caboto tried to calm his nerves for it seemed the king was considering his plan very seriously. Now talking details. He kept his voice steady as he said, "This is the age of new discovery, Your Highness. A most exciting time for kingdoms, such as yours. To go where no explorer has gone before. To benefit in the opening of new trade routes. And to claim new lands."

The king stood. "You will hear from the court soon, John Cabot. Please attend here in Bristol, so that we should know where to find you."

Chapter Twenty-One

On March 1, 1496, Henry VII sent a message to Caboto to come to Westminster Palace, the king's royal residence in London. The entire Caboto family made the five-day journey by carriage from Bristol to London—all were excited and hated the thought of having to wait in Bristol to hear news. Fra Carbonariis had arranged for the family to stay in the Augustine Abbey and they quickly settled in.

The next day, Caboto rode in a carriage directly to Westminster. There, he stood before the king's royal council in a long hall that was draped with tapestries and lit by the gray light of the London day that peeked through thin mullioned windows and dozens of candelabra. Fra Carbonariis now stood, in his favored place, with the council. He gazed at Caboto kindly, but gave no hint at the king's intention that day. The rest of the council, their faces dour and distant, stood silently, awaiting the arrival of the king.

Caboto's knees were weak; he knew a decision must have

been reached that would change his life forever. It might be the best news, or news that could devastate him. But he had been called to London—would the king have called him there just to deny his dream? He remembered how Colombo had been called to Queen Isabel's court, only to be given hope but no official support, and had waited for more than two years. Would he be asked, like Colombo, to promise not to sail under another kingdom's flag and wait for the king's further consideration?

The king entered, guards at his side. All bowed as he settled on a massive wooden chair that was padded with velvet cushions. He did not keep Caboto waiting. He showed Caboto a document and nodded for his advisor to read its contents. "Greetings. Be it known and made manifest that we have given and granted to John Cabot, and to Lewis, Sebastian, and Sancio, sons of the said John, and to the heirs and deputies of them, full and free authority, faculty, and power to sail one ship to all parts, regions, and coasts of the eastern, western, and northern sea, under our banners, flags, and ensigns, with an exploratory ship of whatsoever burden and quality it may be, and with so many and such mariners and men as needed, at their own proper costs and charges, to find, discover, and investigate . . ."

Caboto listened to every word. He had imagined this moment, these words, this permission, but all exceeded every element of his dreams. But only one ship? Colombo's first expedition included three ships. One ship surely meant shorter time to explore once land was reached, because there would be less space for provisions and the bounty he hoped to bring back from Asia.

The advisor was still reading. ". . . And further we have given and granted to John Cabot, his sons, and to their heirs and deputies, that all main lands, islands, towns, cities, castles, and other places whatsoever discovered by them, may not be frequented or visited by any other subjects of ours whatsoever without the license of the aforesaid John and his sons and of their deputies."

The words echoed and spun in Caboto's ears. Here it was declared that, if the expedition was successful, he and his family would likely be landowners, set up in a noble fashion, as protectors of the new lands claimed for the king. Surely, this would mean a place of honor at court. A secured future for his family. He would make due with one ship, and accomplish all he could. Caboto listened as the advisor came to the end of the document. "Witness ourself at Westminster on the fifth day of March 1496."

A silence filled the hall.

Caboto's heartbeat was loud to his own ears. Could everyone hear it?

The king stood. "This is my decision. Make good on your intentions, John Cabot."

The family celebrated with Fra Carbonariis at the Abbey. A roasted leg of lamb was sliced and eaten as the serious work of drafting letters to the identified investors, alerting them it was time to commit funds.

Mattea excused herself. "Husband, I have to find a seamstress. You and I are to attend the king's ball at the end of the week, and I don't want to disappoint you."

Caboto shared a warm look with her. "You could never disappoint, wife. Please, do as you need. It is time to enjoy the moment. Find the finest fabric for the most magnificent gown."

Fra Carbonariis arranged for a young friar to help Mattea hire a ladies' maid to take her to a respected London seamstress.

The men continued working on the strategy for gaining the financing needed to make the planned voyage a reality.

The night of the ball, Mattea was dressed in a velvet silk gown in vibrant azure with a silver- and ivory-colored brocaded overskirt. Her hair was braided and pearls studded her finely wound coils. In the carriage with Caboto on the way to the palace, she had worried about her English. "People in Bristol tell me my accent is charming. I hope London finds it so."

Caboto assured her she would be the most beautiful woman at court. She kissed him. "And you will be the most gallant husband there, Gio. You are too kind to see your forty-year-old wife as the most desirable of all."

Caboto said, "I'll always see you as the finest woman ever to marry an unworthy man."

Mattea leaned into him, happy for his good fortune and the excitement of attending the ball. Caboto gazed at her. "You could have married a rich noble in Venice and been a regular at the doge's parties. You sacrificed many fine nights in beautiful gowns for me."

"I would not have it any other way, my husband."

They arrived at Westminster Palace and were ushered into the ballroom. They circled the massive gilded room, taking in the sparkling chandeliers and silk draperies. Mattea subtly nodded towards a man in a flashy waistcoat and colorful breeches. "Who is that, Gio? He watches you like a hawk."

"William Weston, a trader, mostly of sugarcane from Madeira—an archipelago to the south of Portugal. Fra Carbonariis has told me Weston has petitioned the king, multiple times, for patronage of his own expeditions."

"Has the king not favored him?"

"I have heard there are quite a few lawsuits against Weston," Caboto told her. "Even his father-in-law is not happy with him. Perhaps he is not totally trustworthy."

"Is he envious of your good fortune?"

"I have yet to know the man," Caboto said.

Fra Carbonariis joined them. "Good evening, Cabots." He leaned into Caboto. "Everyone wants to talk with you, especially potential investors." He smiled mischievously at Mattea. "Perhaps Mrs. Cabot and I can speak Italian—quietly—while you mingle."

Mattea's face lit up. Even though the Milanese and the Venetian tongues were different, they were close enough, and it would be relaxing to speak her native tongue. Caboto bowed and left them together; he must use the evening to gain more financial support of the voyage.

As the weeks flew by, financing was put into place. Caboto and a royal council member, Sir Whitman, met with the bankers of London and received promises of monies, but not enough to fully secure a ship, and gain provisions and crew. The wealthy and unpopular Englishman William Weston, who had felt stung by the king's decision to support Caboto's plan and not his own, added financing in exchange for a berth on the voyage. Fra Carbonariis sent letters to the Republics of Italy, specifically to the Bardi, Peruzzi, and Frescobaldi banking families, and received promises of healthy monetary support.

"And good news, my dear," Caboto said, his face beaming with excitement as he joined Mattea by the Abbey's large fireplace.

"What is it, Gio?"

"Fra Carbonariis and I have received word that the doge and the council in Venice will consider the dissolution of my debts there, in return for an investment in any profits from the journey for King Henry."

"And that can be accepted?"

"Already signed for and approved. One day we can return to Venice, the place of your birth."

Mattea moved into Caboto's arms. "Who knows where our journey will take us, husband? But this is very good news."

Caboto could not sleep that night. He knew that all investors hoped to gain riches from items brought back from the Far East. His excitement grew, as did the pressure to make good.

He and his family soon headed back to Bristol. A ship had to be chosen, one that would fare well in the cold waters, winds, and heavy currents Caboto expected to face.

At the wharf, he and Sebastiano sought out sailors who had made voyages to Iceland. Caboto made a connection with a ship owner and potential investor, and determined he would captain a five-day voyage to Iceland to speak to sea captains there. He would find out exactly how far west Icelandic ships had traveled and what charts he might be able to purchase that would illuminate the waters he planned to travel. This journey was fruitful, and Caboto returned to Bristol with a few Icelandic sailors who had agreed to commit to the expedition.

His next task was to finalize the choice of the ship for the voyage across the Ocean Sea to the shores of the land once inhabited by the Great Khan.

Chapter Twenty-Two

Caboto settled on a ship, *Matthew*, a ninety-ton, caravel-style navicula of just under sixty feet. Built in Bristol's shipyards, its single deck made of pine was bookended with a high, reinforced bow and stern that would provide protection from the high waves in the northern waters of the Ocean Sea. It had three sails: two front masts with square sails and a square lateen sail rigged to the rear mast. Caboto had inspected the keel, made of English oak, and the masts that were made of hundred-year-old spruce fir. The canvas sails were made of imported woven flax. Caboto had watched workmen use hammers to drive oakum, a material made from saturated hemp, into the spaces between the pine deck planks and sides of the ship; this was to keep the ship watertight. He inspected the hull to make sure it was sealed with black tar, for he knew the frigid waters would test the ship's structure.

Sebastiano begged to be included in the venture, but Mattea and Caboto decided against it. The risks were high and Caboto did not want the distraction of worrying about his son's safety. He also knew Mattea was not ready to let her young, adventurous son leave the family nest. Caboto now understood his own mother's trepidation and slow agreement to favor his first voyages over unpredictable seas to the Middle East and Greece.

Sebastiano was not satisfied with their decision. As father and son strode through Bristol's port, Sebastiano continued to plead his case. "Papà. I have studied the charts and the celestial markings you will follow. I know how to use the compass rose, the traverse board, and the astrolabe; I can update your rutter as many times during the day that you wish."

"Son, this first voyage may prove problematic. I cannot have your mother worrying about both of us. Be patient." Caboto saw his son's disappointment, ached for him, for he understood it completely.

"Pardon, Giovanni Caboto, the intrusion." A tall, thin man in a brown woolen coat stepped out of a doorway.

Surprised, Caboto stepped in front of Sebastiano, naturally protective. Who was this stranger? The man noticed Caboto's wariness and quickly introduced himself. "I mean no harm."

Caboto straightened, thinking, *How does this man know my birth name?* He had relaxed his vigilance after being told of the doge of Venice's dismissal of his debts. Perhaps he had been wrong that he was no longer sought by the *condotierri*. He said, in a strong voice, "My name is John Cabot."

"I know of you from Admiral Colombo, thus my knowledge of your Italian origin. I will introduce myself. Hugh Say, of England." The man's face was lean, his skin weather-beaten. He wore thick leather gloves and a scarf was wound tightly around his neck.

Sebastiano, never one to back away from a confrontation, asked, "What is it that you desire of my father?"

"To offer my services. I served Admiral Colombo on his first voyage aboard the *Santa María* and I helped to prepare the charts for the second voyage. I know, Signor Caboto—Mister John Cabot—you sailed on the *Rodriga*. And now you will head your own expedition into the Ocean Sea."

"A much smaller expedition. One ship; the goal is to reach the shores of Asia, determine a successful route there, and then return. There will be no time for exploration, depending on how the provisions fare. If all goes according to plan, a following expedition will be larger and more extensive."

Hugh Say's eyes were wide, clear. "I am a man who can read and write and who feels most alive while at sea." He reached into his pocket. "I carry recommendations."

Caboto took the papers. "I'll look these over. I'll be at the Hatchet Inn tonight. I'll expect you there at sunset. I'll give you my decision then."

Hugh Say nodded, doffed his cap. Caboto and Sebastiano continued on. Sebastiano asked, "What do you think of him, Papà?"

"I had hoped for sailors with extensive experience to join my crew. But few have dared sign on. I'll meet with Hugh Say tonight, and perhaps he will prove to be honorable as well as experienced."

That night, over pints of ale, Caboto realized Say shared his passion for sea exploration. They talked of ships, navigation, supplies, and the excitement of discovery. Caboto made his decision, and offered Say the quartermaster position aboard the *Matthew*.

~

Only days remained before the voyage into the uncharted waters of the Ocean Sea. Caboto had Hugh Say take stock of his supplies: the cannon, the crossbows, and muskets for safety as well as bells, scissors, knives, coins, beads, needles, pins, and mirrors for trade. Say checked on the large store of food: sea biscuits, salted meats, cheeses, raisins, beans, honey, rice, almonds, sardines, anchovies, water, wine. Three goats, a dozen chickens, and one rooster were brought aboard. Firewood was stored. And, Caboto insisted, cats to take care of rats.

Caboto strode across the deck, returning nods and salutations from the eighteen sailors who formed his crew. They were getting the decks and riggings in order. He entered his small cabin, where he kept an iron box to which only he had the key. Inside were his astronomical and sea charts and the medicines of the ship's doctor. Medicines were very dear and needed to be distributed carefully, only as needed. Two astrolabes sat on his shelf, for Caboto had found that using them in pairs aided in calculating the position of stars. Next to them was a brass quadrant to aid in measuring the height of Polaris. Compasses, projected tide tables, and instruments to measure the altitude of the sun were also in place.

Hugh Say assigned the crew their shifts and tasks. The sailors wore their own clothes and most had arrived in loose trousers, woolen socks, and long jackets with hoods—all in different colors. Caboto knew most of these men did not own a change of clothing or boots. He wanted to do his part in keeping the sailors dry and warm, so he had used part of his budget to purchase woolen coats to protect them from the cold, wet weather they were sure to encounter on the northerly route.

William Weston arrived with a personal manservant who would share his small cabin. "Captain Cabot," said Weston, his voice high-pitched and dripping with elegant pronunciation. "I look forward to an uneventful journey and a most eventful landing in . . . China. That's what you've promised."

"I hope you'll be comfortable, sir." Caboto felt relieved that Weston's small cabin was not on the afterdeck, that he was far from the captain's quarters.

Later in the day, Caboto gave instructions to the crew. "Do not offend God by swearing or telling lurid or scandalous stories. God is looking after us; we do not want to disturb his sensibilities."

The sailors looked at each other and grinned. This new captain was setting rules that were rarely adhered to on other ships.

"Is that understood?" Caboto pressed, his voice louder.

"Aye aye, Captain!" The sailors shouted.

Caboto continued. "No gambling allowed. Every morning and evening there will be a prayer and a hymn to God, asking him to give us fair weather."

"What about rations?" a few sailors shouted.

"Each day, you will receive a pound of biscuit, and a small amount of butter and honey to eat with that biscuit. Also, a half a pound of cheese, dried peas wetted into a mash, and half a pound of pickled meat. On Fridays and holy days, you will be given dried codfish if no fresh catch is available."

"What if we're thirsty?"

"Every day each of you shall receive a pint of water and a gallon of beer."

Cheers followed this pronouncement. Perhaps, the sailors thought, this Captain Cabot was not as strict as they had thought.

Caboto could see William Weston standing at the rails, taking in the scene. His nose was raised high, his lips curled. He nodded to his young manservant, and the youth cleared a path to Weston's cabin. Caboto knew that Weston would be taking notes, just as he himself had done when he sailed with Colombo. He hoped that Weston had no other designs on the journey, for Caboto did not desire any trouble.

It was May 20, 1497.

"Are you ready, Captain?" Hugh Say said to Caboto as he approached the afterdeck.

"Almost," Caboto said. He laid his hand on his heart and faced his family—Mattea, Piero, and his three sons. They stood on the pier, watching the final preparations. They all put their hands over their hearts, signaling the love that had kept them together through many years.

Then Caboto motioned to Fra Carbonariis, who stood on the pier, near the bow of the ship. "Father Carbonariis will bless the ship."

As prayers were spoken, Caboto held the precious boxwood rosary he'd received on his twenty-fifth birthday from his parents. Fra Carbonariis made the sign of the cross and raised his hands into the air. "Godspeed!" Church bells rang.

Caboto wedged a coin, for good luck, at the base of the mast.

The crew hoisted the sails, and moments later, the ship moved down the Avon River toward the Mouth of the Severn, making its way to the Bristol Channel toward the Ocean Sea.

Looking back at his family, Caboto realized he was not afraid for his life. He was most afraid of failure.

～

Caboto ordered the pilot to steer the *Matthew* past the southern shores of Ireland and then north-northwest, expecting to travel the nearly one thousand nautical miles to Iceland in less than a week. "Aye, Captain, the course is understood," said the pilot.

Soon there was nothing but water on all sides, and no guarantees of land ahead. Caboto walked the decks, checking that all ropes and riggings were in place. Weston stood outside his cabin, leaning against the rails.

"Mr. Weston," Caboto said. "I trust you are comfortable."

"No, I am not. But then this ship is quite small."

"The winds have been favorable," Caboto said, ignoring the complaint.

"May they stay that way. Until we reach the land of great riches." Weston nodded and slipped back into his cabin.

Aspar, an Icelandic sailor who had joined the crew, stood in his assigned spot near the pilot, ready to jot notes in the ship's log of daily temperatures and winds. Hugh Say teased him that he was a man of few words; Aspar grunted and replied that a sailor did not need to talk, only to be constantly on watch.

Once they left the west coast of Ireland and steered north-northwest to Iceland, Caboto and Hugh Say shared nightly suppers of dried sausage and boiled potatoes in the captain's quarters. They went over Aspar's logbook, the daily traverse board markings, and kept records on the ship, the currents and the crew during each of the eight-hour watches.

Every night, Caboto slept fitfully, listening for any signs of problems. He was keyed into the sounds and movements of the ship: the hull slapping against water, the roll of the vessel, the thumps and clinks of sailors going about their tasks, the whistles of wind.

During the day, Caboto took turns around the ship, checking on work, on the state of the ship and the sailors' states of mind. Memories of Colombo's troubles with his sailors weighed on Caboto and he wanted his crew's respect. A young boy of about fourteen was mopping the deck. Caboto remembered asking his father to set off on a sea expedition at that age and not gaining permission. But now, looking at the young lad, he thought he comprehended a loneliness he himself might have felt. "Your name, sailor," Caboto asked.

Caboto saw the boy's dark freckles deepen as he gulped. "Angus McLennon, sir. Did I do something wrong?"

"No, Angus. I've noticed you're diligent with all your tasks. Do you have a cousin or uncle or father or brother on this ship?"

"No, Captain. I'm alone." He looked around at the other sailors. "Well, not alone, but alone without family."

"Have you always wanted to be a sailor?"

"Yes, Captain."

"Angus, I, too, am traveling without family. Shall we watch out for each other?"

"Yes, Captain. Yes." Angus's face brightened.

Caboto asked Hugh Say to assign Angus to the galley, where the warm and good-natured cook took the boy under his wing, and let him eat the infrequent extra portions available at the end of the day.

The *Matthew* sailed on from Iceland and into uncharted waters. It had been more than two weeks since leaving Bristol. The winds had blown hard against them, slowing progress. When the air temperature dipped to near freezing at night, the coats that Caboto had procured were handed out to the grateful crew. But hands and noses and chins were raw as the wind whipped into their eyes and whistled cold air into their ears. Quartermaster Say shortened the shifts, and the crews huddled below when not needed on deck. Rain began to fall, thick like sleet. The winds caught the piercing, nettle-sharp raindrops and anyone who was on deck wrapped scarves tight against their faces.

"Captain! Ahead!" The sailor, strapped in a lookout position, called down to the deck. "Captain! Starboard!"

Caboto and Say quickly moved to the rails of the afterdeck and looked out. Thick, square chunks of ice floated on top of the choppy gray waters. Waves exploded over the ship's bow. The pilot yelled, "We're going straight into the swells, Captain. We'll be hitting the ice! I'll do my best!" The ship lurched against the watery hills and valleys, and ice chunks cracked against the ship's wooden sides, breaking into smaller pieces. Some of them tossed up into the air and landed on deck, sending sailors scurrying for safety. The boatswain blew his whistle and yelled, "Tie yourselves down, men!" Sailors grabbed for ropes, tied them around their waists, and attached themselves to the mast or to the icy rails.

The ship forged on; finally, the waters calmed, and the skies cleared. Caboto ordered the cider barrels to be accessed and the brew to be heated and distributed to the crew. He sent Angus McLennon to knock on the door to Weston's cabin. The man-servant answered, took the mugs of cider, and quickly shut the door.

Caboto and Say sat in the captain's quarters, a large piece of vellum stretched on the table. They were trying to work out their location to mark the rutter. Could it be that the area they'd just passed in the open sea was a place of continual storm? If so, could it be avoided in the future? Or was it only Mother Nature—and God—reminding them to be vigilant and not take life for granted?

And then after forty days, in the middle of June, measurement instruments noted a change in the depth of the waters. Caboto, Say, and Aspar surmised that the ship might be crossing underwater plateaus, some shallow, others deep. The air became warmer, and then suddenly cold again. Aspar suggested that this was the result of currents meeting—the fast-running currents off the western coast of Greenland and the streaming waters coming from the warmer gulfs in the south. Caboto wondered if the underwater plateaus indicated that they were close to land. And then, to everyone's surprise, the waters filled with silver-skinned fish that jumped high into the water as if at play; they splashed back down into the waves and swam around the ship as if they were curious about its size, breadth, and weight.

"Fresh fish, Captain!"

The sailors quickly lowered nets into the water and pulled in the bounty. The cook, aided by Angus, quickly gutted one hundred codfish and cooked them over the fire in huge iron pots. Caboto ordered the musicians to play and the festivities, under a full moon, raised the spirits of all on board. Caboto sighed. Tonight was a respite from worry. "We'll call these the Grand Banks," he said to Say. They looked down into the water; the fish still swarmed, as if they wanted to assure the sailors that they were not alone.

The next morning before dawn, Caboto moved around the ship. A few sailors slept on deck, their heads heavy from the previous day's celebration; they were wrapped in blankets and coats against the cold. He spied a sputtering candlelight from a corner near the bow, and approached to see Hugh Say writing in his own notebook.

"I did not know you were keeping your own rutter, Say."

Say closed his book, speaking quickly. "Captain Cabot. I do so for safety's sake. So that if you would need it, we could compare. That if yours would get lost, I could provide the backup."

Caboto hesitated, wondering why Say had not told him this before. "Not ill-advised."

Say held up his quill and looked sheepish. "My rutter, I'm afraid, also contains more than just the details of our journey. I am a poor writer, but I fancy myself a bit of a poet. The diary holds facts—and flowery odes to the sea."

"You are a poet? Like Dante, the great Italian?"

"I write verse about the sea, the moon on the dark water, the feeling of being a small part of a very big world. I have no poem finished to share at the moment, but when I do, I will ask your patience to hear a recitation."

Caboto laughed. "Poems are always a good distraction." He looked out over the water. Again, it seemed to stretch forever. "I am fearful that patience is what I must hold most dear."

Thick dark clouds filled the moody sky. The water, reflecting the sky, was gray. The sailors' faces also seemed to reflect the gray of the water. All their jokes had become old, spirits too tired for laughter. Caboto calculated how long the provisions could hold; he knew the biscuits had become damp and moldy in storage. Aspar lifted the wooden tops of the rice barrels and showed Caboto the eggs of insects that were now hatching; small worms were munching their way through the precious grains. Rats had multiplied. If caught, they were tossed overboard, but most were quick to find strategic hiding places.

And then a surprise jolted everyone out of lassitude.

"Whale! Starboard side!" Say cried. The crew rushed to the rails to look. Three humpback whales broke the surface, their snorting exhalations snapping through the air. Faces brightening, the sailors hooted and waved at the creatures that quickly disappeared under the surface of the waters after their noisy salutations.

Chapter Twenty-Three

Caboto, in his captain's quarters, marked his calendar at sunrise, noting that the ship had been fifty days at sea. His mind was spent; he'd been harboring a persistent fear that he was wrong, that this was a fool's journey of nearly two months. Had he risked the lives of his crew as well as his own? If so, for what? Glory? Greed? To accomplish a childhood dream? To what end? He remembered Signor Penzo's lectures at Scuola Grande di San Giovanni Evangelista in Venice when he was a student, and the professor's persistent question: Are riches and glory more important than knowledge? Caboto had answered: knowledge. But what had he learned? That the Ocean Sea seemed to stretch forever, that its northern waters were cold and formidable. And that possibly this route led to nothing?

In the top drawer of his desk he kept sketches of Mattea and his three sons that he himself had drawn. He had captured something about each of their faces that tugged at his heart. *Will I ever see them again?* He shrugged off the question; he had to maintain a confident face for the crew. He dressed in his warmest tunic and fur-lined cloak, for the morning air was cold, and headed to the deck.

Hugh Say stood near the pilot. He told Caboto that the water and beer casks were low, despite their strict rationing. Caboto nodded, "Last night I heard the sailors complaining. Seems their appetite for fish is as tired as mine. We all fantasize about beefs and gravies and puddings." Caboto knew that dissatisfaction and longing could quickly turn to disgruntlement and disgruntled thoughts could turn to ideas of mutiny.

Caboto surveyed the horizon. More water. More of the same. He checked the charts once again. Colombo had reached the southern Indies in a month; what did it mean that the *Matthew* had not seen land in more than forty-nine days? For a moment, Caboto contemplated defeat. Should he turn around, return to Bristol with his tail between his legs like a dog that knows it has disappointed? Caboto forced the thoughts from his mind.

"Bird! Starboard side. Bird!" A young sailor, high in the lookout position, waved his arms and yelled. "Captain! A flyer above! A big bird!"

Caboto looked up. He saw a large gull flying high above the ship. Another gull swirled around the ship's mast.

"Two of them, Captain!" Aspar, his eyes on the sky, shouted.

All those on deck were mesmerized. They knew sea birds often headed into open water to dive for fish, but they always stayed close enough to shore so they could nest and rest their wings. Caboto could feel hope fill every fiber of his being.

Hugh Say hurried to join Caboto. "Birds are an excellent sign, sir. With your permission, I'll assign the men to their stations and fill all three of the lookouts."

Caboto nodded. "Give the order, quartermaster. I want

continuing depth measurements. And sailors with keen eyes for rocks and reefs to stand the rails."

Hugh Say shouted the orders and signaled the boatswain to blow his whistle, then headed below to wrest men from their sleep. "All hands on deck! All hands on deck!"

The wind that night was steady for an hour, and then fell off suddenly into the doldrums. The ship slowed. Caboto covered his impatience with assurances to the pilot. "The wind will return. We are close. We must be close." The last light of day slipped away. The moon was three-quarters full, stars shone. But still, to Caboto, the growing darkness and lack of visibility was frustrating. The crew, who hours ago had stood eagerly attendant, eyes searching in all directions, were now slumped, many half sleeping, grumbling under their breaths.

As dawn spread its light over the ship, the breeze picked up. The ship's sails were soon full again and the vessel raced across the waters.

"Land ahoy!" A sailor shouted from above.

Caboto quickly moved to the forecastle. Dark buzzards and small gray birds with deep bellies swooped low to the deck, buzzing past sailors, circling the sails as if curiosity led their flights.

The crew celebrated. Caboto moved to his cabin and fell to his knees and sent a prayer towards heaven. Then he grabbed for his rutter and wrote:

June 24, 1497. On the fiftieth day. Land.

Caboto assigned roles for the landing party. Weapons—crossbows, cutlasses, broad swords, and pikes—were loaded into the captain's skiff along with the flag of England, a crucifix, and a flag of St. Mark.

Caboto, Hugh Say, and Weston and a small entourage sat in the captain's skiff. Oarsmen rowed them to shore. Caboto noticed that the currents and tidal streams were gentle. The weather was temperate; the heavy coats worn through the storm had been left on board the ship. The oarsmen slowed as they steered into a small alcove-like indentation along the bank.

Caboto felt a grand sense of accomplishment that was mixed with gratitude and awe. He had done it. They had done it. They had reached the shores of Far East, the homeland of the Great Khan.

But it was so quiet. The rugged coast before him was not what he had expected. Where were the temples? Where were the Chinese ships, the ones with deeply dyed sails that were called junks? Where were the people he had seen drawn in pictures, some with conical hats and robes made of silken threads? Where were the farmers who tended the trees that provide cinnamon bark? Where were the weavers of silk? Where was the gold?

There was only silence.

Caboto nodded to the marksman beside him, and told him to send a shot into the air to announce their arrival. The marksman fulfilled the order. The sound reverberated. They waited. No response.

Caboto could hear the scraping of sand against the bottom of the boat. "Low tide, Captain," the oarsman said.

Caboto stepped into the shallow water. He could feel its coldness through his leather boots. He strode to the bevy of rocks, climbed onto them, and then moved to the compact, solid earth. He reached down and scooped up a handful of dirt; it was part sand and part rich and black soil. Thick spikes of grass had taken hold in areas around the weather-beaten trees near shore. Caboto gazed up at the massive pine trees. So many were of great height and girth, they could be used as masts on large ships. He kneeled, sending his grateful thanks heavenward. Then he stood and took hold of the staff of the Tudor flag. He felt the weight of it and held it high, letting the thick material, sewn in honor of King Henry VII's reign, fly in the crisp air.

"I, John Cabot, plant the flag of England on these shores. Long live the king!" Caboto's voice rang out in the quiet and a priest uttered a prayer of blessing.

Weston stood to the side. Caboto heard his sneer, "Not exactly what I imagined the exotic, rich, exciting Far East to look like."

Caboto and Say surveyed the area. Say said, "The villages we seek could be inland." Caboto nodded and looked toward the wooded areas. "The season has not warmed the banks enough to make for easy fishing. This time of year, the natives may be closer to hunting grounds."

"Our provisions are enough to get us home, Captain," Say said, "if we don't face another great storm. And I don't see anything we can gather here to bring on board that will add to our food stores."

They looked around. There was no edible vegetation.

Caboto was frustrated, but he knew that the original plan must be followed. "The king wanted us to reach the shores of Asia, to find a path to it through the northern waters. We have done that. With only one ship and a small crew, everyone knew it was impossible to spend time in exploration or to leave men here to build a fort." Caboto wanted to make the most of his time. "I'll have Aspar organize a crew to chart and take notes on what they can on these shores. Tomorrow, the *Matthew* will head south for another day—along the banks, take measurements, record observations, and identify possible landings and harbors. Then we'll head back to Bristol and trust that the king will send us on a return voyage, with a grand number of ships."

Caboto, with an armed sailor at his side, walked the tree line and noticed notches dug into the bark. He carefully eyed the ground and noted snares hidden under thin brush, remnants of broken arrows, a carved wooden bowl, and bones shaved and sharpened into needles. There was a trail that led inland. Following it for a few hundred yards, he noticed animal dung and a clearing with what looked like a fire pit. Caboto thought about the people who must live near and hunted on the land. But there was no sign of these Chinese. Surely he was in China, wasn't he?

Angus McLennon, stepping lightly, hurried to Caboto and whispered. "Captain, the quartermaster wants to tell you he has spotted a deer." He pointed to a clump of trees. "Over there."

Caboto followed Angus and they joined Say and others of the landing party who were pointing into the trees. Two deer—large and fearless—sniffed at the air, sensing the foreigner's presence. Two sailors raised their crossbows.

The deer were skinned and bled as Caboto ordered the oarsmen to collect more members of the crew and bring them onshore. They were to collect the snares, broken arrows, bone needles, and other proof of the land's inhabitants.

Aspar organized a small group of sailors who boarded the skiff and rowed the shoreline, taking measurements for rough charts. Caboto oversaw a crew taking samples of the seabed. Strips of bright cloth were attached to iron stakes the crew pounded into the sand to mark the depths near the shore. Caboto made rough drawings of the shoreline; he'd take all the information to his cabin and start to work on charts.

That night on board ship, chewing on pieces of rich venison, the crew wondered if this was all there was to see. Caboto knew they were disappointed, that many of the men had thoughts of filling their pockets with gems and gold. Next morning, Caboto stood next to the pilot and ordered a steering south, close enough to keep land in sight, anchoring only long enough to plant England's flag on points of land he named Cape Discovery, Island of Saint John, Saint George's Cape, England's Cape, and the Trinity Islands.

On July 20, the *Matthew* turned toward home using the Gulf Stream and strong westerly winds.

Caboto, though he had found no hard evidence of Asia's people or resources, was sure they had landed near China's promised riches. He had accomplished what was expected on the voyage. Perhaps he had not found the desired goods, but he had found and claimed the land for Henry VII. A larger, second expedition had been pledged and he hoped the king would keep his promise. A larger number of ships, crews, and more provisions would be needed for exploration.

The next expedition would be the one to reap rewards. Caboto wanted to get back to Bristol to ensure this opportunity.

Chapter Twenty-Four

It was August 5, 1497, and the *Matthew* entered the mouth of England's Avon River. The tide helped move the vessel towards Bristol, and the next morning, the ship docked at Bristol Bridge. The crew completed the unloading and cleaning of the ship and were released, most rushing off to the arms of their loved ones or to the nearest inn for pints of strong ale.

Aspar and Hugh Say stood with Caboto, overseeing the final needs of the ship. "We've passed the king's first test, proven we can reach the northern coast of Asia by sailing west from England and claim New Found Land. If all goes as I hope, we'll be gaining patent for a full expedition to find the source of riches in the king's name."

"And all sailors are accounted for, all back in one piece," Say said. "That bodes well for gaining crews for the next."

Caboto wanted them to know he appreciated their knowledge and demeanors. "I want you both to be part of the next voyage. I'll send word, after I meet with the king, to the map-maker's shop on Broad Street, near Saint John's Church."

The men shook hands. They did not need to speak of the bond that had been created while spending long days at sea, sailing into the unknown. Say and Aspar headed into the crowds. Caboto saw Say veer off towards the markets and wave goodbye to Aspar.

And then Caboto was surrounded by Mattea and his sons. Caboto kissed his wife, and breathed in the scent of her hair, feeling deeply that this was the smell of home. His sons, now all surpassing him in height, threw their arms around his shoulders. Piero, his beard now speckled with gray, had a huge grin on his face. "Why do you look like the man who has swallowed the sweet canary?" Caboto asked.

"Because I have my brother back," Piero said. "What could be better?"

That night, Caboto sat near the warm fireplace in the family's stone cottage. His eyes grew heavy; it felt good to close them and relax into a safe sleep. Mattea, who had learned the art of making a perfect cup of English tea, put a cup next to him on a side table. She touched his shoulder. He opened his eyes. She held a flyer in her hand. "Look, my husband, you've made the city's announcements. It's signed by the mayor and sheriff of Bristol."

Caboto took the thick piece of printed paper and read:

This year, on Saint John the Baptist's Day, June 24, the new land was found by a ship of Bristol called the Matthew, *helmed by one Mister John Cabot; the ship departed from the port of Bristol the second day of May, and came home again the 6th day of August next following.*

Mattea teased. "You will be famous, Gio."

Caboto could not hide his pleasure. "It is now a matter of record." He chuckled. "They have made it sound much easier than it was."

Mattea knelt beside him and put her head on his shoulder. "I never worried I would lose you. I had faith, my husband."

"We leave tomorrow for London," Caboto said, sipping his warm tea. "To see the king and gauge his pleasure. I'm not bringing gold to him, Mattea. But I hope he sees I'm bringing him glory and opportunity to rival Spain and Portugal."

A week later, Caboto, with Sebastiano beside him, walked toward King Henry VII's residence in the Tower of London. Ludovico and Sancius walked next to the horse-drawn cart piled with wooden crates filled with the found snares, needles, fragments of nets, samples of earth, and sand, plants, shells, dried fish, and animal hides, as well as Caboto's notebooks of drawings, and his charts.

"Papà, may I stand by your side in front of the king? I've never met a king."

"I must go in to see him alone, Sebastiano."

"But if I can meet the king, it would bode well for my future. As an explorer."

"Now is not the occasion to plead your case." Caboto was kind. "I'm sure your time will come, and especially so, if my discovery of this New Found Land is considered a success. But today I must concentrate on my presentation."

Sebastiano bit his lip. Caboto knew his son was frustrated, but he could not worry about that right now.

∾

King Henry VII's eyes moved over the contents of the crates. "Why so simple, Cabot? There is nothing of value here."

"Your Highness, the value of the expedition is, I believe, that we landed in a northern area of the Far East, where the cold keeps many from settling and creating the riches that thrive in the more southern territories where the Great Khan once lived and where Marco Polo ventured. But even in its barren state, this land is of great benefit. The sea is rich in fish, enough to feed a country for generations. There are animals to hunt—you will see their mighty size when you inspect the deerskins I have brought back with me. We anchored along the shores and did not have the opportunity to explore inland, for our crew was small, and our provisions not enough to sustain the time needed for longer scrutiny. We accomplished all that one ship could do, a fine ship allotted by our most high king. To the south, as we traversed the coast for a few days, I could see the deep orange bark of what is sure to be brazil wood, very valuable for its dye and fine grains. I could see signs of communities where silkworms could thrive." Caboto felt guilty for stretching the truth. But he was certain that he could find these things if he were given permission for a longer expedition. He pressed on, "Our lone ship accomplished the set goal, my king, which was to reach the shores and claim this New Found Land in your name."

Caboto rolled out a map he had completed; he'd drawn it during the final days of the return voyage. He pointed to an X with the English crown drawn above it. "Your flags rest in these territories, Your Highness. With large crosses, to give God thanks for your wisdom."

King Henry looked at the map for a long moment. Then he spread his large hand over it. "So. This now belongs to England.

We will build colonies here. Where Englishmen can prosper. And you, John Cabot, have claimed it for us, without a stroke of a sword."

"Yes, Your Highness."

"No battles. No deaths." The king looked tired.

"It is serene and beautiful, Your Highness."

"Good."

Caboto continued, "Settling these territories with colonists, Your Highness, as you envision in your wisdom, is advised. It is the best way to assure no one moves in on England's claim. Spain has done that in the West Indies, where Colombo claimed land for Queen Isabel. With another expedition, I could transport settlers that could make the land their new home."

King Henry VII motioned to his advisor. The advisor handed Caboto a leather pouch. The king said, "This is ten pounds, our payment to you for the voyage." Caboto, pleased, took the purse, and felt its heaviness. The king continued, "And for claiming land for England, we also award you a yearly pension of twenty pounds." Caboto knew this was enough to finance a larger and finer home for the Caboto family and would raise his family's stature in Bristol. But this was not of utmost importance to him. He wanted to hear of the king's decision on the next expedition.

However, Caboto did not want to appear to be pressing, so he spoke softly. "Much preparation is needed for a second journey, Your Highness. The waters are cold in the months close to winter and great islands of floating ice would make travel difficult. Early summer departure, for a fleet of ships, would be optimal, and to do that, plans need to be made as soon as possible."

King Henry VII frowned. "John Cabot. You will have our

answer when we choose to give it." The royal stood and strode out of the room. Stung by the abruptness, Caboto quickly bowed low, bending his knee nearly to the floor.

News of Caboto's voyage spread throughout Europe. Lorenzo Pasqualigo, a Venetian merchant who had settled in London, wrote a letter to his brothers in Venice. It detailed Caboto's journey and predicted Caboto would be awarded a second expedition of ten or more ships. Pasqualigo wrote of great honor that was now paid to John Cabot, who was being called a great admiral. He wrote that Caboto dressed in silk, that the English ran after him like insane people hoping to gain his kind eye.

Caboto received letters of congratulations from Venice— from Fernando, Carlo, and Rizo. There were even notices from the doge's council stating that charges against him had been officially dropped and that Venice would welcome the great explorer into the Republic again.

But not all were happy. In Bristol, Weston told tales of unrest on board the *Matthew*, of navigational mistakes. He grumbled to the nobles and merchants who supported the journey and reminded them they all had hoped for riches, for spices or gold or bounty that could be traded, goods that would increase their bank accounts. Caboto had to combat Weston's stories and assure the investors that the king would surely give his patronage to a longer expedition, one that would reap the deserved rewards. Weston, often nearby, would curl his lip, and wait for another opportunity to discredit Caboto.

Weeks went by and Caboto had not received any messages from the king. He wrote Fra Carbonariis and received a note stating that great things were accomplished by standing strong in purpose and practicing patience.

One night, Caboto entered the Hatchet Inn, where Sebastiano sat with a group of Bristol's merchants, sea captains, and nobles. He saw that Sebastiano was on his feet, enjoying attention as he spoke. "The king is a great admirer of my father, John Cabot," Sebastiano called out. "He will soon send my father to set up a colony in the New Found Land, and it will become a grand trading port. Yes, a title will surely be bestowed on our family." He grinned. "But for now, you may address me as, well, let me see . . ." He laughed and held up his pint of ale. "Earl of New Found Land or Sir Sebastian, Duke of New Found Land." He took a large swallow of ale and bowed to the raucous applause of his fellow drinkers.

"How about we call you the braggart?" someone shouted from a back table.

Sebastiano took it all in good humor. He looked toward the door and saw his father. "There he is—Admiral John Cabot! Head of the expedition west to reach the abundant and fragrant land of China!"

The applause grew. Caboto felt uncomfortable and calmed the cheers. "There is no patent yet. We must wait on the king's good graces."

Sebastiano shouted over Caboto's humility. "Only a matter of time, Papà! Twenty ships, maybe even thirty! Larger than the fleets of Cristoforo Colombo!"

As father and son walked back to their home that evening, Caboto gently advised Sebastiano. "It is good to have confidence, my son, but perhaps not good to promise too much. It is better to temper your assurances so that the end product will seem even grander than expected."

Sebastiano shook his head. "I disagree, Papà. Expect the best, shout it to the world. It is a better way to get what you want."

A few days later, Caboto received a message. Henry VII had arrived at his Bristol court and he wanted to see him. Caboto hurried to the royal hall and waited with others who had business dealings with the king.

Finally, his name was called and he was bowing to King Henry.

"Stand, Cabot. We present you with letters of patent."

Caboto quickly stood, trying to keep signs of relief from his face. He wanted to exude confidence.

The king continued, "You will have your second voyage, John Cabot. We will allow you six ships."

"Six?" Caboto's excitement deflated. Colombo's second expedition included seventeen ships.

The king's gaze was level; he sounded irritated. "Is there a problem?"

"No, Your Highness. I will, of course, be glad of as many ships as you see fit."

The king continued, "We are pleased, John Cabot, with your maps and your assurances. So much so that I have decided to finance one of the ships myself."

Caboto knew this was unprecedented. "I am honored to have your confidence, Your Highness."

"You are authorized to identify six English ships of not more than two hundred tons, in any port in the realm, and use them to travel to the land and islands that will be of benefit to the king of England. You will, as before, arrange financing for the voyage. We will send details of my expectations and perimeters by messenger." Flanked by his military advisors, the king strode out of the room.

As Fra Carbonariis joined Caboto and walked along the wharf, Caboto shared his disappointment with the size of the expedition. Fra Carbonariis replied, "The king is in a foul mood, I'm afraid. The revolt in northern Wales has taken his attention. His message to you is to focus on finding the wealth in this New Found Land and bring back riches that will help him finance soldiers to fight insurrections."

Caboto's chest tightened, as the pressure to find gems and gold began to increase. "I always strive to please the king."

"His Highness has asked me to relay another aspect. He will order the release of as many prisoners from England's jails that you may need to serve as sailors. These men will be promised their freedom for undertaking—for no pay—a dangerous and long journey. They will also be given the option of settling in this New Found Land."

Caboto nodded. "First, I must identify the ships. And find sailors who are experienced. Then I shall see how many prisoners will be needed to fill out the posts."

Fra Carbonariis stopped and smiled. "And I have more excellent news for you. I have been given permission to sail with this next expedition of yours."

Caboto, surprised, looked questioningly at Fra Carbonariis. "You?"

"Your mission is to find riches and claim new lands. Mine will be to help find these natives who we know exist there, and introduce them to the one true God."

Caboto shook his head, smiling. "Piero will discuss with you the idea of one true God."

Fra Carbonariis laughed. "It's always good to talk to Piero, for his questions keep me on my toes."

Caboto took the friar's hand. "That is magnificent news, Fra Carbonariis. I look forward to sailing with you. And, as you say, you have your mission and I have mine."

Snow was blowing, and the temperatures were freezing. It was New Year's Eve and Caboto visited the mapmaker's shop on Broad Street near Saint John's Church. There was a note from Aspar, congratulating Caboto on gaining the king's patronage for the next expedition and committing himself to the voyage. But there was no word from his quartermaster, Hugh Say. Caboto asked for him at the inns and along the wharf, but no one had seen him.

Piero and Ludovico focused on the accounts, the costs of sailcloth, ropes, oakum, foods, blankets, navigation equipment, and all other elements needed for six ships on a long voyage. Caboto mingled with the merchants and nobles, finalizing their continuing investments. But his favorite activity was working on the maps, considering various changes in the route back to New Found Land, going over his rough charts of the inlets that might serve as landing points and potential harbors. Sebastiano often worked by his side.

One night, Sebastiano put down his quill. His voice was low. "I have Mother's permission, Papà. And now I want yours."

"For what?"

"I am almost twenty years old. I want to sail the Ocean Sea with you."

Caboto leaned back in his chair. "It is not all excitement,

Sebastiano. Each day can bring danger. Danger that brings with it the possibility of not arriving back home to your mother—to your beloved brothers."

Sebastiano did not back down. "You take the risk, Papà."

"Sometimes with a heavy heart. For our family is of great importance to me."

"Papà, I understand that. I also know that sometimes you think you waited too long to fulfill your dreams of exploration. Do you not want more for me?"

Caboto chuckled, aware that Sebastiano had worked out his arguments and was now using them as cannon fire to get his way. "Parents always want the best for their children."

"Papà, I know you think I want glory. I do like attention, that is true." He laughed, but quickly grew serious. "But my love of the mystery of the sea and the unknown world is paramount. Haven't I proven that to you?"

Caboto thought of the hours Sebastiano had spent learning chart-making. Reading of the adventures of the Portuguese sea captains, of Marco Polo's travels, of the travels of the Moroccan Ibn Battuta and other explorers, and how he had nearly memorized every word that had been written about Colombo's expeditions. He knew Sebastiano spent hours at the wharf every day, talking to sailors and merchants, gleaning every detail of their latest finds. He could name every boat in the harbor, knew each of their strengths and weaknesses, which sails were optimal, which pilots were most highly regarded, which sea captains had reputations for harsh management, and which ones had the respect of their crews.

Sebastiano leaned forward. "If you were not the admiral of the expedition, I could have signed on already. I don't want to be held back just because you are my father."

This plea hit home. Caboto realized that Sebastiano was of age, that he could have signed on to work on a ship heading to foreign ports years ago. But he, like his father, had put the desires and needs of his family first.

Caboto stood and looked down at Sebastiano. "My son, you have great tenacity. And yes, I understand the passion you've inherited from me." Tears filled Caboto's eyes. He pulled Sebastian to him, embracing him in a solid grip. "I would be honored if you would sail aboard my ship. And stand by my side as we plant the flag of England in the lands we will find together."

"Papà," Sebastiano said, his voice tight with emotion. "I will not disappoint you."

A week later, Piero settled in the chair that was placed in front of Caboto's desk. "I have tracked down Hugh Say."

"Good. Tell him we will sail in June."

"Unfortunately, he is committed to another ship."

This news stopped Caboto. He asked, "Going where?"

"Hugh Say is sailing on Colombo's third voyage."

"Queen Isabel has approved it?"

"Yes. Colombo promised the queen he'd capture a bounty of slaves for her to sell, to make up for the lack of gold. She denied that request; she didn't want slaves. She has told him he may sail again, to find the actual path to the rich shores of the Far East. It sounds as if the queen is giving him one last chance."

"And Hugh Say will be at his side."

"Yes."

Caboto did not like the possibility of betrayal. "When will this expedition take place?"

CHAPTER TWENTY-FOUR

Piero hesitated in giving Caboto the bad news. "The end of May."

"Before ours."

"Yes, brother."

Caboto pressed, "Have you word of Colombo's planned route?"

"It is thought Colombo will, once again, sail the southerly path. Following his former voyages."

Caboto took a moment, then he grabbed a chart from a cubbyhole and laid it out on the table. "Piero. We must get our second expedition on the water. I want my ships to depart before those of Colombo."

Chapter Twenty-Five

It was near the end of May in 1498. Caboto knew that Colombo's departure from the coast of Spain was imminent. He was frustrated, for only five of the six chosen ships had proven seaworthy. The late spring winds were favorable and he wanted to reach the waters during the summer months. He made the decision to cut back his plan and sail the northerly route with only five ships. He reminded himself that one of the ships had been financed by the king himself; that responsibility lay heavy.

Cabot and Piero oversaw the loading of provisions for a full year, in addition to large quantities of cloth, caps, laces, and other items to use for trade with any natives that they might encounter. Two hundred men had volunteered for the journey, so Caboto did not have to rely on the consideration of the prison population. Fra Carbonariis was set to sail on the ship named *Dominus Nobiscum* and he watched over the loading of Bibles, rosaries, and crucifixes.

On the night before the expedition's departure, Caboto and

Mattea huddled together, the candlelight dim in their room. "This journey will be longer, wife. I will think of you every day and want to hold you close. You must stay strong and healthy and watch that Piero does not eat too many beef pies and that Ludovico gains confidence to court the young lady I see him watching as she strolls through town . . ."

Mattea laughed. "I'll encourage love, Gio. You know I will."

"And that Sancius finishes his schooling. And does not try your patience."

Mattea kissed him. "My love. We will be here when you and Sebastiano return."

Caboto met with Aspar under the high afterdeck, outside the captain's quarters. They shared a solid handshake and were soon intent on carrying out the final check on the preparations. Everything was in place. The five ships were ready.

The cannon on the flagship was fired. Sails were raised, anchors hoisted. The ships moved through the river and out towards the open ocean.

Caboto's planned route varied from his first voyage. The expedition was to head toward Ireland as before, but then bypass Iceland and steer toward the southern coast of Greenland; Caboto hoped to shave days off the voyage. But three days into the journey, an unexpected storm raged in the rough Celtic Sea; winds and heavy rain pounded the ships. Sebastiano clung to the rails in the early hours of the storm, vomiting the contents of his stomach. Caboto watched the heaving of his son's shoulders; he wanted to help him but knew he could do nothing. Even the most experienced sailors were seasick as the winds whipped and the swells tossed the ship. Caboto tried to keep all the ships in sight for he did not want to consider the possibility of the entire fleet being wrecked and ruined.

When the storm dissipated, the ships entered an inlet in southern Ireland to assess damages. One of the ships had a cracked mast so it had to be left behind to be repaired, with most of its crew and some provisions staying with it.

The fleet was now made up of only four ships.

Back out in the open northern waters, blocks of floating ice were once again seen. But the sun was warm, the breezes steady, and the pilots of each of the ships were able to steer clear of the deeper islands of ice. Caboto stood with Sebastiano and Aspar as they sighted the shores of Greenland. Aspar told them, "Very few people live here. Explorers from Iceland—they were called Vikings, and were led by Erik the Red, one of the most famous of all Norsemen. They landed here centuries ago. Erik the Red gave the island an inviting name—Greenland—to convince more of his tribe to settle here. But most of the Vikings found it too cold, too hard, and eventually moved on. The ones who stayed like to tell the legends of their land."

Sebastiano prodded Aspar to continue. "Can you tell us one?"

Aspar wove a story. "There is a legend of an island that used to be situated right here, where we are about to pass, off the southwest corner of Greenland. It was called Round Island. The legend is that two Inuit seal-hunters wanted nothing in the way of their endeavors. They got frustrated with having to traverse around the large Round Island to find the seals that liked to swim in the colder, more northern waters. They tied a long piece of incredibly strong hair from a child onto a large rock on Round Island . . ."

"Long hair from a child? How could they . . ." Sebastiano interjected.

Caboto chuckled. "Just listen, my son."

Aspar continued, "The Inuit seal-hunters tied this piece of strong hair from a child onto a large rock on Round Island and, holding on to the other end of it, they got into their low boat. They prayed for wind and their prayers were answered. A great wind blew at their backs and the seal-hunters towed the island north and out of their hunting path."

Sebastiano laughed. "The whole island towed by a strand of hair? No one really believes that, do they?"

"These are the stories told around the fires." Aspar shrugged, a twinkle in his eye. "But the tale doesn't stop there. The seal-hunters wanted to banish the island as far north as it could go. But a witch in the village of Ilulissat saw the island approaching and became angry the seal-hunters would disturb nature, so she cast a spell. The ground rose up and blocked the island's northern path. So, Round Island is no more; it is a jut of land connected to the mainland and cannot be moved again."

"Do you think it is true, Papà?" Sebastiano turned to Caboto. "That we have seal-hunters and a witch to thank for pulling an island out of the way so we can have a straighter line to the shores of the Far East?"

Caboto sighed. "Legends are morality tales, I think. The truth is in the lesson they teach."

Days later, a cold fog engulfed the ship. Visibility was gone. The sounds of the ship, its wood creaking, the cats and rats fighting, the chickens squawking, altogether created an eerie and strange atmosphere. The sailors were becoming restless; some were distraught and full of fear. Caboto was proud to witness Sebastiano spread good will; he moved from sailor to sailor on the flagship, engaging them in stories and asking of their families and hopes and dreams. Aspar arranged for musicians to play up-tempo music.

All they could do was wait for the wind.

Finally, the winds found them and the ships' sails filled. Fresh air blasted the sailors' faces for they now began traveling at good speed and soon entered the area of the Grand Banks. Stores of cod were caught in the nets and lifted onto the ships. Sailors salivated, for this meant meals of fresh fish for days.

And then, only a week later, Caboto heard the sound of a rigger shouting from high on the mast, "Land! Land ahoy!"

By Caboto's calculations, this land lay south of the New Found Land first claimed in the initial voyage. He could see imposing pines trees as they approached, but the beaches at this site were less rocky and their white sands glistened. Caboto gave orders for the ships to anchor. He eyed the shore and saw a lone deer, as big as a fine horse, standing on the shore gazing back at him.

The skiff was lowered into the water. Caboto and Sebastiano took their places at the bow. The standards of England were loaded onto the skiff, the flags waving in the air.

The sand under Caboto's feet was firm. There were mounds of empty oyster shells, and wooden stakes were stuck into the ground. *Perhaps*, Caboto thought, *these are remnants of a temporary shelter.*

Sebastiano joined his father next to the flag and participated in claiming the land for England.

And then Caboto felt movement behind him. He turned to see natives stepping out from behind trees. They looked strong, but they were not of high stature. Some wore coats made of animal skin, and feathers hung on leather cords around their necks. Their feet were wrapped in pounded leather and tied with leather cords around their ankles.

"They are armed, Papà," Sebastiano whispered.

The natives held bows in their hands and caches of arrows were attached to their belts. Several of the younger boys held slingshots. Others carried thick wooden clubs.

"Sebastiano, stay still. We must show them we mean no harm."

Caboto motioned for his landing crew to bring forth a crate that had been loaded onto the skiff. Inside were woolen hats, eating utensils made of copper, glass beads, and brightly colored trinkets. Caboto took an armful of items, walked toward the natives, and put the gifts on the ground.

One of the sturdiest natives turned his back to Caboto and raised his arms. In a moment, men appeared with several cages of live partridges and primitive wooden boxes filled with dried fish. Caboto accepted the offerings and bowed again.

The natives picked up the gifts that were offered to them, and disappeared back into the thick trees.

Caboto ordered the ships to continue south. At each anchoring, the crews of his ships explored the shores. Often natives watched the sailors from only yards away. When Caboto approached them, they looked up at his tall frame and full beard as if he were a great oddity. He always showed them gold coins and made it clear that he wanted to know if they had something similar. He would receive shrugs—and sometimes baskets of their prized shellfish.

As the ships continued south and anchored to plant King Henry's flags, more natives came to greet the sailors. Caboto was asked into natives' shelters, conical tents made of animal skins, decorated with paints created from wild fruits or crushed shells mixed with tree sap. But there were no fine temples adorned with jewels, no mines of silver or gold.

Fra Carbonariis and his friars often sat with the natives to learn their language. The friars shared their religious icons and finally, when the natives understood their significance, they brought out small statues carved from tusks and woods. These were tributes to their gods—gods of the sea, of the earth, of the sky, of family, and of rain.

One of the small inlets, with its waters protected by land filled with strong pines, became a special spot for Fra Carbonariis and his cohorts. They gazed at the terrain and were transfixed.

"This is our place," Fra Carbonariis said. "We like the mosses and scrub brush that cover the ground. And the natives are open and friendly. They seem to believe that all things have a spirit. People, animals, and objects, and all forces of nature. Their ritual dances, the ones they perform for us to the beat of drums covered with animal skins, are celebratory, welcome dances. They know many things, but they do not know of our God or that all comes from Him. This is our opportunity to save their souls. We will stay here and build our church." He smiled at Caboto. "On your third expedition, you will visit us and see how well we are doing."

"This is your wish, Fra Carbonariis? To build your church here?"

"We Augustinian friars will build the first Christian settlement on these shores. It will be named after the church of San Giovanni a Carbonara in Naples."

"Our Italian peoples will be proud."

"Yes, Giovanni Caboto. They will be proud."

~

The next months were full of more southerly travel along the coast. Sites were claimed for England. Caboto was swept away with the beauty of the land and the skies, but he longed to find proof that he was in China. At each stop, he gave orders for the crew to trek into the woods to look for signs of gold, spices, or exotic items that would please King Henry VII. The sailors found tools made of stone, tusks, bones, and horns of mammals. They found spears, bows, arrows, and traps. They saw caribou, fox, deer, and hare. They saw that the stitched sealskin floats attached to fishing lines were filled with air and used as buoys to keep caught fish from sinking and disappearing into the waters. At every site, sailors were able to lower their nets into the water and easily pull up salmon, sole, cod, and plaice fish, many more than three feet long.

But no temples. No farms of silkworms. No ancient sailing vessels. No sign of the land of the Great Khan.

Nearly two years passed. Sebastiano sat with his father in the captain's quarters. "Papà," Sebastiano said, "this land of Asia goes on forever. We have made so many maps and charts. Is it time to go home to our family and plan a new route for our next expedition?"

Caboto agreed. It was time to return home to his king, to his brother, to Ludovico and Sancius—and to his beloved Mattea.

Chapter Twenty-Six

Back in England in 1499, after the two-year expedition, Caboto was worn out. His body ached and he constantly felt chilled. His mind and spirit were also spent. King Henry VII had not found his charts and maps and memorabilia from the journey sufficient. The king had a country that needed funds. He increased Caboto's pension, but no longer invited him to court.

The nobles and merchants who had championed Caboto and petitioned the king on his behalf no longer stopped him in the streets to ask of his adventures. Was it only a few years ago that he was followed by the masses cheering him? When Caboto visited the map shop on Broad Street, he heard the news that William Weston had secured a patent from King Henry VII to sail Caboto's route, for he promised to find the riches Caboto never could.

Caboto had little appetite. Mattea prepared warm soups for him, but nothing could bring warmth back to his body.

One morning, Caboto walked into his library and saw Sebastiano going through the charts and maps. "Son, we have not seen you of late. What are you looking for?"

"I've been talking to rich nobles about financing an expedition. I would lead it."

"This is news," Caboto said, surprised. He wanted more details.

"Papà, Germany and France are both wishing to claim new lands. And I have heard that Spain is open to new proposals. I'm sending letters of my experience, requesting meetings. Trying to get financing together in case I am awarded patronage."

Mattea came to the door, a frown on her face. "Sebastiano. I thought I heard your voice."

Sebastiano moved his mother, and kissed her cheeks. He looked at her, confused. "Why do you look unhappy, Mamma?"

"I've heard rumors," Mattea said, "that you have let it be believed that you alone planted the flags of England in the New Lands. That you take credit for your father's glory."

Sebastiano did not take the time to look sheepish. He shrugged. "I do not say exactly that. I cannot help what people, who are not fully educated on seafaring and expeditions, assume."

"Sebastiano, your father's legacy is not to be tampered with." Mattea's voice was stern.

Caboto held up his hands. "Dear wife, in the world of expeditions, we know that perception is of great importance. Sebastiano, if he wants to captain great voyages, must assert himself and his abilities. History will sort things out."

"Papà, I only want to build on your legacy. Look what I am wanting to explore . . ." Sebastiano was excited; he showed Caboto an area on a map. "What if there were a passage in this northern area that you claimed for England? What if a ship could sail further inland—to territories of Asia?"

"A northwest passage?"

"We noted in our charts waterways that we were not able to explore. No one knows their length, or where they might lead."

Caboto was interested, but concerned. "The ice in the cold months could make it impassable."

"I would target a summer expedition."

"You'd have to turn around in a short amount of time—so as not to be caught in the ice on the way back."

"I will find even more new lands. I feel it, Papà. First, I'll try to get an audience with King Henry, but if that is not successful, I will not give up."

Mattea sighed. "I want your promise, Sebastiano, to always acknowledge your father's work as his own. His part in opening this new world."

Sebastiano kissed his mother's cheek again. "Trust me, Mamma. I'll always make it clear that I'm the son of John Cabot, the able and fine explorer."

Months passed before news arrived at the wharf of Cristoforo Colombo's sad fate. Near the end of Colombo's third voyage to the West Indies, his crew revolted against their tyrannical admiral, citing cruel treatment and reckless endangerment. Queen Isabel had sent Francisco de Bobadilla, a knight of the court, and five hundred soldiers to Hispaniola to shackle Colombo and send him in chains back to Spain. There he was stripped of his Governor and Viceroy titles. Humiliated and angry, Colombo spent time and energy to right this wrong, but from that time on, Queen Isabel was no longer open to his entreaties.

Caboto was saddened to hear of Colombo's misfortune. The man had accomplished much, and had great talent. For his reputation and stature to be so diminished was disheartening.

One day, Mattea answered a knock on the door of their home in Bristol. She opened it to a man who looked much older than his fifty years, a man with eyes that never seemed to rest. He said he was there to visit Giovanni Caboto of Genoa. Mattea invited the man inside and moved to the library.

Caboto looked up when he heard Mattea enter. "Wife, tell me who has come to our door."

"I think, Giovanni, you will be pleased."

"I do not wish to see anyone," Caboto said, rubbing his forehead. Headaches had begun to plague him.

"And what if I told you it was Admiral Cristoforo Colombo?"

Caboto was surprised. He thought perhaps he was dreaming. "Cristoforo Colombo?"

"Yes, my husband."

Caboto straightened his back and he sat two inches taller in his chair. "Wife, please show our visitor in. I'll receive him here. And would you ask the servant to bring us mead?"

"I shall bring it myself."

Colombo entered the room and sat in the chair opposite Caboto. The fire licked the wood, giving warmth to the room.

Caboto said, "Look at us. Now we are fifty years old."

Colombo nodded his head. "*Sì*, Giovanni. When we first met, you were talking about sailing into the Ocean Sea. A boy just like me in Signor Fallio's shop."

"Yes. He predicted our paths would cross."

"And they did. I met you as Johan Caboto Montecalunya. A harbor designer."

"Yes. And bridge-builder to King Ferdinand," Caboto said.

"With an ache to test yourself on the Ocean Sea."

"Yes."

They were both quiet for a moment. They stretched their hands toward the fire.

Caboto finally spoke. "I'm sorry for your troubles on board the ship, on your most recent return to Spain . . ."

Colombo rubbed his wrists as if to remember the chains that had bound him. "A captain must have the strongest faith, an iron faith. And if he cannot instill it in others, that is his failure."

Caboto nodded. "We cannot know men's souls."

"I accomplished much."

"Yes. There is no doubt." Caboto could hear the impatience and anger under Colombo's tired exterior. How he ached to be held up as a hero, not as a man who had been shackled and sent in shame back to Europe.

Mattea entered with a tray. She poured mead from a pitcher into two glasses and exchanged a glance with Caboto. He took a moment to appreciate that his wife had never lost faith in him.

The afternoon grew darker and the two men shared the details of rising from the lower classes of Genoa to being feted by kings and queens. Of making their way through storms and doldrums and seeing new lands for the first time, making grand discoveries.

"We understand each other—perhaps better than anyone else," Caboto said. "We never found the silks and gems or huge stores of gold; we never sailed to the Asia of Marco Polo."

"No," Colombo said. "And our kings and queens, who coveted that wealth, were never satisfied."

"Perhaps the new territories will be appreciated one day." Caboto sipped his mead. "Perhaps the land is the real wealth that has been added to their kingdoms. Shiny baubles can distract. But land can be colonized and made into homes, farms, and places for people to live well."

"There are riches in those lands, Caboto," Colombo said, his voice growing steely. "The Catholic royals have gone back on many of their promises, not understanding the problems I faced in the New World. I will not give up trying to prove them wrong."

"You desire another expedition?"

"I have not given up," Colombo said. He looked around. "You have a home. A good family. I seem to have only my ambition."

Caboto was silent. He knew that Colombo's ego and single-mindedness had allowed him to do great things, but also pushed Colombo, at every turn, to put his desires before others.

Caboto was grateful for the friendships and love he had found in the people around him, in all his endeavors—in Venice, in Catalonia, and in England. He wondered if Colombo had nurtured relationships, and found fairness and kindness more useful than harshness and punishment, if he would be more at peace.

Finally, as the sky darkened, Colombo grunted and rose to his feet. "You've been kind, Giovanni Caboto."

"And you, Cristoforo Colombo, have been an inspiration," Caboto said. "A man one step ahead of me for so many years."

Caboto stood and poured one more glass of mead for both of them. "The Ocean Sea pulled us into its mystery."

CHAPTER TWENTY-SIX

"*Sì*, very true," said Colombo.

The explorers clinked their glasses. "To the Ocean Sea."

One week later, Piero, his hair and beard now completely white, sat next to his brother's bed. Caboto had grown weaker, his breath shallower. "Gio," Piero sighed. "We were scruffy boys from Genoa, not a noble coin to our names. You accomplished your goal, to sail into uncharted waters."

Caboto, who had wound his precious boxwood rosary around one of his hands, reached out to Piero. "This journey through life, with my brother always as my support, was a good one."

Mattea entered, and sat in a chair near the bed. She stroked her husband's face. "Gio. My love."

That night, in early 1500, Caboto was deep into a dream; he was sailing on a fine vessel trimmed in gold leaf, a ship worthy of an accomplished captain. The passage was smooth through the immense Ocean Sea. Saltwater was fresh on his face. He scanned the horizon for any sight of land, and there was hope in his heart that he would indeed find a new paradise. That it was within reach. Beside the ship, schools of sparkling, silver-skinned fish rippled the waters, their path straight and sure, as if they were determined to guide the voyage. From a distance, high up on the mast, he heard, "Ahoy! It is found!"

As the early morning sun brightened the room, Giovanni Caboto, the explorer John Cabot, took his last breath. Mattea, Piero, and his three sons, his beloved family, were at his bedside.

Afterword

Where did John Cabot actually make landfall? Even though Cabot was convinced he was in Asia, we know his ships reached the eastern coast of Canada. The exact locations of where Cabot planted the flag of England for the Tudor King Henry VII are still subject to debate. Most historians believe that, on his first voyage, he landed on Canada's Cape Breton Island or the mainland of Nova Scotia. There are also researchers who believe that he landed in Labrador and Newfoundland (where the Christian settlement was founded), and may have even moved south through what is now Maine, the most northeastern state of the United States.

The exact landfall locations of Cabot's second voyage remain a mystery. One noted scholar suggests that Cabot, during the years of his second voyage, explored much of North America's east coast. Some suggest Cabot sailed as far as Virginia and Florida, even to Venezuela (its name means Little Venice); however, to date, no definite proof has been found. One of the earliest maps of the regions was signed by Juan de la Cosa in 1500. Cabot's own maps and his logbook are no longer in existence.

Documentation of both voyages was not of high priority at the time, for the riches that were expected from reaching Asia were not realized. However, when England moved seriously in colonization in the late 1500s, Cabot's voyages and his claiming of territories for Henry VII were finally appreciated.

Interest in John Cabot has grown in the last decades. The University of Bristol, in England, is an excellent source. Its Cabot Project, in the Department of History, was set up in 2009 and continues to search for more clues on John Cabot's life and his voyages.

About the Author

Jule Selbo is an award-winning screenwriter, playwright, and novelist. She has written feature films, and written and produced television series for major studios and networks. Credits include George Lucas's *Young Indiana Jones Chronicles*, HBO's *Women Behind Bars—Prison Stories*, and the feature *Hard Promises*, starring Sissy Spacek; her Disney credits include the animated features *Hunchback of Notre Dame Part Deux*, *Cinderella II*, and *Ariel's Beginning*. Her plays *Boxes* and *Isolate* have won regional theater awards. Her novels include *Piazza Carousel* (2018) and *Pilgrim Girl* (2005, co-written with Laura Peters). In addition, she is a professor of film and television at California State University, Fullerton, and has written books on screenwriting and film history, including *Screenplay: Building Story Through Character* (2015), *Film Genre for the Screenwriter* (2015), and *Women Screenwriters: An International Guide* (2016, edited with Jill Nelmes). She has contributed to *Journal of Screenwriting* as well as anthologies on film writing. She holds a PhD in film from the University of Exeter in England and holds seminars on writing in the USA and internationally.

NOW AVAILABLE FROM THE MENTORIS PROJECT

America's Forgotten Founding Father
A Novel Based on the Life of Filippo Mazzei
by Rosanne Welch, PhD

A. P. Giannini—The People's Banker
by Francesca Valente

The Architect Who Changed Our World
A Novel Based on the Life of Andrea Palladio
by Pamela Winfrey

A Boxing Trainer's Journey
A Novel Based on the Life of Angelo Dundee
by Jonathan Brown

Breaking Barriers
A Novel Based on the Life of Laura Bassi
by Jule Selbo

Building Heaven's Ceiling
A Novel Based on the Life of Filippo Brunelleschi
by Joe Cline

Building Wealth
From Shoeshine Boy to Real Estate Magnate
by Robert Barbera

FUTURE TITLES FROM THE MENTORIS PROJECT

A Biography about Rita Levi-Montalcini
and
Novels Based on the Lives of:
Amerigo Vespucci
Andrea Doria
Antonin Scalia
Antonio Meucci
Buzzie Bavasi
Cesare Beccaria
Father Eusebio Francisco Kino
Federico Fellini
Frank Capra
Guido d'Arezzo
Harry Warren
Leonardo Fibonacci
Maria Gaetana Agnesi
Mario Andretti
Peter Rodino
Pietro Belluschi
Saint Augustine of Hippo
Saint Francis of Assisi
Vince Lombardi

For more information on these titles and
the Mentoris Project, please visit
www.mentorisproject.org

Made in the USA
Las Vegas, NV
11 January 2024

84243334R00184